# SUNDAY'S CHILD

## *by Edward O. Phillips*

A Geoffry Chadwick Misadventure
Book 1

*Nominated for Best First Novel Award
Books in Canada 1982*

Foreword by Alexander Inglis

**ReQueered Tales**
Los Angeles • Toronto
2022

# Sunday's Child

## by Edward O. Phillips

A Geoffry Chadwick Misadventure, Book 1

Copyright © 1981 by Edward O. Phillips.
Foreword: copyright © 2019 by Alexander Inglis.
Cover design: Dawné Dominique, DusktilDawn Designs.

First Canadian edition: 1981

This edition: ReQueered Tales, July 2019

ReQueered Tales version 1.62
Kindle edition ASIN: B07TTF2JNQ
Epub edition ISBN-13: 978-1-951092-01-6
Print edition ISBN-13: 978-1-951092-60-3

*For more information about current and future releases,*
*please contact us:*
E-mail: *requeeredtales@gmail.com*
Facebook (Like us!): www.facebook.com/ReQueeredTales
Twitter: @ReQueered
Instagram: www.instagram.com/requeered
Web: www.ReQueeredTales.com
Blog: www.ReQueeredTales.com/blog
Mailing list (Subscribe for latest news): https://bit.ly/RQTJoin

ReQueered Tales is a California General Partnership.
All rights reserved. © 2019 ReQueered Tales unless otherwise noted.

# Praise for
# SUNDAY'S CHILD

"The feelings run deep and it speaks sensibly, amusingly,
and passionately."
— Marian Engel

"A masterful and original novel."
— *The Globe and Mail*

"Edward Phillips has produced something unique in literary
history – a comic thriller about gays, set in Westmount.
I read it with mounting appreciation and laughter.
A highly promising debut."
— Robert Fulford

"A witty, wonderfully poised, poignant, self-pitiless book."
— *Montreal Gazette*

"The book is so good it deserves a wide readership and
a place on the bestseller's list, and parts of it – Phillips' lovely,
wise and black puns and home-grown homilies – should
make it into everyday language."
– *Toronto Star*

# BY EDWARD O. PHILLIPS

## THE GEOFFRY CHADWICK MISADVENTURES

Sunday's Child (1981)

Buried on Sunday (1986)

Sunday Best (1990)

Working on Sunday (1998)

A Voyage on Sunday (2004)

A Month of Sundays (2012)

## OTHER NOVELS

Where There's a Will ... (UK/US: Death is Relative) (1984)

Hope Springs Eternal (1988)

The Landlady's Niece (1992)

The Mice Will Play (1996)

No Early Birds (2001)

Queen's Court (2007)

# SUNDAY'S CHILD

*by Edward O. Phillips*

# Table of Contents

SUNDAY'S CHILD

Copyright ................................................................. 2
Praise for Sunday's Child.................................... 3
Also by Edward O. Phillips ................................. 4
Foreword by Alexander Inglis ........................... 9
Dedication ............................................................ 13
Epigraph ............................................................... 14

Chapter 1 ............................................................... 15
Chapter 2 ............................................................... 33
Chapter 3 ............................................................... 51
Chapter 4 ............................................................... 75
Chapter 5 ............................................................... 87
Chapter 6 ............................................................. 107
Chapter 7 ............................................................. 133
Chapter 8 ............................................................. 159
Chapter 9 ............................................................. 185
Chapter 10 ........................................................... 207
Chapter 11 ........................................................... 219
Chapter 12 ........................................................... 237

About the Author .............................................. 245
About ReQueered Tales ................................... 246
More ReQueered Tales .................................... 248
One Last Word ... .............................................. 259

# Foreword

When *Sunday's Child*, the first of six Geoffry Chadwick novels arrived in print from McClelland & Stewart in the fall of 1981, Canada's best known man of letters, Robert Fulford was effusive: "Edward Phillips has produced something unique in literary history – a comic thriller about gays, set in Westmount. I read it with mounting appreciation and laughter. A highly promising debut."

Let's do a little reset. Though Justice Minister Pierre Trudeau had quipped "The government has no business in the bedrooms of the nation" as he led his government in 1969 to decriminalize homosexuality, a dozen years later LGBT Canadians still had no specific civil rights protections under law. The 1970s produced several high profile firings, including a well-known jockey, solely on the basis of sexual orientation; the employers won and all the rest of us lost. The year *Sunday's Child* debuted, Toronto's gay community was under siege fighting court battles stemming from police raids on the local newspaper, *The Body Politic*, and an egregiously overplayed hand of the provincial Attorney General who authorized a February raid on several bathhouses using violent tactics. That led to thousands of people in the streets in the following days, a progressive mayor who in trying to bring calm lost his job, and the galvanization of gay activism as a mainstream Canadian pursuit.

Into all this turmoil a 50-year old out gay Montreal corporate lawyer, settled comfortably in Anglo Westmount, waltzes onto the stage, with a seemingly unending supply of WASPish cliché observations of people, life and his community. Wry, affable and accident-prone, Geoffry Chadwick is experiencing a mid-life crisis – wanting a relationship but pushing one away, wanting sex but not willing to work for it, too bored to go to clubs and bars: he's feeling quite verklempt. His solution on a snowy New Year's Eve at the cusp of 1980 is to pick up a parka clad hustler on Dominion Square and bring him home for a drink and other necessities.

But all does not go well: the hustler turns nasty and, in a split-second, the young man tumbles down the stairs and unluckily breaks his neck. Geoffry, in a panicky noir-drenched mode, proceeds to make all the wrong decisions – beginning with hiding the body in the freezer.

Phillips never abandons our hero (anti-hero?), nor do we ever lose sympathy for him. The story unfolds on two tracks: Geoffry dealing with the cleanup of his accidental deed, and the rest of his life including unexpected house guests, his archly amusing mother (a Westmount Lady Bracknell if one could ever exist), a queenie friend still awash in the 1940s homosexual life, and a musical 20-year old nephew visiting from Toronto in the throes of coming out.

No wonder Canada's leading feminist novelist of the day, Marian Engel, praised *Sunday's Child*: "It's real, and it's moving ... emotional range is wide, the feelings run deep and it speaks sensibly, amusingly and passionately of and for its community." Make no mistake, it's not quite as sombre or dour as Engel might hint: it is laugh out loud funny and the skewering of Montreal's Anglo Westmount, and its equally snobby Toronto Rosedale, is perfectly played. The author was launched with a stunning debut. The *Toronto Star* said "a wise novel about homosexuals" and "deserves a wide readership and place on the bestsellers' list". The Toronto *Globe and Mail* was more colourful: "[Chadwick's] observations are grumpy, bitchy and savagely funny; he reveals himself a master complainer of the true Canadian school." And more bluntly the *Globe* concluded: "*Sunday's Child* is masterful, original, and absolutely Canadian."

There is a masterful author's voice here: while the prose is awash with wit, literary allusions, puns and keen observations which put meat and bones on the characters, the book takes an unexpected and memorable turn at Chapter 7 as the tone grows darker, deeper and full of pathos. It is this shift which elevates *Sunday's Child* above a raunchy Oscar Wildean romp or a Donald Westlake bumbling crime caper. Without doubt, Phillips's first novel was justly nominated for Best First Novel by *Books In Canada* Awards.

Although the follow-up, *Buried On Sunday*, did not arrive for five more years – gay rights in Canada having been enshrined in the meantime as well as the onslaught of the AIDS plague upon a generation of gay men – Phillips' reputation continued to grow. He published a non-Chadwick book of mystery fiction in the interim – *Where There's A Will* (US title: *Death is Relative*) – and saw *Sunday's Child* issued for an American audience: first at St. Martin's Press and, a year later, in the same imprint's Stonewall Inn division as the first Canadian author in its catalogue. Geoffry Chadwick continued to amuse the public with four more adventures ending with *A Month of Sundays* in 2012 – more than three decades after his debut. The world had changed, Canada had changed (same-sex marriage had been law for nearly ten years nationwide, AIDS has been downgraded to a "chronic condition"); and our favourite gay Westmount lawyer finally retired, as did Phillips himself.

In all, Edward O. Phillips produced 12 novels of quietly perceptive and often hilarious observations about Canada, and in particular, that odd mix of gay WASPish soft-hearted folk as embodied in Geoffry Chadwick (one or two of whom we all know personally, if we aren't that person himself).

*— Alexander Inglis,*
*July 2019*


Alexander Inglis is a Founding Partner at ReQueered Tales.

*For K.S.W.*

*... but a child that's born on the Sabbath day*
*Is fair and wise and good and gay*

# 1.

I HAVE ALWAYS DETESTED BUYING traveller's cheques, a task worse than any of those punishments in Greek mythological hell. Worse than rolling a stone endlessly uphill, only to have it roll to the bottom; worse than reaching for grapes always out of reach or filling fathomless wells with broken pitchers. Far worse than burning or freezing or torture by demons is writing one's name repeatedly across the upper left-hand corner of a self-replenishing stack of cheques. Writing Geoffry Chadwick on so many tens, twenties, fifties, I found my name fracturing into nonsense syllables: Geoff-ry Chad-wick, Geoff-ry Chad-wick, like a group of children chanting mindlessly in the street. And it's not as if there are no banks in Toronto, too many if anything. But a branch of one's own bank always turns out to be several long blocks away. Traveller's cheques are more efficient, although many places are getting awfully sticky about cashing them. They want you to produce a driver's licence, a urine specimen, and a note from your high-school principal or the mayor.

The girl selling me the traveller's cheques reminded me more of a cocktail waitress than a teller in the Westmount office of a major Montreal bank. Her topaz wig badly needed resetting and she had outlined her puce lipstick with heavy black pencil. She couldn't wait to finish with me and go back to poking her bust across the counter at her boyfriend, a surly lout in a quilted nylon parka. This same bust was piled loosely on the counter within inches of my hand as she stared impatiently over my left shoulder. And then to discover my fountain pen had slid down into the lining of my jacket, which meant I had to use the pen provided by the bank, lashed to the counter by a chain. As if anyone would want to steal it. Every word begins with a viscous gob of blue ink which never dries but lurks, dormant, waiting to smear itself onto finger and cuff.

The cheques signed, I watched the girl try to fit them into a vinyl wallet. Her fingers were stubby and covered with busy little rings of ten-carat gold. She fumbled, folding the cheques twice instead of once down the middle, making the wallet twice as bulky as necessary. I hoped she had thick ankles. She handed me the wallet of cheques and told me tonelessly to have a nice day. For a second I was tempted to reply that a nice day was the last thing I intended to have, but decided she wasn't worth the trouble of a reply. And if my cup wasn't already running over and down the front of my trousers, who was tottering into the bank at this very second but Millicent MacLean, the nosiest senior citizen in captivity. I tried to sneak by.

"Geoffry Chadwick, as I live and breathe."

"Why, Mrs. MacLean, you're looking very spry for December." Even though it was New Year's Eve I did not wish her a Happy New Year.

"Touch wood. But I always say the lovely thing about Montreal is the change of seasons."

"Isn't it though." I did not feel it necessary to point out my retirement project called for three hundred and sixty-five days a year of hot, unadulterated sunshine in some place where they have never even heard of a Celsius thermometer. I have never relished freezing my buns for three months a year in the Paris of North America. "Mind you, I could do without winter. If only we could skip from December right through to April."

"Perhaps. But that would be cheating. How's your

mother?"

"Coming along nicely, thank you. She's learning to manage on crutches. I had lunch with her yesterday and she walked right across the room, don't you know."

"Good. Does she often have these – dizzy spells?" From her pause I could tell she knew – wasn't it a public secret? – that Mother fell down drunk and broke her ankle.

"Not really. I think she found the fall a sobering experience. She'll be more careful in future."

"Isn't that encouraging. I really must get in to see her one of these days. Did she get my get-well card?"

"I expect so. One gets so many cards at this time of year." I did not feel it necessary to explain that Mother detests get-well cards as they only serve as reminders of her imperfect health.

"Where are you going?"

"Going?"

"You were putting traveller's cheques into your pocket as I came in."

I smiled my Stegosaurus smile. "I haven't really decided. I thought I'd just call my travel agent and go somewhere sunny."

"How very fortunate. With all that money you can do whatever you like." She pulled off angora gloves to show hands covered in liver spots. "Not like a poor widow on a pension." Her tweed tarn and ratty muskrat vibrated with impecunious indignation above the hem of her pleated tartan skirt, hanging comfortably below the bottom of her coat.

But why should I have told her I was going to Toronto to look for an apartment. She would have just bobbed that pointy little face up and down and announced the English ought to stay in Quebec. I couldn't be bothered to explain it wasn't for me but for my firm because we were doing more and more business in Toronto. Where I chose to go was none of her effing business, even if she does claim to be one of Mother's oldest friends who saw me naked as the dawn in my layette.

"I guess. But do you suppose the poor get to heaven any faster than the rich? Have a reasonable day. I'll tell Mother I spoke to you." That was my signal the conversation had finished. "I'll tell Mother I spoke to you." Like royalty rising it signals the end has come.

I turned on my heel to leave the bank, but it is not easy to turn on one's heel in overshoes several sizes too large, the result of a mix-up at a Christmas Eve party. Much liquor, wrong overshoes. There has been a lot of liquor in my life for the past few months, ever since Chris and I split up and I moved into a kind of emotional black hole, no light, no time, no motion, where the inertia of depression envelops one with a gravitational pull impossible to overcome. Booze didn't quite fill the hole; but at times, after a few drinks, it seemed a little less dense, not quite so black. My advice to the world: don't mess with schoolteachers. In fact, I'm surprised that sex with schoolteachers is not against the law. Every teacher I ever met was frozen into a state of perpetual adolescence; the forty-year-old body has a sixteen-year-old mind. One is, in effect, having sexual relations with a teenager. When the world censures the Latin master, caught diddling one of his pupils, who incidentally gets excellent grades, he is branded as a pervert, a dirty old man, a corrupter of youth. All these accusations are far from the truth. One small boy is simply playing pecker pull with another small boy who inhabits an adult body. I had to go and fall in love with an assistant headmaster who teaches history – the lessons of the past really teach us nothing – furthermore, I wasn't even an old boy of the school. My parents thought public schools taught democracy. They were wrong; it is difficult to learn the principles of democracy in a fascist environment, but I did learn a number of useful survival skills.

About four years ago I was invited to this exclusive private boys' school as part of a career counselling program to give a talk on what it's like to be a corporation lawyer (punk!). The name of the school was Haddley Hall. Among rival institutions it is known as Haddock Hall; Haddley boys are known as fish. Arriving promptly – I am always on time – I was ushered into the headmaster's office, a treasure trove of ugly Victoriana. The headmaster himself was out of town being awarded an honorary Ph.D. by a small agricultural college, and I was turned over to the head of the history department who also acted as assistant headmaster. "How do you do. I'm Christopher Pratt," said a voice; and I turned to look into the most luminous hazel eyes I had ever seen. By the time I left the school we had a date for dinner that night and by the end of the week those sexual coloured lights were blowing their fuses. Can that really have been four years ago? *Tempus fugit*, to coin a phrase.

My next stop after leaving the bank was to pick up clean shirts from a counter draped with swags of tired tinsel. From somewhere behind the racks of dry cleaning a radio played the song about Rudolph the Red-Nosed Reindeer, the one with hypertension. The woman behind the counter had decided to let her shoulder-length hair go natural; salt and pepper brown faded into magenta behind eyebrows pencilled black. "Happy New Year," she said, handing me change.

"The same to you," I replied.

I was just crossing the street to the supermarket when I was nearly run down by that neighbour of Winnifred's. Winnifred is my aunt; I was looking after her house for a month. She has this neighbour who jogs, in granny glasses. Oh, he has all the usual gear: the jogging suit, the Adidas, the matching tuque. But it was the granny glasses that really got to me. Foolish! He has a trim body and the snappiest little backside on the block; he'd probably be swell in the sack. But I don't know if I could get past those dipshit glasses. And there's something really looney about runners; they're the Born-Againers of the health-nut set. If they have a twisted knee or a pulled tendon they pamper themselves by running only five miles instead of fifteen. And they make life creepy for pedestrians. I belong to the generation who believes footsteps and heavy breathing coming up behind you means trouble. My neck still prickles. Now it's just some fitness nut trying to stop the clock. And we're all getting there at exactly the same rate. To think that Mickey Mouse is fifty. Teddy Bear is seventy-five. Winnie-the-Pooh is sixty, if he's a second. Even Kermit the Frog's getting a bit long in the flipper. I'll wager even Peter Pan has grown up – to be Peter Pansy. I'm fifty on the nose. Half a century old. Trouble is I feel about twenty-five in my head and about eighteen when a pair of buns like those on that granny-glass nitwit goes jogging by.

A few minutes later I pushed out through the supermarket door with a feeling of genuine accomplishment. Not only had I bought my groceries, sneaking nine items through the six-item express cash; but I had avoided the Potter sisters, Edith and Edna, by scrutinizing a bottle of Mop and Glow. They rattled past without seeing me, talking in tandem as they always do, neither listening to the other, one near-sighted, the other deaf. They make heavy weather, always asking "How's your mother?" and never waiting for an answer. I was so grateful to the Mop and Glow I felt almost guilty putting it back on the shelf. Another woman had run her shopping cart over my foot as she barged down the aisle. She did not stop to apologize, so intent was she to reach the store manager, whom she harangued rudely in a thick, Middle European accent. One hand gripped the handle of her cart, heavy sausage fingers covered in diamond rings. While her attention was occupied I tucked a box of Stayfree Maxi-Pads under a bunch of bananas in her cart, thinking with satisfaction how it would bring her up short at the checkout counter.

Crossing the street with my bag of groceries and box of shirts I headed for my car. At least I had something to eat over the holiday. There's nothing to eat at Winnifred's, only a deep freeze full of leftovers and a kitchen cupboard filled with cat food. I put my parcels onto the passenger seat of the car for the drive back to Winnifred's house.

\* \* \*

## SUNDAY'S CHILD

WINNIFRED CHADWICK IS my father's younger sister. I call her Winnifred instead of Aunt Winnifred because she's only sixty. In fact, she hates being called Aunt. I once introduced her as my Aunt Winnifred at a party and she nearly crowned me with a bowl of hummus. It was that kind of party, full of people who had been turned down by the Canada Council. Hummus and guacamole and about five different colours of wine. Also sangria. It made one long for the days when one washed down onion soup and sour cream dips with rye and ginger ale.

Winnifred is just about my favourite relative, not that I have that many or that they offer any real competition. She married an absolute prick, and after the kids were launched, she divorced him. I admire her for that. Most women of her generation would have just hung in there and been miserable. Not Winnifred. She knew her husband was running around so she put a private detective onto him and got the goods, divorce and a big alimony settlement. She even took back her maiden name, Chadwick. She's a sketch. She speaks with one of those truly Westmount voices; you could hear those quasi-British vowels through a brick wall and know she came from the Westmount ghetto. Not quite plummy, not quite nasal – somewhere in between. The colonial voice. She picks up bits of slang to pepper her conversation, only she can't lose that last trace of self-consciousness. Her slight pause before the term puts the words into relief, the conversational equivalent of italics. Last year she was getting it all together and now she's trying to get a handle on things. When she's ready to serve dinner, all systems are go and she watches educational television for intellectual input, the Boston Symphony playing yet more Beethoven with a hockey game bleeding through.

She turns on and off like a dishwasher. Winnifred is useful though as a kind of linguistic barometer. By the time she's picked up an expression you know it's passe. In effect she collects antiques.

Anyway, now that Winnifred has unloaded her husband

and shed the children she has taken to touring. She climbs onto charter flights with gaggles of leftover women and flies off to clamber over Grecian rubble or shuffle through Versailles or absorb cultural input to the level of overkill at the Edinburgh festival. This Christmas she decided to sail through the Panama Canal and asked me if I would keep an eye on her house. Montreal weather is usually unpredictable around Christmas. Temperatures can plunge, furnaces fail, pipes freeze. Having someone come in to check an empty house is the responsibility of a prudent administrator, to use the windy legal term.

Chris and I had planned to go skiing, which meant he intended to ski while I sat in the bar drinking Bloody Marys and reading *War and Peace*. I have never read *War and Peace* but I feel about it the way Sir Edmund Hillary must have felt about Everest; it is there. Chris's wife Audrey was taking the children to Kingston for Christmas with grandmother. Chris and I seldom had whole days together and the prospect was pleasing. But that was then.

Winnifred has about thirty-seven plants that need watering. They block out the light and breathe up the oxygen and shed leaves and collect dust and spiders and are generally repulsive. But, what the hell, *de gustibus*. She also has a cat, not a bad little creature I suppose, but pretty wild. She tries to jump into my lap when I'm standing up. There's something creepy about people who have city pets. I have nothing against animals in their native habitat – the squirrel in the tree, the deer in the forest, the polar bear in the garbage dump. But an animal in the same house with people, on the chairs, on the beds, on surfaces where food is prepared. Not nice, not nice at all. Worst of all, pets are a substitute for children. Mind you, I'd rather be around pets than around children. At least pets don't talk back.

However, one can survive anything for a few weeks, and since my own holiday plans had gone up in smoke, I had said sure. Even though I was pretty numb at the time, I did lay down a few ground rules. Winnifred talks to her plants and plays them music: Vivaldi and Scarlatti and Couperin, all that music that makes you want to scratch. I told her they weren't getting a word out of me, not even a "good morning." As for the cat, I would feed it. I don't need to water it; it drinks from the toilet bowl. Another plus. If the beast did not bother me, I would not bother it. Her name is Norma – after Shearer, not the Druid priestess. Her? Somehow animals seem divorced from gender, although the cat spends a lot of time walking into the room backwards.

My apartment is tastefully furnished in just the right combination of traditional and antiques. In fact, it is so tasteful that some days, or evenings to be more precise, after I'm into the Rob Roys, I want to lay about me with a cricket bat. (You can't smash up a tasteful apartment with a baseball bat; it would be coarse.) The apartment's not so bad, I suppose, and it does wonders for the image. The muted gleam of old silver, the quiet sheen of brocade, the understated palette of Kalibar at God only knows how many knots per inch. A lot of stuff came from Mother's house after we moved her into an apartment downtown. She had fallen asleep smoking and set the bed on fire. It was a close call. The security patrol noticed smoke pouring from an upstairs window. They could hear the smoke detector blaring right out into the street but it didn't wake Mother. That's when I decided she couldn't live alone any longer. But nobody wanted to go and live in a mausoleum way up on top of the mountain. It's just about inaccessible during the bad weather. Also no help today is prepared to climb stairs, and Mother's house had a staircase that was pure Hitchcock, wide, majestic, with an elaborate balustrade and a small greenhouse off the landing.

Mother hadn't been at all keen on the idea at first. Old people resist change. So do I, for that matter, and I'm not old. She had wanted me to move in with her. A package deal: the widowed mother, the widower son. I pointed out that Susan had died over twenty years ago and by now I had reverted to terminal bachelorhood. To be fair to Mother, she didn't push the guilt. She's far too busy being the Widow Chadwick to bother much with the children. "My life ended when your father died," she says, reaching for the gin bottle. She's never been happier. She really didn't much like Father when he was alive. He was energetic and organized; his very presence rebuked her soft-core incompetence. But once dead he grew an aureole. She wears her widowhood the way other women wear chinchilla. She must have a liver made of corfam. And her lungs; the non-stop cigarette.

I had hit her with the idea of moving around five in the afternoon. It's the best time to broach anything new; she's tight enough to be malleable and not yet drunk enough to be stubborn. She moved into a fashionable downtown apartment chock full of rich retired drunks. The insurance premiums are staggering; someone is always setting himself alight, or letting the tub overflow, or neglecting the oven. But there are sprinkler systems and smoke detectors and a nimble janitor. Of course, in that kind of building he's called the superintendent. Some banana republic bought mother's house to use as a consulate with maybe a little rum-running and white slavery on the side.

Before going to Winnifred's, where, for a slight change in scene, I'd been sleeping over from time to time while she was away, I decided to drop by my apartment to leave my clean shirts and check out mail; it was, after all, the last day of the year. Maybe there were messages from my answering service. I pried mail from the jammed letterbox in the lobby and carried it up to my apartment. The brown telephone bill could wait, so could the cleaner's bill and the T-5 slips. I finally got around to opening a stack of Christmas cards, including my sister's predictably dreadful one. This year it was a potato print made by my youngest niece, the artistic child. At least it was an improvement over the family snapshots in carefully choreographed spontaneous poses she used to send. I remember visiting one summer in Muskoka. We were all having as good a time as could be expected when my sister dashed up to the house, threw on a smock over her wet bathing suit, thrust a camera into my hands, and ordered everyone out of the water onto the dock for the Christmas card. Another year the family posed in their Sunday best, my sister wearing an enormous cameo brooch. The pin was as big around as a tangerine and profiled an eighteenth-century damsel with one of those improbable, no-sex hair-dos. (Not tonight, dear, I just had my hair done.) My sister loved that cameo. Whenever anyone asked about it she would finger the brooch at her throat and say in a low voice that it was a family piece, suggesting by tone and demeanour that it had been thrust into her trembling hand by a dying grandmother. The truth was that Mother bought the cameo while on a Mediterranean cruise from some beady-eyed Italian shopkeeper, who realized Mother's sales resistance was zero. My sister quite literally nagged the cameo out of Mother, then wore it constantly until her youngest daughter, the artistic one, decided the cameo needed a bit of sprucing up and went at the white profile with a purple crayon. Now my sister wears bits of jewellery made from Connemara marble. Even though she hasn't a drop of Irish blood in her veins you would still think the earrings and bracelet and pendant cross came special delivery from the wee folk.

I glanced briefly at the other cards before tossing them into the wastebasket. On the bottom of the pile lay a large envelope, heavy, cream-coloured, and obviously an invitation. It opened to reveal a second envelope inside; seemed to me like a waste, but there wasn't any glue on the inside envelope so I guess we really need the one on the outside.

"Mr. and Mrs. Richard D. Hamilton announce the marriage of their daughter Leslie Ann ..." Leslie Ann Hamilton getting married? And why not. She's twenty-five, the same age as my own daughter Allison, were she alive. But March strikes me as a poor month for a wedding, dragging the train through slush, shaking sleet from the veil. And I don't really much want to go. It's so long since I received a wedding invitation I wonder if I remember the codes. "Mr. Geoffry Chadwick regrets that he will be unable to attend, no, accept the kind invitation –"

## EDWARD O. PHILLIPS

I tossed the wedding invitation onto the desk and went into the kitchen. The place was spotless, my cleaning woman having been in last Friday. Her name is Maria, but then all cleaning women call themselves Maria. I think they come from a giant cloning machine. They all have accents and thick red arms and wispy hair and a husband who ran off, and they clean for twenty-five bucks a day plus round-trip bus fare and whatever they can scrounge out of the refrigerator for lunch. I poured myself a drink and carried it into the living room.

Somebody, I guess it was Eliot, wrote that April is the cruellest month. Maybe so, but December thirty-first is the cruellest day. Instead of looking forward to a shiny new year I found myself looking backward and listing all the things I didn't get done during the past one, principally going on the wagon. I would like to beat fate just once in my life and cut out liquor voluntarily before the doctor tells me I have to. But so far no luck, or no will power, depending on the level of severity. The Jewish New Year makes far more sense. September is a month for beginnings: autumn, schools, symphony. Rosh Hashanah marks the end of summer. January first is just one more in a succession of grey winter days. It marks nothing but the end of that dreariest of seasons, Christmas.

With Chris out of the picture only a few months I did not find it a season to be jolly. Not that I ever am around Christmas. It is a togetherness festival predicated on hordes of children who wear jammies and hang up stockings and leave out cookies and milk for an outrageously dressed old man, who needs both a barber and a dietician. Yes, Santa Claus, there is a Virginia. The idea of being hauled from bed at 6:00 A.M. with a Christmas Eve hangover to open presents is as close to hell as I will ever come in this life.

I had Christmas dinner this year with Mother. My sister didn't come up from Toronto, which was a relief. She's younger than I am, for which I already dislike her; and she's such a tightass I'm convinced her daily b.m. is a major trauma. And she's a snob. The first thing she wants to know about anyone is who his parents are and whom he married. She's worse than the unemployment insurance commission. A casual introduction at a party always turns into twenty questions. Even as a girl she never played house, only mansion, or palace. She never wanted to play mother, only queen; the other little girls, usually relegated to playing aunts and daughters, became princesses or ladies-in-waiting. When other children broke out in goose bumps my sister developed swan bumps. She grew up to be a debutante, St. Andrew's Ball in a dress that made her look like a boudoir lamp. Then she married a skinny little doctor who's a hypochondriac. He's a double doctor, a pediatrician with a Ph.D. in something or other, and lectures at the University of Toronto.

My sister Mildred (what a ghastly name, and she refuses to answer to Millie) married him because of his mind. At least so she says. I believed her until I saw him in trunks; he's got a dork the size of a cucumber. But he's always got something wrong with his this or that, mostly his back. You'd think he invented the disc. I've always believed there's nothing wrong with his back a good blow job wouldn't cure; but Mildred telephoned before Christmas to say George was in terrible pain and she couldn't leave him over the festive season. She's like that, so loyal and honest and true you want to slap her.

As a result Mother and I drank our way quietly through Christmas Day. The housekeeper received a bonus to thaw out a little Butterball turkey and cook it for the two of us. It came out of the oven hot and sat getting cold while we had another little drink, and another. It was pleasant without my sister. She doesn't smoke and spends her time jumping up to empty Mother's ash tray. By the time we got to the turkey it could have been cardboard stuffed with sawdust. But we didn't care; we had nothing better to do.

I'm really quite comfortable around Mother. She's made a whole career out of being rigorously uncritical. She does not sit in judgment on her children, like most still-extant mothers I know. At times her refusal to take issue was infuriating; one longed for some kind of support and found attitudes with the consistency of chocolate mousse. I guess it was the only way she could cope with my father, hard-edged and diamond-cut in his thinking. Not that he wasn't a kind man. He was a true Christian who found it impossible to believe in God. But his intelligence cut through muddy-mindedness like a laser. Mother had been terrified of him and made herself deliberately amorphous. He had tried to give her shape but she leaked and melted and oozed, a snow lady during January thaw. Finally he gave up and treated her with the kindly tolerance one might display toward a retarded child. She looked at him the way a mountain climber without pick or rope or boots might look at the Matterhorn, longing to ascend but totally unequipped. She drank a little. Then he died. A light went out in my life but a soft glow began to suffuse hers. I lost the dearest man I had ever known; she gained status. In her own eyes she had become important as the widow, the grieving widow, the brave, grieving widow of Craig Chadwick. Instead of a panacea against loneliness her drinking became an almost religious libation, a toast to the departed shade, naturally roaming jocund in the Elysian Fields, while she, mourning like Niobe, longing to play Alcestis (Why did he have to be taken when he had so much to live for?), silently and drunkenly reproached the Fates for cutting his thread of life. She had even wanted to keep Father's ashes on the mantelpiece but I put my foot down.

The rest of Christmas week had passed somehow. I watered Winnifred's plants and ducked the cat. I nearly broke my neck because she left the remains of a catnip mouse with a Christmas bell around its neck at the head of the stairs. I stepped on the damned thing and was so surprised I nearly took a header down the staircase. The cat was lonely without Winnifred and followed me around like a bad conscience.

Well, now at least it was New Year's Eve and the so-called festive season was almost over. I have always disliked New Year's Eve parties; after the round of Christmas festivities most people are exhausted. They drink too much, and I have yet to be at a New Year's Eve party that was not packed with noisy incident: the crash of breaking marriages, the tinkle of terminated engagements, the thud of people falling down drunk. I knew this particular New Year's Eve was going to be worse than most and I had already decided to spend it alone. I had had invitations to any number of parties because I am any hostess's dream guest, a single Caucasian male whose socks match. I am tall and trim and still have my hair, which actually looks better since it turned from mouse brown to grey. In fact, for years I was described as prematurely grey, the young face, the old hair; but fifty is the cut-off point. I am now maturely grey. And although not handsome I have the kind of bony features generally described as interesting. My eyes are grey-blue, the colour of honesty; and I have learned to focus them on bores as if I were really listening when in reality my mind is far away. In short I am very waspy looking, so much so that whenever I'm with French Canadians I look like a coelacanth in a goldfish bowl.

Nor am I an obvious fag; no more than I'm a jock, a species I would gladly see as extinct as the Dodo. And to cap it all there is a dead wife in the past. "Tragically killed, my dear, in an automobile accident. Very sad. They were no more than children." I can hear it now. A fifty-year-old bachelor in our society is open to suspicion. Is he gay? If not, what's his giggle or bag or trip? Young girls? S and M? Flashing? Swinging? Jacking off on a groundsheet covered in vaseline? Rubber boots filled with cold cream? But to be fifty years old and a widower is like having one of those pale blue government stamps on your dork. Grade A heterosexual.

As a result I have floated through dinner parties on a sea of widows. Westmount is awash in widows, too conservative to leave the ghetto, too timid to go where the men are, prepared to settle for lives of dun-coloured loneliness rather than take the risk of bringing a little technicolour into their lives. Many of them are rich, rich enough to buy the best studs in the business; but they are so brainwashed by their upbringing, they want relationships. They refuse to face the reality that sex, like anything else, is a commodity to be bought and sold or bartered. I'm old and fat and rich; you're young and virile and poor. Let's make a deal. I'm young and beautiful; you're young and beautiful. If you will let me enjoy your youth and beauty I'll let you enjoy mine. I'm an impresario who's into leather and discipline; you're a young dancer who's into a career; ergo.

Finally I know how to use a knife and fork; I can tell the finger bowl from the soup; and I can hold my liquor. That's one of our better Westmount euphemisms. Hold your liquor. Get as drunk as you want only don't let it show. Drink half a quart of behaviour-altering fluid but don't let it appear to alter your behaviour. I'm good at that. The drunker I get the more I encourage other people to talk. That's my awful secret. Most drunks hog the conversation or the floor or the spotlight and make it blatantly obvious they're well on the way. I play wallpaper, present but inconspicuous. My father once said to me, "You can get away with murder if you wear a shirt and tie." He had meant it as a joke.

Anyway I had decided to pamper myself on New Year's Eve. Having already bought a forty of Black Label, I intended to spend the evening at Winnifred's. She has a huge colour television, which I enjoy after my own tiny set; it's like watching animated postage stamps.

I finished my drink and mentally scrubbed the rest of the day. I had already been to my office, although why I had bothered to go in I'll never know. Everyone I wanted to reach was either skiing in Vermont or snorkelling in the Bahamas. Nothing was pending one of my partners couldn't handle, and I was more or less supposed to go to Toronto. It had been my idea that renting a small studio apartment would cost the firm less than paying for hotel rooms each time one of us went there. But with the responsibility of Winnifred's house, I could only go for a day, two at the most.

I was just folding a bathrobe to toss into my overnight bag when the telephone rang. I picked up the receiver and said "Hello." It has always struck me as a safe, non-controversial way to begin a conversation with the unknown party.

"Meanwhile back at the oasis the Arabs were eating their

dates. There's a rumour going around that you're a mean old queen, but I know you're only a petulant principessa. How's your mother?"

"Larry!"

"You guessed."

"I'd know that gin-soaked rasp anywhere. Are you in Montreal?"

"Just arrived. You're the third to know. If you don't have dinner with me I'll stamp and pout and make a scene."

For just a second I hesitated. My scenario called for a quiet evening, and Lawrence Townsend II is anything but quiet. He's an outrageous, ageing queer-the kind other homosexuals call queer-sometimes amusing, often tedious. But I've known him a long time, and within his huge limitations he's a good friend. I didn't feel like going out to dinner, not with Larry certainly. New Year's Eve is the last stronghold of the heterosexual date. Two unescorted men out together in a restaurant on New Year's Eve might just as well wear sandwich-boards. It's years since I left the closet but I still don't advertise. And Larry doesn't exactly hide his light under a bushel. He winks at waiters and gropes busboys and cruises the adjoining tables. I once heard him ask the headwaiter if he liked to fool around. That *maitre d'* was cool. He said, yes, he fooled around but never on the job. Larry was floored; he wanted to shock and ended up with egg on his face.

"I had planned a rather quiet evening – as befits a person of my age and station. And I'm house sitting for my aunt. Why don't you come over there and I'll make dinner."

"But I was going to sweep you out into the glitter and glamour of beautiful downtown Montreal. I've packed my Lana Turner sweater over which I'm wearing my Dorothy Lamour sarong, finished off by my Carol Landis net stockings and Joan Crawford fuck-me ankle strappers."

"Well put on your Ann Revere housecoat and spectator pumps and come to Winnifred's around 7:00." I gave him the address and rang off.

The second after I hung up I was sorry. Not that I minded

seeing Larry – in a laboratory-controlled environment – but now I had to produce a meal. And I hate to cook. Cooking is the ultimate waste of time. Good, bad, indifferent, food always gets eaten. At predictable times people sit down to eat predictable amounts of food. You can spend five hours or ten minutes on dinner and within fifteen minutes it is over, the main course at least. Another big drawback to cooking is all those millions of other people who like to cook. Everybody these days has to be creative, in my vocabulary one of the dirty words. Any nitwit who can't sew on a button or screw in a replacement fuse can take a pound of hamburger and a tin of tomato sauce, adding this or that with a heavy hand, and all in the spirit of free-wheeling creativity. What this free spirit ends up with is a pot of liquid heartburn to be ladled onto overcooked spaghetti. Fortunately Winnifred has a deep freeze the size of a steamer trunk, and I was sure to find something, some old beef burgundy or elderly lamb stew I could toss into a double boiler. Mix two tins of soup with a cup of sherry; shred some lettuce; drop by the deli to pick up dessert and a piece of cheese that wasn't Kraft. A meal more nutritious than memorable; no crossed forks in the restaurant guide.

# 2.

LARRY ARRIVED AT WINNIFRED'S on the stroke of 7:00 with forty ounces of gin in one hand and a bottle of Chateauneuf du Pape in the other.

"I don't care what you say," he announced with an exaggerated lisp, "I'm going to see in the New Year with grape and grain."

"1979 was the Year of the Child. Don't you think we ought to be seeing it out with milk?"

"Milk? Did I hear you say milk? You're not a well woman. And they never did get around to organizing that children's crusade against the OPEC countries. Another wasted opportunity. Now to business. I'm launching right into a martini. *Et tu, Brute?*"

"Why not?" Everything sat ready in the kitchen in double boilers and casseroles. Even under stress I knew I could cope. But was I going to begin '80 by breaking my '79 resolution? No more dry martinis. The most delicious, the most tempting, the most lethal drink ever to pour out of a jug. As I watched Larry splash and stir with the expertise developed over years of splashing and stirring my resistance crumbled. Tossing a sop to my conscience, I had my drink over ice in a water goblet. Winnifred kept no cocktail glasses. Larry filled a wine glass to the top with the colourless, fragrant fluid.

## EDWARD O. PHILLIPS

We went back down the passageway to the lounge, as Winnifred calls it. You couldn't call it a parlour, not even a living room. Perhaps waiting room comes closest, but it really defies description. Between the plants and the curios the occasional bits of furniture virtually disappear. A giant rubber plant in a tub shrouds the one comfortable chair. Anyone over four-feet-six sits with his head in a cluster of broad waxy leaves. Three spider plants in hanging sisal planters block out light in the upper bay window while on the window-sill itself sits a row of avocado plants, started naturally by impaling a seed with three toothpicks and suspending it in water, each plant a different height. The window-seat hides beneath dusty African violets separated by reproductions of pre-Columbian antiques from the Mexican trip. The cobbler's bench coffee table groans under a spreading poinsettia, while to go near the desk means brushing into a giant fern, which sheds leaves at a sneeze.

I really quite like the room. It is such a beautiful put-down of the homosexual sensibility. In a subculture where perhaps the only true heresy is to lack taste, Winnifred's front room stands as a proud monument to a total absence of taste. Not bad taste, no taste. Nothing in Winnifred's room could really offend. Taken individually no object is outrageous; and a couple of pieces – the Chippendale desk and art nouveau alabaster lamp, for instance – are beautiful. And it isn't as if she doesn't give a damn; she loves everything in the room. Each curio, every chair, has an association and a story, which her enthusiasm, restrained but nonetheless real, makes interesting. And I give her full marks for not turning the house into a loft. She has not whacked the lath and plaster from the walls to expose stained brick; she has not thrown rooms together to make one large, uncomfortable space. She did not rip out the lovely old bathroom fixtures, tubs with claw feet and real porcelain sinks resting on huge pedestals. Unlike many people of so-called taste she respected the architect's original concept. But scratch a queen and an amateur decorator bleeds through.

Larry struck an attitude of mock amazement. "I don't believe it. I absolutely don't believe it. I'm in a state of schlock. Bring me my machete. I mean do people really put two crossed spears and a shield over the fireplace?"

"Winnifred loved Africa. Sit down, if you can find a place."

A rocker stood free of encumbrance if one discounted the hand-hooked mat in primary colours on the seat. Larry sat. By turning the poinsettia forty-five degrees counterclockwise I was able to clear a sight-line from the end of a loveseat upholstered in Black Watch tartan.

Placing his drink on an old nail keg, serving as occasional table, Larry looked around. "It's truly remarkable. Life imitates craft. I mean it's too eclectic to be even bad. Do you know in my entire life I've never seen a real white elephant." His reference was to three carved ivory elephants, small, medium, and large, grouped under the fern on the desk to make a sort of jungle tableau.

I always drink my first drink quickly. So does Larry. By the time he had taken in Winnifred's lounge it was time for another martini. I took the precaution of turning the oven to low and the double boiler down to simmer. "What brings you to Montreal just like that?" I asked. "Nothing happening in Toronto?"

"There's always something happening in Toronto, the ceaseless round. But the same old faces having it on with the same old faces. I thought I'd see in the New Year with friends, not tricks. That's the trouble with Toronto. Everybody has lovers but nobody has any friends."

"Nobody special in the picture?"

"Nobody. Everybody but nobody."

I suppose if I weren't feeling so sorry for myself I could feel some compassion for Larry. He's going the way of the dinosaur into total extinction. A man who discovered he was gay during the 1940s, when every young man paraded himself as a tireless screwer of women (or else was considered "shy"), he developed into a divided personality, conservative on the surface, outrageous in private. He picked up all the then-current catch words and phrases: "Get you, Mary. Up yours, Maud. Wait till your son turns nelly." Groups of men were always "the girls," and whoever he slept with at the time was always "she." When he was hung over, which was most of the time, he was "not a well woman," or else having "that time of the month." Decades passed, but the patter never changed. To look at, he's Mister Medium: medium height, medium build, medium features – regular but forgettable – medium brown hair, medium brown eyes, medium intelligence. Totally unthreatening. He has made a great deal of money selling real estate. His appearance is so bland prospective buyers trust him. He has limitless energy and a shrewd, almost instinctive sense of how to close a sale. To see him with clients one would never suspect a "Get you, Mary" lurks just below the surface.

He goes through tricks the way most people go through Kleenex. Of course, it's much easier to sleep with a person than talk to him, or her, as the case may be. And when conversation time comes around all he can offer is the 1940s patter, smooth as lacquer, formal as a sonnet, impenetrable as Saran Wrap; to perforate is to tear. He's spent the last twenty years lamenting the absence of true love. He wants romance the way a spotty pubescent girl longs to dance *La Sylphide*. Love is a distant city, Oz, or Shangri-la; and it goes without saying love is a constant high, an endless orgasm, a jugful of martinis without the hangover, a whiff of amyl nitrate that lasts forever.

One day Larry woke up and realized the love that knows no name had become a sub-Olympic sport. Being gay no longer carried an aura of decadence or even of off-beat. Homosexual men and women were banding together to march, picket, lobby – for civil rights, equal housing, similar job opportunities. No longer secret and forbidden, homosexuality turned strident and political. Like many gay men, Larry is an arch conservative. His attitudes on everything but sex hover somewhere to the right of Frederick the Great. And even about sex he has lived a double standard, straight to the world, gay to the charmed circle. He has lived a lie, or so he likes to think; and the thought gives him a little jolt of pleasure. Most North Americans of middle age, brought up in a kind of moribund puritanism, like their pleasures seasoned by a little guilt or at least the feeling they are pulling a fast one. And now those who shared Larry's awful secret are marching five abreast down Sherbrooke Street and Yonge Street and Park Avenue and Beacon Street and Michigan Boulevard. They are publishing weekly newsheets and glossy magazines to which one subscribes even if one does not have a post office box. They play baseball games with cops, complete with cheerleaderettes in drag. (Shake your ass. Shake your tits. San Francisco is the pits!) They form their own churches and lobby for those politicians whose public utterance suggests tolerance. If not respectable, homosexuals have become visible, and Larry doesn't quite know how to react.

We settled ourselves around the second drink.

"How's business?" I asked.

"Booming, absolutely booming. All those frightened English ladies from the Province of Quebec are scrambling off to Toronto and buying up all the houses. We're thinking of putting out contracts on old people living alone – the old lace and spats set – simply to get places to sell. I could have sold my own house fifty times over, but who wants to live in a high-rise with a doorman who keeps tabs on comings and goings. Do you suppose this gin has been cut? I'm not feeling a thing."

"Give it time. What are you doing for excitement these days? Wait. Let me rephrase the question. Are you doing anything else for excitement?"

"You mean like tickets to the symphony or a night course on French existentialism in translation, or maybe introductory ceramics. Come, now. I'm off to Key West in a couple of weeks. I understand it's the place."

"What's the change in that? Same old thing in a new locale. Why don't you take your mind off your box and have a real vacation?"

"My, aren't we sententious tonight. Since when were you so averse to a little push-push in the bush?"

"I'm not averse; it's just that I'm-well-let's have another drink."

I wasn't in the mood for explanations. One of the few advantages to growing older is losing the need to justify oneself. The young are forever explaining themselves away. But as years pile up one learns, or one ought to learn, a measure of self-acceptance. And with a walking case of arrested development like Larry it always seems easier to change the subject. Besides, Larry doesn't know about Chris, not that we had split up, not that he even existed. I don't put out bulletins on my private life. And Larry wouldn't have been at all pleased with the news. In fact, his reaction would have been jealousy; not the jealousy you feel when someone you love is running around with somebody else but the jealousy arising from a possessive form of friendship.

I have been able to deal with Larry largely because he moved to Toronto and I see him only sporadically. Otherwise I would have to be firm, even unpleasant, about defining my boundaries. Typical of Larry was his tacit assumption I was free New Year's Eve. In fact, he would not even have considered my having a prior engagement. If I had had I must somehow disengage myself to be at liberty for him.

By the time we were into our third martini I knew for certain I was drinking gin. The silver bullet strikes again, diffusing that special detached euphoria which is almost but not quite worth the price one must ultimately pay. Larry too began to show his several ounces of gin and French.

By now he was fully animated and telling a lengthy story of an argument he had in a bar with his latest ex-lover, if one can use that term for liaisons measuring themselves in hours. "So I said to her, 'Mary, you're not a well woman. Now get your skinny little ass over to that bar and get me a double scotch with lots of ice.' And do you know what that cunt said to me?"

"Larry!" Gin makes me impatient, among other things.

"Let's talk about me for a bit. Do you suppose you could find me a decent centrally located apartment in Toronto?"

"What for?"

"To live in, that's what for. I know you deal mainly in houses, but maybe you know someone who knows someone who slept with someone. I don't want to be in the suburbs, nor do I want two cozy rooms over a massage parlour on Yonge Street."

"You're really moving up to Toronto? Cross your heart?"

"Yes and no. The firm is doing more and more business in Ontario and I figured out a studio apartment would cost us less per annum than hotels. As it was my suggestion I got stuck with finding the place. Just as well. At least I'll be satisfied with the digs when I use them."

"Why don't you come and stay with me for a few days? I could show you what's available. I might have a few leads."

"I'd like to come up and look around. Maybe I'll just book into a hotel. I don't want to be a nuisance."

"Of course you'll stay with me. And with all the money you'll save your firm we can eat out every night. There's a rash of new restaurants, serving real food ..." The cat, who had been crouching behind the rubber plant, leaped several feet in the air to land precisely in Larry's lap. "Jesus Christ! I mean, mercy me," he exclaimed somehow managing not to upset his drink. Larry never spills drinks. I've seen some close calls, but around alcohol he has the dexterity of a five-orange juggler.

"Larry, spare me the obvious joke."

He laughed. "You mean it's a long time since I had this much pussy in my lap?"

"Precisely. Are you ready to eat?"

"Eat? After only three drinks? On New Year's Eve? You're not a well woman. Why don't you fix the next round. I can't disturb her ladyship."

By now the cat had colonized Larry's lap. And she was doing all those things cats do when they want to be adorable: purring, extending and retracting her front claws, half-closing her eyes. It was all I could do not to whack her with a rolled-up newspaper. By now I had reached a point I always reach when drinking gin; I know I've had enough to drink and I don't give a damn. I should stop and eat, but I know perfectly well I won't. As a gesture of conciliation to my better judgment, I used the jigger to measure the gin, then poured in a shot freehand for good luck.

"Growing old is a real pain in the ass," Larry volunteered out of the blue from the kitchen door.

"Amen."

"That's why I'm going to Key West. When the sun shines and I'm on the make I have an illusion of time standing still. Sex stops the clock, for a while anyway. All the people I used to hang out with are taking it easy because they're afraid of the second heart attack, or they're on the wagon because of an ulcer, or they're having chemotherapy. I'm sorry. I really am. I wouldn't wish illness on anyone. But they've become so preoccupied with themselves it isn't real. Even those boring old farts who used to talk nothing but politics and business are going on about their jogging and their fibre intake and how long since they last had a cigarette. I know, I know. I'm one of the lucky ones. I should have cirrhosis of the liver and all those unpleasant diseases they used to warn the troops about in World War Two. But I don't. Nor do I get out of bed in the morning thinking: praise de Lawd; I don't have cancer or angina or Legionnaire's disease. I don't suddenly gaze out the window in an orgy of gratitude because I'm not blind. I'm pissed off because I need bifocals. I hate those capillaries growing in my cheeks. I hate hair that looks like dirty pewter, and I won't admit I'm old enough for Grecian Formula."

As I could not come up with a suitable response I made moves to serve dinner.

By this time Larry was more or less propped against the kitchen table drinking neat gin over ice. "You know something. I met this number in a bar a couple of weeks ago; chicken but cute."

"You mean chicken frightened, or chicken young."

"Young, but post-pubescent. I thought we were hitting it off just fine, so I asked him home. Do you know what that little prick said to me?"

"No, but I believe I'm going to find out."

"She said, 'I'll be back on Wednesday night. If you're really interested I'll see you then.' Can you imagine? Me, hot to trot, and 'I'll see you on Wednesday.' I said, 'Sweetheart, you're not a well woman.' And she said, 'I thought that line went out with button boots.'"

"Larry, it did. Look, I'm about as contemporary as an antimacassar but even I know the gay scene has changed. Now that young people are more up front about sex they don't feel they have to take everything that's available. When we went to bars in our younger days it was to pick someone up and dash off somewhere to hump. It was the urgency of desperation. God, the number of times I checked into seedy tourist rooms with tricks, no luggage. But attitudes have changed, right across the board. It's not just gay life. Jesus, I hate that word. For me 'gay' will always be the antonym of 'morose.' Look at what's happened to women. They're really in there and pitching. And high time too." By this time I had managed to set the kitchen table with an elegance so casual as to be almost non-existent. Larry pulled the cork on the wine. Wine on top of gin, real kamikaze drinking; and I'm sure as hell old enough to know better.

Almost immediately I was sorry I had made the observation about women. Never having really known any, Larry treats women, all women, as some kind of strange, untrustworthy, and barely rational species, domesticated, even at times useful, but never to be treated as equals. He has the British colonial mentality toward women, only the wogs are broads and the yellow peril has been superseded by militant feminists.

"You know something, Geoffry, you're going a little soft in the head. Do you mean to tell me those stunned cunts with the floppy tits and the loud voices and the lard arses stuffed into pants are really getting to you? I know; it's because they all have such a terrific sense of humour."

"Larry, I'm not talking about strident, militant, cryptodykes. I'm talking about your mother of three who's a dermatologist, and a good one."

"Show me a broad who'll reach for the cheque, and I'll show you an emancipated woman."

"I've known plenty. Clients – female-type clients – often buy me lunch."

"They're only after your body, Chadwick, and don't you forget it."

"Much as I'd like to believe that it simply isn't true. I'll grant you I have areas of reaction. I like to have my hair cut by a man and I like men serving food. For the rest I respect whoever does his or her job well. I don't care whether it's driving a taxi or transplanting a cornea. I respect competence. And thank God hundreds, thousands, of women are now able to admit their abilities without feeling apologetic."

"Geoffry, you know as well as I do there's nothing a man can't do better than a woman except have babies."

For a moment I hesitated. Was it worth getting into an argument? But the first glass of wine on top of gin in an empty stomach saw fit to disagree. "Larry, you're full of shit. Furthermore you're a walking encyclopedia of stale attitudes. If those little green men got you onto one of their flying saucers and grilled you they'd think the world was stuck back in 1945. You're a human time capsule. And I'm bloody well sick and fucking tired of being talked down to by someone whom I do not consider my intellectual equal." When I'm angry my diction goes profane-Edwardian.

"Well, listen to you, Maude –"

"Be quiet. I haven't finished. You have turned into a bore. When you're not talking about your dreary, repetitious sex life you're putting down women. When did you last go to a movie? I know you haven't read a book since high school. You don't even watch television with any discrimination. You're fifty-five going on fifteen. Now place your arms akimbo and tell me you did not come here to be insulted."

I must confess even I was a bit surprised at my outburst. There's no reaction like overreaction. Larry rose to his feet only a little unsteadily. "In a word, fuck you, Chadwick. I'm sorry I don't have the world's greatest ideas at my fingertips but I don't jerk off reading the *Encyclopedia Britannica*."

"As a matter of fact neither do I. But I don't have to move my lips to read 'Keep off the Grass.' "

"Perhaps not. But you can certainly move them fast enough if there's a prick, or a pussy – *faugh!* – in the vicinity that wants to be eaten. Remember, darling, you are who you eat."

I found myself laughing out loud. Secretly I adore true vulgarity even though I was annoyed with myself for letting Larry breach the palisade. When one is trying to be haughty one ought not to guffaw.

However, my laughter appeared to annoy Larry. "If there's one thing I can't stand it's a closet straight," he said with a toss.

"No one will ever accuse you of that, my dear Lawrence. The only straight thing about you is the part in your hair. But that is beside the point. The real reason you never read is because you have dyslexia of the soul." I wasn't entirely sure what I meant, but it sounded pompous. "Has it yet occurred to you that you are trembling on the threshold of becoming a dirty old man?"

"Is that right. I shall apply to Dirty Old Manpower for work. And I shall write a book about my visit to Key West. I shall call it *The Dirty Old Man and the Sea*." Larry was quite obviously taking me off and I had to admit it was pretty funny, at least to me. Gin magnifies reaction. He continued. "Why, you might even consider collecting a few of your deathless percus into a slender volume. *The Daring Middle-Aged Man on the Flying Trapezium*, subtitled *Sodomy for Suckers*."

"That's gross! But I suggest you repent before it's too late. If you die with your legs in the air they'll have considerable difficulty fitting you into a coffin."

Larry aimed himself at the door. "On second thought why

don't you call your memoirs *The Dormant Dork*. It will be a companion volume to *The Vacant Vagina*. I, however, shall leave you to write. I intend to see in the New Year with cheap sex."

"You'd better eat something first." I wasn't prepared to back down, nor did I want to see Larry lurch into the night with nothing in his stomach but liquor. He gave me a withering, slightly out-of-focus look. "You can take your Dr. Ballard's daube and stuff it." With the exaggerated dignity of the drunk he heaved himself into his raccoon coat.

"One last word of advice." I could not resist one final dig. "When you use bronzer I suggest you put it on your hands as well as your face. You look like 'Pale hands I love beside the Shalimar.' "

Larry pulled open the front door. "Have you ever considered a sex-change operation? It might turn you into a human being." He banged the door shut.

"You forgot your overshoes," I called as he was halfway down the walk. "Shall I pin your mittens to your sleeves?"

Larry walked stiffly back and took the proffered overshoes as though they were a pair of rotten fish. "I just puckered up my anus so you can kiss me goodnight."

"Good luck with your mouth," I replied sweetly as I shut the door; but Larry, trying to pull on his overshoes while standing up, was too preoccupied to reply.


UNLIKE CERTAIN WINES AND BRANDIES food does not improve with age. I did my best to eat some of Winnifred's daube, but it had a dark-brown taste to match the colour. I pushed it around my plate and drank some more wine and wondered whether I should call Larry before he returned to Toronto. He can well afford the Ritz but as often as not he stays at the YMCA (*Y'a Mayen de Coucher Avec*). Not that I intended to apologize. Once I outgrew my childhood I vowed never to apologize for anything unless I was truly sorry. All children, at least the ones I grew up with, swam through childhood on rivers of apology. If we weren't being made to say "I'm sorry," our mothers were apologizing for us. "So sorry," one mother would call across the street to another. "He's full of the devil today." She would then laugh, a hollow laugh, before hauling the kid inside and bouncing him off the walls.

I longed to be grown up. Being grown up means never having to say you're sorry. And I was certainly not sorry about telling Larry off. I suppose if I were honest with myself I would admit I couldn't care less about Larry's views on women. No resourceful feminist is going to be dashed because an ageing faggot thinks she ought to be scrubbing floors with a cake of yellow soap. What really annoyed me, and still does, is that after years of calling me a friend, Larry knows practically nothing about me. We have never had a single conversation in which my point of view was ever considered, much less solicited. Larry is totally self-centred. As a result he has become above all else trivial. That kind of highly personal triviality is a waste. And I hate waste.

I forced myself to finish what was on my plate before I started getting maudlin. Gin exaggerates all those tendencies that sober I won't even admit to having. It has been called Mother's ruin, only far from ruining my mother it is making her old age infinitely more palatable. Alcohol has been referred to as pain killer more than once during the ages. Even more than physical pain it can ease the mental. Between the gin and the wine I found the thought of Chris had become a dull ache more than an open, uncauterized wound. But Larry, blast him, had put a bee in my bonnet. That's silly; men don't wear bonnets. A bee in my bowler, actually more like a hornet in my Homburg. His lofty announcement that he was going to see in the New Year with cheap sex made me realize in that department there had been next to no activity during the past weeks. A little listless masturbation in the shower hardly measures up to the orgiastic fulfillment promised by the glossy sex-peddling monthlies. And along with everything else gin makes me randy. I really wasn't much interested in sitting surrounded by Winnifred's plants watching 1980 arrive on the television screen. The night was young, and I had to admit the idea of cheap sex sounded quite attractive. Of course cheap sex is what the North American puritan mentality calls good sex, the kind you no longer have with a tired wife or stale mistress or shopworn boyfriend. Ordinarily North Americans blame sex on other countries: French kissing, Greek love, the English vice. Perhaps cheap sex ("It's so good I feel guilty. What was your name again?") is our ethnic contribution to world sex mores. Into every life a little anthropology must fall.

As I checked and double-checked burners and oven to see they were safely turned off, I poured myself a brandy. That was in itself a sporting gesture. Ordinarily if I so far forget myself as to drink brandy in the evening I am still doing the insomnia waltz at 4:00 A M. No wonder it is given to people who faint. Wash down a couple of brandies with two or three cups of strong black coffee and if you fall asleep at the wheel the manufacturer promises to give your life back. I turned off lights, a legacy from my childhood. Father was stern about lights burning in empty rooms, all part of his attitude towards money. Stingy with petty cash, generous with large amounts, small economies brought out his banal side. "A penny saved is a penny earned," which anyone who works for a living knows is bullshit. "Look after the pennies and the pounds take care of themselves." Also bullshit. And I did not have to be told, even as a small boy, that money doesn't grow on trees.

Everything seemed to be in order. I had just slid my right arm into the matching sleeve of my overcoat and was struggling to find the left when the telephone rang. Five steps took me from the passageway into the kitchen, where I glared at the offending instrument attached to the wall like a giant roach. The telephone ignored my disapproving stare and went right on ringing. I had no idea who it could be. Larry did not know the number and anyone else would logically call my apartment. Probably a friend of Winnifred's calling to wish her a Happy New Year. The black box continued to ring. Still half-in, half-out of my overcoat I plucked the receiver from its chrome cradle. "Hello," I said in a tone suggesting I would give Winnifred a message, nothing more.

"Happy New Year, Geoffry." That flutey, farty voice could only belong to my sister.

"Mildred! How did you know I was here?"

"Mother told me you would be. I called to wish her a Happy New Year and she told me you were house sitting for Aunt Winnifred. How is she, by the way?"

"Winnifred? Fine I expect. She promised to send me a card, but you know the lamentable state of the mails. She'll be home long before the card arrives."

"Not Winnifred, Geoffry, Mother. How is Mother? She sounded on the telephone as though she had been drinking."

"I expect she had. If you want her sober, call before noon."

"Geoffry, we've simply got to do something. You really should. What can I do down here in Toronto?"

"Nothing. Unless you can persuade the liquor board employees to go on strike. But then she'd get the housekeeper to drive to Ontario. Maybe I could hide all the glasses in her apartment."

"You're being silly. You know she has a problem and you refuse to do anything about it. But then you always were selfish. Is she still smoking as much?"

"I really don't know. I haven't been counting butts."

"Really, Geoffry. Clever retorts will not solve the problem."

"Neither will snide remarks over the long-distance phone from Toronto. Now what is it you want?" I deeply regretted having picked up the receiver. Mildred could irritate me more quickly than anyone else I knew. Her voice swarmed with mosquitoes, every vowel a black fly, each consonant a gnat.

"I would like you to take a more constructive attitude towards our mother. She's slowly killing herself and you won't lift a finger to stop her."

"Mildred, has it ever occurred to you that life is a terminal illness. Why do you want to keep Mother alive? Is it because she lives such a rich and productive life? The world can't carry on without? Why don't you get your ass onto the Turbo and truck on up here and point out to her the error of her ways, over a drink and a cigarette. She's an old lady, Mildred. The kindest and most moral thing I can do is just to leave her alone to live out her few remaining years as she sees fit."

"You are begging the question. I fully intend to come up just as soon as Bruce's back is enough better so he can manage without me."

"Are you fucking him too hard?"

"Geoffry, that's not the least bit funny. I never met anyone who took so much pleasure in the misfortunes of others."

"That's good coming from you, dear sister. If there was a guillotine in front of Toronto City Hall you'd be front row centre, knitting. Now you didn't call at this ungodly hour to kvetch about Mother." I let my coat slide from my arm over the back of a chair.

"You're right, for once. I want you to give Richard a bed at Aunt Winnifred's for a couple of nights. He wants to go up to Montreal during the holiday."

"Richard? The spotty smartass nephew? And you forgot to say please."

"Please." The word came out like a raw egg dropped onto cement.

"Why doesn't he stay with his grandmother? She has a spare room and plenty of liquor and cigarettes – and a housekeeper."

"I don't want to bother Mother. She has all she can handle with her ankle. That's why I'm asking you."

"You don't want to bother Mother. You have just finished telling me I should hang over and harangue her about smoking and drinking, yet you won't let the first born grandson use her spare room. She'd love to have him; I wouldn't."

"I don't suppose you would."

"And furthermore I'm thinking of –" Just in time I stopped myself from saying "coming to Toronto." Mildred would have nailed me for dinner on the spot. And since I would probably be there only one evening I didn't want to waste it eating underdone beef and overcooked vegetables with my sister and her boring brood. Maybe Toronto could wait until Winnifred got back.

"And furthermore why can't the child – young man – creature – ask me himself?"

"He hardly knows you. You must admit, Geoffry, you haven't exactly fallen over backwards getting to know your nephews and nieces."

"I admit nothing. And you know perfectly well I never talk to anyone under four feet tall." Mildred has always resented my never having played uncle.

"There's another reason." Mildred paused. I knew we were getting down to the real reason for the call. Mildred seldom, if ever, hesitated before she spoke. Not for her the thoughtful pause, the reflective instant before an appropriate answer. Her speech came out as atonal music without rests.

Words formed into phalanxes on her tongue and marched out of her mouth with military precision. Many people thought her intelligent when she was merely articulate. "I'd like Richard to talk to someone else, a member of the family – an adult – who isn't a parent, if you know what I mean."

"You mean he's behaving like a pain in the neck and you want me to straighten him out."

"Well – sort of – yes." Her uncharacteristic pauses told me she was troubled. But I was not prepared to let her off the hook just yet.

"If I can't straighten out my own mother, who's an adult, how do you expect me to deal with a twenty-year-old who isn't. Have you tried putting him into the stocks for a day?"

"Please. Geoffry, if you would only talk to him. I don't know what to do. He's been acting so strange, withdrawn. Neither Bruce nor I can get through to him any more. Oh, dear, I hope he's not on drugs."

"Has he been stealing spoons and selling them to support his habit?"

"No, nothing like that. It's just that we seem to be – so out of touch. Will you at least talk to him?"

I heard the siren song of downtown Montreal. "All right, Mildred, I'll talk to him. Words are cheap. But don't expect any miracles. If the boy's taking a downer on family it may well include me too. And I have a very weak wave length with the young. But I will give him a bed for a couple of nights. And I will talk to him. When is he coming up?"

"Wednesday."

"Tell him to call me from the station. Is there anything else?"

"Not at the moment. Thank you, Geoffry." Mildred's thank you was another egg on asphalt, but I could tell she meant it. Mildred says thank you's all over the place, but her thank you's come from the head, not the heart. The very fact that this thank you came out stiff and ungracious showed it to be genuine. I think Mildred was born toilet-trained.

The second I replaced the receiver I forgot about Richard. Like Scarlett O'Hara I decided to think about that tomorrow, or the day after. I scrambled into my coat and overshoes fearful lest the telephone detain me a second time. I prefer not to drive when I've been drinking, at least most of the time; so I left my car in Winnifred's garage. Luckily for me, she disapproves of the internal combustion engine; she has no car. A block from the house a cruising cab picked me up and took me downtown.

# 3.

THE ONLY DIFFERENCE BETWEEN New Year's Eve and any other Monday night downtown was in the large numbers of people milling about. Xmas decorations were in evidence everywhere, some of them having been up since shortly after Thanksgiving. I did my best to avert my eyes, most especially from the department store window filled with electrically animated stuffed toys doing adorable things, driving trains, and milking cows. How I would love to put a brick through that window; if only I thought I could get away with it. I trudged along, uncertain of where to go or what to do, conscious that everyone else on the streets was in groups or at least pairs. I don't like discos, gay or straight, although I confess it's getting more and more difficult for me to tell them apart. Not that it matters. But young men today are so much more pulled together than when I was twenty, when really caring about how you looked branded you as a sissy or a queer. What I mind about discos is the punishing level of noise, the pounding monotonous beat, and repetitious, raucous lyrics whose performers sound drunk, doped, or demented. Whatever happened to the big band sound – Glenn Miller, Tommy Dorsey, Count Basie – when people held onto one another on the floor. I used to be a good dancer. God, how I loved to waltz, and tango, except when I had a partner who talked nervously, didn't count, and stepped all over my highly polished shoes. Music was mellow then, sex still a mystery, and we all believed change was progress. Now music has grown strident, sex aggressive, and change just another source of dislocation. Gin also gives me a bad attack of the ain't-it-awfuls. Everything from shoe laces to the post office has degenerated since I was a boy. Even gin ain't what it used to be.

I turned the corner at St. Catherine Street onto Peel and skidded on a small patch of ice, executing a buck and wing right into a lamp post.

"Hey, take it easy," drawled a soft, southern voice as I straightened myself out like someone about to make a stage entrance.

The speaker was young, that much I could tell. The face under blow-dried hair shone smooth in the light from the street, and the posture, even muffled by a down-filled parka, crackled with energy. I straightened my grey lamb hat. "A broken leg is a great way to start the New Year," I said half to myself, half to the speaker. I was fine but my dignity suffered a bruise.

"I guess so," replied the young man. "Say, what does one do for excitement in this town? I just got in."

That, of course, was my first clue, more exactly the second. As I played that meeting through the television screen of memory, as I was to do many, many times, I could not countenance how I had been so obtuse. Clue number one: the Peel-St. Catherine corner and the strip down to Dominion Square is a hangout for hustlers. I was an obvious score, a well-dressed, middle-aged man alone on New Year's Eve. Clue number two: how come somebody with a voice full of Georgia or Virginia or Tennessee has just arrived in Montreal yet is fully equipped for winter cold.

But my radar, up to now pretty good, lay dormant, perhaps rusty from disuse. Some years had elapsed since I last made a street pickup, and that is exactly what I did. "Depends what you're looking for." That line was so obvious that if it had been a brick it would have landed on my foot.

"Nothing very pricey," said the young man. "Even with the exchange, I'm pretty strapped."

"How about a drink at my place? I was just on my way home," I lied glibly.

"Suits me," came the soft, slow reply.

Right on cue an empty cab stopped at the light and the two of us climbed in. I was just about to give the address of my apartment; then for a fraction of a second I hesitated. The doorman at my building was no fool; he knew a trick when he saw one. As I was not in the habit of bringing people home off the street I must confess I was reluctant to march this number past the consciously neutral gaze of the night porter. One of the many drawbacks to living in a democracy is being tyrannized by the help. My car sat in Winnifred's garage, and the key to the garage door of my apartment building on the ring with my car keys lay on the spare room dresser. That way was shut. Why not go back to the privacy of Winnifred's house, through the secluded front door, nobody the wiser. I gave the address to the driver.

"What brings you to Montreal?" I asked the young man beside me. I would ordinarily have asked his name, but that would have told the driver I had just picked this person up. In sex, as in just about everything else, I am not democratic.

"I wanted to see Canada – the winter. I thought I could find a job, but I don't speak French."

"You'd be better off in Toronto."

"Right. I plan to go as soon as I can raise the fare."

My father used to talk about people being asleep at the switch. I certainly was. The young man was unemployed and broke. I was just about twice his age with the outward trappings of prosperity, fur hat, expensive overcoat, Gucci gloves. Sober, I would not have touched him with an eleven-foot pole. But I was drunk, lonely, randy. As if that was not enough I found myself excited by the very unfamiliarity of the situation. The element of novelty, not to mention risk, gave zest to what in my youth would have been a routine pickup. I was revisiting my past, a cruise down memory lane; four, five, six, pick up tricks.

In the semi-dark of the back seat the young man's knee found mine. The electric shock of physical contact made conversation superfluous. The cab skidded slightly turning a corner; centrifugal force pushed us together. By the time we pulled up in front of the house my distant early warning system had been totally short-circuited by acute hot pants or crotch fog or plain stupidity. I paid the driver, peeling a five from a sandwich of money in my left trouser pocket, and told him to keep the change. We climbed out of the dirty back seat, stepping on torn newspapers put down in a vain effort to sop up slush. I could see my visitor giving the street and its houses a quick appraisal before following me up the front steps and through the door.

I hung my overcoat on a hook in the passageway leading to the kitchen; the young man tossed his parka onto the oak bench in the hall, to reveal the uniform of all tricks under thirty; jeans with a cotton-polyester shirt over a T-shirt. "Why don't you take off your boots?" I asked, prompted less by a sense of hospitality than concern for Winnifred's floors.

"They aren't dirty," he replied, the refusal softened by the low, gentle tone. I have always found the practice of wearing shoes or boots from the street into the house extremely distasteful and dirty, but I decided not to pursue the subject.

"Drink?" I offered.

"Do you have a beer?"

"Yes."

He followed me into the kitchen while I poured a beer and a highball for myself, which I certainly did not need. "What's your name?"

"Dale."

"I'm Geoff." We shook hands briefly. The homosexual introduction. The instant intimacy of a first name without the responsibility of a second. And if the first name is not already short-Dale, or Rex, or Jean – it is lopped into a nickname – Larry, Dick, or Jim. I'm Geoffry to my friends, Geoff to my tricks.

I led the way back down the passage to the front room. I suppose someone coming into Winnifred's house for the first time, someone who did not make snap judgments on furniture and colour schemes, would consider it a substantial place. The entrance hall is spacious and feeds into a handsome staircase, which leads straight up to a small landing, where it takes a sharp right onto the upper floor. The hall furniture, of oak the colour of strong coffee, strikes me as heavy, as does the bronze chandelier with eight bulbs moulded to resemble candle flames. But the overall effect, and the fact that the detached house is on a quiet street in a good neighbourhood, suggested money, the kind that has been in a family for more than ten minutes.

I could see Dale calculating his surroundings and I had the opportunity to appraise him more closely, now that he had shed the camouflage of an amorphous parka. I could remember birthday parties as a child where favours wrapped in waxed paper turned up mysteriously in the cake. With stubby little fingers we picked the limp waxed paper from the favour, always to be disappointed by the reality of the tawdry little object.

Dale had that assembly-line kind of clean-cut look, which is predicated on plenty of soap, water, and blow drying. His features were regular, skin clear, teeth white and even. It was the kind of face you could see Monday, Tuesday, Wednesday, Thursday, and forget Friday. For all its handsome regularity something around the eyes struck me as not quite right, but it was only a fleeting impression. He carried himself like an athlete, although that too could be blamed on youth and the assembly line. Too short for a basketball player, too light for football, too muscular for track, he might have been a swimmer. But the combination of gin and juxtaposition turned him from just another slightly seedy young man in the street into that obscure object of desire.

"Let's sit down." I indicated the loveseat.

"Nice place you got here," he replied, sitting to rest forearms on knees.

By way of answer I reached out my right hand and let it fall lightly on the nape of his neck. He did not respond. I rubbed his right shoulder; the muscle felt like a ridge of granite. "You must be in pretty good shape," I said. "Do you work out?"

"Karate." The word came out in three leisurely syllables. "I just passed my brown belt."

"I thought black was the highest."

"It is."

"Did you fail the written exam?" I laughed just a shade too hard.

By way of answer he stood and moved past the poinsettia to the centre of the room. Thoughtfully he picked up one of the Mexican figures from the window-seat, a dog with pointed ears and round, bulging sides in red terra cotta from Colima. It happened to be the one genuine piece in Winnifred's collection. I know because I had given it to her for Christmas some years ago.

"This old?" he asked.

"Yes," I replied. "It's from Mexico."

"It's so fragile. How did it last this long without getting broken?"

"Good question. I suppose it's a result of twenty per cent careful handling and eighty per cent good luck."

"You know," he began, "I sure would appreciate a stake to get me to Toronto."

"You need a temporary job. Have you tried Manpower?"

"I don't want to wait that long."

"You could rob a bank, I suppose, but banks don't open until the day after tomorrow."

He smiled, a long, slow smile that was decidedly appealing. "I thought perhaps you could help me out."

"Perhaps, but I don't even know you. Now, why don't you come back and sit down and we'll remedy that." I was beginning to get impatient. After all Dale had made overtures in the cab and now he was beginning to turn me off. I glanced at my watch; 1980 was still about forty-five minutes away, and I decided to forgo watching it sneak in on television.

"I sure would hate to think you were stingy. Why, that watch alone would get me to Toronto and the bills in your pocket would carry me until I found something."

"Is that right. You mean just like that I'm to hand over my watch and wallet in prepayment. You must be dynamite in the sack."

"Who said anything about the sack? I mean you're old enough to be my father." By now he had begun to toss the ceramic figure lightly into the air, to catch as it fell.

"You'd better put that down." I was stung by the crack about my age and my voice had a distinct edge. "Before it gets broken."

By way of reply he tossed the Colima dog high into the air and took one step backwards. The piece fell. Hitting the side of the cobbler's bench it did not so much smash as disintegrate into a small heap of dust and shards. Through the initial shock of seeing something old and valuable deliberately destroyed my mind filtered out two ideas. First, I was being shaken down. Second, I was swept, engulfed, drowned in a red rage that quite literally had me shaking. But through the raw fury I could hear a warning bell. A fifty-year-old man in pretty good shape is no match for a man half his age in top condition. Even if he did not know karate, which I could not tell, he would be a mean opponent. Also, the slightest scuffle would devastate Winnifred's crowded room.

Even as I sat clenched on the loveseat, struggling for control, Dale picked up the alabaster lamp. I knew I could explain away the dog, knocked over by clumsy me as I watered the plants. But if anything happened to that lamp I was dead.

"Okay, okay, put it down," I said, trying unsuccessfully to make my tone conciliatory. "Sit down – in the rocker." After only a momentary hesitation Dale obeyed, although he did not so much sit as crouch on the edge of the seat.

"Now let me get this straight. You want me to hand over my money and my watch and then what?"

"And then I'll leave."

"What if I call the police?"

"I could break your arm before you picked up the phone. But you won't call them anyway. People in this kind of neighbourhood don't bring hustlers home. Even if the cops came what would you say?"

I had to admit he had a point. I was trapped. Sober, I would have been apprehensive, frightened even. Of course sober, I would not have been in this situation. My reaction was not fear but anger. Good judgment dictated I give him the watch and the money. But drinking and thinking don't mix. I should have played it in low – but I didn't. Instead I was swept with the oddest sensation, as if I were in some kind of movie. This was not my life, not the life of Geoffry Chadwick, dull, secure, predictable. I was suddenly living a script, writing it as I experienced it, second by second.

"Very well," I said, "here's the money." I reached into my pocket to take out the roll of bills, which I proferred. Dale stood to reach out his hand; I noticed his nails had been bitten down to the quick. "Would you pass me my cigarettes?" I asked, as he pocketed the money. I did not smoke; the cigarettes and lighter belonged to Larry. But an idea was taking shape in my mind. I lit a cigarette, my hand trembling from tension and anger, and placed the cigarettes and lighter beside the heavy glass ash tray on the cobbler's bench. I puffed deeply, holding the smoke in my mouth for a second or two as if I were inhaling.

"You should give those things up," said Dale. "Bad for you, very bad." He sat.

"Look," I began, "this watch – the one I'm wearing – has a good deal of sentimental value. Besides it's only gold-filled." Both statements were lies. "However, I do have a gold watch upstairs. Would you take it instead of this one?" My tone was pleading. I almost gagged.

"Why not."

"Come on upstairs and have a look." As I rose to my feet I heard a soft click as the switchblade flicked from the handle in Dale's hand. "No tricks," he warned, the threat softened by his mellow drawl.

"No tricks," I replied as I casually picked up the cigarette in a left hand rigid with rage. With my right hand I reached for the ash tray. I walked from the front room and started up the stairs, conscious that my armpits were drenched with perspiration. "It's not cool to sweat," I remember thinking as Dale rose to follow, carrying the knife. But not for nothing had I seen every Hitchcock movie ever made. "You're right," I began as I started the climb. "I should give these things up." I butted the half-smoked cigarette in the ash tray. "I've tried a few times, but you know how it is." I struggled to keep my voice from shaking.

At the landing I paused just long enough to plant my feet firmly. Using a smooth tennis backhand, formed by three years of lessons, I swung the heavy ash tray hard. With a crunching thud it hit Dale on the right temple. His arms flew up, sending the switchblade bouncing down the stairs. Slowly, as if under water, he tilted backwards, struggling without a sound against the momentum of the blow. Flailing arms could not save his balance as he fell away from me; the soles of his boots lost purchase with the step; his feet rose lazily into the air. The back of his head hit the large square newel post with the sound of someone punching a watermelon. Then the body described a graceful half-turn before hitting the floor face downward to lie absolutely still in an obscene sprawl, a Raggedy Andy doll dropped from a great height. From my position on the landing I could tell he was dead. Taking the limp arm to test the pulse was no more than a formality.

As I felt for the non-existent pulse I realized that I had never touched a dead man before. I laid the arm gently back on the floor, suddenly sober; perhaps not cold sober, but all dizziness fell away as my mind clicked suddenly alert. A dead man lay at my feet. And he was dead all right. Dead people do not look as if they are asleep; they look dead. Blood oozed slowly from the gash where his head had hit the newel post. I wanted to turn him on his back but feared getting blood on Winnifred's worn oriental. I hurried to the kitchen and pulled a plastic garbage bag from a drawer. By the time I returned, the cat, her pupils like olives, was sniffing the wound. I whacked her away with the plastic bag, which I then spread beside the body. I wanted to roll it over. It! Alive Dale was he; dead he became it. I hesitated. Perhaps I shouldn't touch the body until the police arrived. Also before they came I thought I had better examine the bulky wallet in the rear pocket so I could at least come up with a last name. I was struck by the wallet itself, elegant pigskin, which folded in two, gold brackets reinforcing the corners. As I slid it from the pocket of the jeans the wallet sprang open as a result of being stuffed to capacity. The slot for bills burst with money, American and Canadian. A cursory glance showed at least three hundred dollars. An Alabaman driver's licence gave his name as Dale Lawton, as did all the major credit cards in polyethylene envelopes, along with an address somewhere in Birmingham. A photograph of a middle-aged couple, the man about my age, showed them in front of a development house in dowdy, respectable clothes. A few business cards, a parking receipt, and a slip for shirts at the laundry were also inside.

I stuffed the wallet back into the jeans pocket. Struck by a sudden idea I hurried into the passageway leading to the kitchen, where on a high shelf I had noticed several summer handbags belonging to Winnifred. I looked in a shapeless straw bag with Nassau sewn across the flap, then through a braided nylon pouch. Finally, in a red plastic envelope I found a small hand-mirror. But how could I test for breath moisture without turning the body over? My sense of decorum made the decision; the dead must lie tidily on their backs. Grasping the body by the left shoulder I made two attempts to roll it over. A lesson in physics: inertia and dead weight, although I was hardly in the mood for jokes. The body undulated slowly onto its back, almost as if the skeleton had turned to plasticene. The eyes were open, expressionless. A foolish observation. Eyes have no expression. The face surrounding the eye animates iris and pupil. Now they were just two eyes in a slack, dead face. But I noticed for the first time why the eyes had bothered me initially. In the harsh glare of the overhead fixture I could see the eyes did not match; one was green, the other blue. Green and blue also figured prominently in a large bruise beginning to form on the right temple. Gingerly I held the small, square mirror in front of the mouth. Not a trace of moisture clouded the glass. I straightened up. About to slide the mirror into my pocket I reconsidered and put it back in the plastic purse, which I returned to the shelf. Break a mirror and you will have seven years' bad luck.

Even someone who didn't watch all the police shows on television could have figured out that a person does not fall backward down the stairs and end up with a large bruise on his temple, a large gash on the back of his head. That bruise would blow a hole in the story that Dale stumbled on the stairs and lost balance to fall back. Even dead he did not look like someone who slips on stairs. Another nice question: Which blow killed Dale Lawton? If he died as a result of a blow on the back of his head the verdict might well be accidental death. But what if he died from the blow on the temple? My stomach turned over at the recollection of the terrible, sickening sound, glass against bone. Was I guilty of manslaughter, maybe even murder? The blow was certainly premeditated. I asked Dale to hand me Larry's cigarettes so I could pretend to smoke and thereby pick up the ash tray without suspicion. What exactly was I going to tell the police? I had better call them soon. The downstairs telephone hung in the kitchen, where only an hour or so ago I had been talking to my sister.

I froze at the sound of the doorbell. Who could be ringing minutes before the old year faded into the new? Would it seem more suspicious not to open the door? Lights blazed throughout the ground floor. Should I pretend to be out? Whether I acted without thinking or whether my mind went into overdrive I'll never know. Grabbing the body under the armpits I dragged it down the passageway, down the basement stairs, heels thumping on each step, past the laundry tubs to dump it, without ceremony, behind the furnace near the hot-water heater. There are times when simile fails. It was not like dragging a giant puppet or a sack of bran or a rolled up rug. It was like dragging a dead body.

The doorbell rang a second time. At this point the scenario began to fall apart; there ought to have been a blanket or a sheet or a drop cloth to throw over the body. But Winnifred ran a tight ship; her basement was not equipped to conceal corpses. I could only hope the person at the door had not come to repair the furnace or tinker with the hot-water tank.

I was back in the hall when I remembered the open switchblade still lying on the floor near the spot where Dale's body had landed. I had no idea how to retract the blade. The doorbell gave a third strident ring. "Just a minute," I called as I wrapped the knife tightly in the plastic bag still lying spread over the rug. Then I ducked into the front room and stuffed the package into the brass coal scuttle sitting beside the desk and serving as wastebasket. By now whoever it was had given up the doorbell and was pounding on the door with heavy, rhythmical blows. Had I been in a movie I would have paused for breath before opening the door. Panting, I fumbled with the latch. Larry stood on the doorstep.

"When two Eskimos fuck is it called Nanooky or just sex on the rocks? As part of my New Year's resolutions I've decided to forgive you. Also I forgot my cigarettes and lighter. Are you going to let me in or shall we see in the New Year on the front step?"

"No – not on the front step – of course not – sorry – I was upstairs. Come in – come inside." I forced myself to pause, to take control. "So you're back. I thought you went off to find true love."

"I did, but he was so zonked out on something or other I split. Drugs and sex don't mix. I'd as soon sleep with a corpse as with someone who's so spaced out he can hardly walk. Remember the one about the necrophiliac? 'Not guilty, Your Honour. I didn't know he was dead. I thought he was English.'" As if drawn by a magnetic field Larry headed for the bar in the kitchen, tossing his coat at a hook as he walked unsteadily down the passage.

"Pour yourself a drink," I called after him as I made a quick check around the foot of the stairs, smoothing out the oriental rug dragged crooked by the heels of the corpse. Then going quickly to the front room, I bent over the coal scuttle and covered the plastic package with the paper debris lying under it.

Larry came down the passageway with two highballs the colour of old tea. Then I remembered the drink I had poured for myself only minutes ago. Too late. And the untouched glass of beer sat in full view beside the fern. "Me-oh-my, we are seeing in the New Year *comme il faut*," he remarked, placing the drink he had just poured beside the one already sitting on the table. "Double your pleasure; double your fun; get pissed on two drinks; they're better than one!" He glanced into the hall, then walked over to the bench.

"Why, Geoffry Chadwick, I'm surprised at you," he said, picking up Dale's parka from off the floor, where it had fallen. He held it up by one sleeve. "A trick? Wearing a parka? A woman of your age and station? I've a good mind to rap you sharply across the wrist with my fan. *Là*, sir, fetch my *sal volatile*. More important: Where is he? Where's the body? Fess up now."

I walked over and took the parka from Larry and carried it into the passageway to hang on a hook. By the time I returned I was ready.

"It's not what you think," I replied, surprised at my own glibness; but necessity mothers invention. "It – actually it belongs to my nephew. He's come to spend a few days. He arrived just after you left."

"A likely story. Is it bigger than a breadstick?"

"How should I know. I'm not into incest."

"You really have a nephew?"

"Yes, of course. My sister Mildred's son."

"I repeat: Where is he?"

"He was tired out. He went to bed."

"How old?"

"Around twenty, I guess."

"You don't expect me to believe someone twenty years old would go to bed before midnight on New Year's Eve. Why didn't he drink his beer?"

"How should I know?"

"Do you suppose I should go upstairs and wish him Happy New Year?" Larry said, making for the staircase.

"No! I don't think you should go upstairs and wish him Happy New Year."

"The trouble with you, Chadwick, is you're a born chaperone."

Weaving his way over to the television set Larry pushed the On button. "Why don't you play the old man with the hourglass and the big butch scythe. I'll rush in wrapped in a shocking-pink ribbon embossed with 1980. Better still, I could be carried in by a pair of muscle-bound blacks. Yum! Enter slaves bearing fruit. I won't wear a diaper, though. I have some fetching leopard skin briefs, not real leopard, mind you. Endangered species and all that. I'm an endangered species myself. We'll do a *tableau vivant* – or is it a *nature morte*? A living picture or a dead nature?"

Superimposed on a haze of dancing figures numbers flashed onto the screen by a computer, whittling away the seconds: 11:55 ... 11:56 ... 11:57 ... 11:58 ... 11:59 ... 1980! Larry sat heavily in the easy chair. "Happy Groundhog Day." Taking a deep swallow of his drink he put the glass on the floor beside his chair. Then he passed out cold.

I remember reading, some years ago, a Dorothy Parker story about newlyweds on a train to New York City for their honeymoon. "Well, here we are," one says to the other who replies, "Yes, here we are." "Well, here we are," and so on. I was tempted to make the same observation. Well, here we are: Larry out cold in the chair, me strung out on the loveseat, Dale growing cold in the basement – not to mention the hypothetical presence of my nephew in one of the bedrooms upstairs. Stealing out into the hall I crept up the staircase like a cat burglar. Once past the landing, I let out an audible gasp as my foot struck the ash tray, the murder weapon, which I had left, without thinking, on the top stair. I carried the ash tray into the spare room and slid it into a drawer in the dresser. From the bed I took a folded afghan, knitted squares crocheted together and fringed with tatting, and stole down to the basement only to discover the cat crouched on the corpse like something out of Edgar Allan Poe at his most lurid. I hissed and she tore away with a snarl. I covered the body. It lay pretty well concealed behind the furnace, but would be hell to move once rigor mortis set in. Rigor Mortis, sounds almost Swedish – or Danish. "How do you do, Mr. Mortis. Come in, won't you? I'm Mr. Chadwick. Rigor? Then you must call me Geoffry. This way to the basement, please." Of course, if I called the police right now they would come at once, before the body lost its heat and flexibility.

And then I realized I was not going to call the police. My reasons, although complex, could be stated quite simply. I dreaded the scandal. For someone to whom privacy is almost as necessary to life as oxygen the mere thought of publicity had me in a cold panic. I could not face the houseful of police asking the kinds of questions I knew they must ask, not least of which was how the body ended up behind the hot-water heater. How was I to explain away Larry, who would wake up and try to put the make on the youngest officer present. I could just hear it: "Do you always carry a gun? I'd love to see it sometime." Winnifred would arrive home fresh from the locks of Panama to discover her house in the papers and her nephew under suspicion of murder.

Nor did I think the firm of Lyall, Pierce, Chadwick, and Dawson would be overjoyed to see the Chadwick part accused of something not quite pukka. "Always had my doubts about Chadwick. Never remarried. No women in his life I ever heard of. Bad business." It was unlikely I could convince the police that Dale's death was accidental now that I had moved the body. And his indisputable presence in my aunt's house was suspect. He was not a client, not even a friend. I did not kidnap him, nor did I bring him back to look at my stamp collection. Even if I never went to trial the story would spread through the grapevine. It would animate many a dinner party and leaven a business lunch. Whatever the social stigma I would have to bear would be nothing compared to the damage to my professional reputation.

One of the few advantages of law, a truly dreary profession except on television, is that it encourages orderly thinking. I sat down at the kitchen table with a glass of milk. My mind refused to settle, shifting first one way and then the other, like a well-oiled weathervane. Sleep was out of the question. I thought of adding a dash of brandy to the milk, only to kill that aggressively wholesome taste, but decided to hang onto what few wits remained about me. The house was strewn with bodies, not to mention the cat, who had taken up sentinel position outside the closed basement door. For her this was some kind of game. Maybe I should try to imagine the situation as a diversion, a game with me the only player, with no rules, and the knowledge that I was to win or lose everything I had. And I realized I could do nothing about the body in the basement before I managed to get rid of the body in the front room. But then what?

One thing I will say for murder: it takes your mind off your other problems. I realized that since I had met Dale at the corner of Peel and St. Catherine, I had not given a thought to Chris. I watched 1979 slide into memory without so much as a backward glance. And 1980 was not off to a shining start. If only Chris had been there to talk things out with, I thought. What would he have said about the mess I was in? If only he had been there, I wouldn't have been in my predicament. If only. But I already knew what he would have said. Call the police and tell them the truth. Take what is coming to you. Let justice be done. Chris believed in the system. How could he not, and be a good teacher? He put more faith in the law than I ever did. He believed if the law was bad it must be changed, but we were not at liberty to disobey. We were handed that line of bullshit during first year law school, windy abstractions and half-truths about natural law and the immutability of justice, making us believe we were embarking on something noble and worth while. I remembered the guest speaker at graduation, in love with his own rhetoric, and quoting Oliver Wendell Holmes: "The Law, wherein, as in a magic mirror, we see reflected not only our own lives, but the lives of all men that have been! When I think on this majestic theme, my eyes dazzle." Then we graduated and the system stepped all over us.

But where did one go to learn the important things: how to get rid of a drunken friend without making him suspicious; how to dispose of a dead body; how to behave for the world as though nothing had happened? Removal, Recycling, Resilience – these were the three Rs I had to learn, and fast!

On second thought, Chris's presence would have been more of a liability than a help. Knowing my general distaste for young people, a distaste I frequently advertised, Chris would never have understood why I sought out a Dale Lawton, even for simple, uncomplicated sex. I do not as a rule seek out people younger than myself. The young make such heavy conversational weather. Either they want to talk in sweeping generalities, like people who work for the CBC, or they tell you where they bought it and how much it cost or, worst of all, they talk horoscopes, signs and cusps and ascendants, and all that drivel. It had been years since I approached a younger man for sex, and the outcome had been, to say the least, unfortunate. I was suddenly engulfed with weariness, a feeling of total depletion. I put my head into my crossed arms and fell asleep at the kitchen table.

A FEW HOURS LATER, stiff and cramped and with a pounding headache and a mouth full of moss, I awoke; not a happy way to begin the New Year. I looked in on Larry, who had moved from the chair to the loveseat, and lay curled up asleep like a foetus. A quick shower and two codeine aspirins helped to get my motor turning over. It would be impressive to say

I took a bracing cold shower, but the truth remains that I have never taken a cold shower in my entire life. To be physically uncomfortable does not make one a better person; and I firmly believe those who sleep on a Beautyrest mattress and wear 100 per cent cotton underwear get to heaven just as fast as those who mortify the flesh. As I wanted to appear as casual as possible I put on my robe. Halfway down the stairs I spotted a cigarette butt, the one I had extinguished before clouting Dale with the ash tray. I dropped it into my pocket.

A hoarse voice came from the front room. "Your mother's not a well woman. But all I want is coffee and an improving book. Shakespeare? Milton? Aristotle? How about a little Plato?"

"How about a plate o' bacon and eggs?" I managed to quip, ever the thoughtful host, hoping desperately he was not hungry. Aside from my anxiety to get rid of Larry I honestly did not think I could face looking at a piece of uncooked bacon or a raw egg.

"You kill me. If that pun weren't enough to gag a maggot the idea of food certainly would. I shall arise and go now – back to my hotel, where I will shower and shave and order toast, coffee, and a Bloody Mary from room service. Maybe the waiter will be cute and not too busy." Larry sighed a long theatrical sigh. "Once, just once in my life, I want to be awake when the Sandman comes. What are your plans for lunch?"

"I'm busy," I lied.

"Your – nephew?"

"No."

"Can't you get out of it?"

"Not really." The lie would have to grow tall and put on weight. "It's a New Year's brunch, or luncheon, to be more precise. Knees under the table at one, pairs, all rather laid on. Maybe later. When do you return to Toronto?"

"Whenever. It's open."

"Call me this afternoon. Coffee?"

"Instant?"

"It's all I have." I lied, hoping he'd leave.

## SUNDAY'S CHILD

"I'll wait. Instant coffee is like masturbation; it's no substitute for the real thing. On that elevating thought I'll leave you." Heaving himself to his feet Larry pulled on his overcoat and stumbled out the door. I realized with a rush of relief I had not given him Winnifred's telephone number and I was reasonably certain he did not know she had resumed her maiden name.

I pulled on a shirt and trousers and went downstairs to confront the cadaver.

It hadn't moved, unfortunately. Besides, the cat had been keeping a sharp eye outside the closed basement door, all night it seemed. I pulled back the afghan to reveal the discoloured face of Dale Lawton, not rouged and powdered as in a funeral parlour, but greenish in places, pallid, and very, very dead. If only I had called the police immediately. If only I hadn't moved the body. If only Larry had not arrived. If only.

But I had not called the police and Larry had arrived, and the rest of my life lay on the line. At that particular moment I did not dwell upon the sanctity of human life and the terrible sin of taking it. I was not my brother's keeper. I was the travelling salesman with a wife and four kids who finds two teenagers vandalizing his car and takes after them with a monkey wrench. That car is far more important to him than the well-being of a pair of punks. My life and the tranquil continuation thereof seemed far more important than confessing to the accidental slaying of a southern street-hustler. But I couldn't think about it tomorrow; tomorrow was today. I had to dispose of the body, and at once.

Being an amateur in the disposal of corpses I was uncertain where to begin. If only I had not answered the door to Larry I could have started up my car, eased Dale into the passenger seat while he was still warm and flexible, and pushed him out on some deserted strip of road as just another New Year's Eve casualty. If only. Disposing of bodies always seems so simple in the movies. The director always provides a handy carpet, which no one will ever miss, to envelop the body. Or there is a wheelchair sitting handily around or an empty steamer trunk below stairs. Sometimes there is a basement, still unexplored and uncolonized, with root cellars and furnace alcoves and a bag of convenient concrete, complete with instructions. Just add hot water and stir.

Some years ago, more years than I would care to count, I, along with the senior students in my law class, was invited to an autopsy to learn just how cause of death can be ascertained. The corpse, an unidentified vagrant we were informed, was wheeled in on a trolley and tipped without ceremony onto a steel-topped table. We were seated on chairs in an amphitheatre belonging to the Faculty of Medicine. The actual tools, however, struck me as odd, not to say crude: a knife, a saw, a pair of pruning shears.

It was a blunt, brutal spectacle, which had many of us bolting for the door. The knife served to make an incision down the front of the trunk, after which the rib cage was cut with the shears and pulled back to expose the lungs, pink, spongy, and in remarkably good condition for a corpse of his years, we were informed matter-of-factly. Pulmonary complications had not killed our mystery cadaver. Vital organs plucked at random from the abdominal cavity next appeared, larger than life, glistening, intimate, obscenely so. The heart, healthy, the liver, an immense purple slab, more vast than I could have imagined would possibly be contained in that emaciated abdomen. Kidney, spleen, all healthy, none offering a clue as to cause of death.

Then came the part that made my palms really sweat. Up to now I had faced everything with only an occasional uneasy squirm. Picking up the knife the white-coated lecturer made a neat incision across the forehead, like Cochise scalping someone from central casting. Peeling back the scalp he took the saw, an ordinary household workbench saw, and cut off the top of the man's head. The sound got to me more than the sight, the rasping crunch of saw tooth against skull. The top of the head opened to reveal the mystery of death to those few students still in the room. A blood clot on the brain, casually poked with a probe, had struck our nameless derelict and caused him to die unclaimed in the street.

Mixed with queasiness I remember being struck with the terrible indignity of the spectacle. Death is undignified, except in the theatre. But to have already undergone the humiliation of the death rattle, the final heartbeat, the final spasm, only to be carved up like a Christmas turkey, struck me as beyond everything, the ultimate desecration, the quintessential rape. Sad, and sick to my soul, I left the amphitheatre.

And now I was about to perform a similar violation. I intended to cut the body of Dale Lawton into portable sections, stow them in the deep freeze, and dispose of them piecemeal. I looked about for tools. Before he moved out, Winnifred's husband dabbled in cabinet making. From a well-stocked workbench had come a stream of occasional tables, curio shelves, straight-backed chairs; heavy, sturdy, ugly, glazed with yellow varnish and pressed upon reluctant friends. Whatever I needed lay at hand.

First I covered the tiny basement windows, already swathed in net, with bathtowels, even though I did not expect the neighbours to begin the New Year prowling about the house and pressing their noses to the panes of Winnifred's cellar windows. Then I pulled and rocked the body onto a bed of plastic bags, spread flat. Using tin shears I cut the clothing from the body, taking the wallet and belt from the jeans. Impeded by my own clothes I stripped down to my jockey shorts. The basement was cold. All older heating systems push heat to the upper floors, but I found myself perspiring freely. The body of Dale Lawton lay naked on the floor except for a large digital watch hidden before by the cuff of his shirt. On each bare forearm a tattooed dragon curled from elbow to wrist. Kneeling beside the body, in a grotesque parody of a loving gesture I lifted his hand in mine and slid the watch with its flexible band from his wrist. Then I stood looking down at the dead man. He had the smallest cock I had ever seen.

I put the watch on the workbench beside the wallet and belt and went barefoot up to the front room, where I fished the plastic package containing the switchblade from the wastebasket. On my way downstairs I shut the basement door to keep the cat away, though it clawed and howled at the door. Kneeling once more beside the corpse I used the scalpel-sharp knife to make preliminary incisions. Anyone watching me bending over Dale would have thought I was about to take him in my arms not, quite literally, to take him apart. I then took a hacksaw and cut through the legs at the knees. I sawed the thighs from the trunk. It was obscene and disgusting but I did it. I cut through the arms at the elbows and again at the shoulder. My hands were sweating so heavily I had to wipe them repeatedly on the cut clothing. Finally I sawed through the neck. Because the body was stiff and the basement cold there was little mess.

I emptied the deep freeze of odds and bits of leftovers, packages of hamburger, sausages on special, and legs of New Zealand lamb, bought, no doubt, on sale and carted them up to the kitchen refrigerator. Then I wrapped the two pieces of each arm, neatly taped together with masking tape, the two sections of each leg, the torso, and the head, each in double garbage bags, one inside the other. For the torso I used the oversized bags one uses to collect raked leaves in autumn. I made one package of the two arms, one of each leg; five packages in all. I lifted the torso into the empty deep freeze and arranged the other packages neatly around it, then shut the lid.

I put the switchblade knife, the saw, and the shears into the dishwasher, which I started. Then, with a jolt, I remembered the ash tray, still in the drawer of the spare room dresser. Taking the stairs two at a time, up and down, I carried it to the kitchen. As I turned the handle the appliance grumbled to a stop. I placed the ash tray on the rack beside the other objects, already coated in a milky, soapy film, erasing all traces of the deed. After restarting the machine I returned to the basement where I rolled the plastic bags on the floor into a tight bundle and thrust them deep into the kitchen garbage to be put out in the garbage for routine collection. I mopped up seepage with paper towels, which I then burned in the fireplace.

As soon as the dishwasher had finished its rinse cycle I took a shower, scrubbing my hands with a nail brush until they were red and sore. I dressed and went back to the basement. I folded the cut clothing neatly after checking it carefully for identification. All was totally commonplace; the shabby garments could have been bought anywhere. Only the boots and belt bore the stamp of a boutique specializing in leather. They looked custom made and expensive; possibly they could be traced. I would dispose of them separately. I rolled the belt into a tight coil and slid it into one of the boots before sliding the pair sideways, one at a time, under the hot-water heater. I retrieved the wallet and digital watch from the workbench and dropped them into my pants pocket, then placed the folded clothing neatly in a shopping bag, which had been hanging on a nail beside the stairs. I carried it up to the ground floor, where I took Dale's parka from the passageway and stuffed it in. The shopping bag of clothing looked like a shopping bag of clothing, nothing more.

I unloaded everything from the dishwasher, making sure each object was dry. I returned the ash tray to the front room, the tools to the basement workbench. It took me several tries before I succeeded in retracting the blade of the knife; in the process I narrowly missed gashing myself across the palm. I carried the digital watch, the wallet, and the knife, up to the spare room and tucked them into my overnight bag. My own money, pushed casually into the pocket of Dale's shirt, was now in my trouser pocket. With a dustpan and whisk broom, found under the kitchen sink, I swept up the remains of the Colima dog from the floor beside the cobbler's bench. Fortunately Larry had been too drunk and too hung over to notice the mess, although I would probably have blamed the cat. Then I folded the bathtowels, covering the basement windows, and returned them to the linen closet.

I dressed to go out, then paused. Men wearing Prince Alberts do not generally carry shopping bags of old clothing onto the bus. Hanging in the passageway I found another parka, which must have belonged to Winnifred's husband, and put it on instead of my overcoat. Carrying my shopping bag, I left the house and shut the front door.

# 4.

NOT A SINGLE HUMAN BEING broke the tranquility of the street, no joggers, not even someone walking a dog. Odd considering the pet population of the neighbourhood is enormous. Every house harbours at least one gigantic dog, whose ancestors roamed the sweeping Steppes of Russia or prowled the melancholy mists of Ireland or raced the scorching sands of Persia or mushed across the frozen fields of our own harsh land. A walk to the bus stop on any day of the week discovers more wild animals than one would ever see during a month in the country. But this morning even the squirrels were sleeping it off.

I walked quickly down to Sherbrooke Street, where I stood for fifteen chilly minutes until a bus pulled up. My mind always blanks out at bus stops. I don't even daydream or woolgather. People waiting for buses lose their identity, like people in airports. When I see someone I know waiting for a bus I hurry past, hoping he or she won't see me, almost as if he were doing something shameful. I infrequently ride the bus. I do not like to be thrust into an indiscriminate crowd of people, most of whom I would not acknowledge on the street and at least one of whom has a bad cold he is only too willing to share. But wearing a parka, its hood framing my face like a cowl, and carrying my shopping bag, I looked and felt suitably anonymous. Thankfully, the bus was sparsely populated, a handful of all-night revellers, beginning the New Year unhappily, and a sprinkling of grim-faced people obliged to work on the holiday. Steam clouded the window, but the warmth of the bus thawed my mind. Try as I might I could not prevent the images from flooding my consciousness in waves. There are times when I envy the so-called baser creatures, like Winnifred's cat, who are not burdened with memory.

Holding a bag stuffed with a dead hustler's clothing on my lap I found myself thinking of Chris. The images dancing around in my memory fine-tuned themselves into recollections of last New Year's Eve. Chris had gone to Kingston with Audrey and the children to spend Christmas with Audrey's mother, a widow who had turned into an absolutely rapacious grandmother. She had spent all year knitting for the family, all of December baking, and the entire week before Christmas cleaning; consequently she exacted such a toll of gratitude that everyone was exhausted. Chris pleaded school business and returned to Montreal New Year's Eve.

To me, Audrey was always an enigma. A cool, beautiful blonde, she had become adept at the social game of using words to conceal her true meaning. She was always conventionally charming to me, not that I saw that much of her. She caused cracks to appear in my poise; I was her husband's lover and her presence made me uncomfortable. Not that I thought she knew. She and Chris had one of those working marriages: home, children, work, church, committees. A good deal of mutual respect and support, a partnership.

I found talking to Audrey difficult; outside of Chris we had surprisingly little in common considering how Anglo we both were. By way of small talk I used to single out something she was wearing for comment, on the lines of, "My, that's a handsome ring. Mexican?" Relating the purchase gave her the chance to manufacture a little conversation. The ploy had worked once; I used it again. "You've had your hair cut. I like the colour of your blouse. Interesting earrings; they look as if they might have come from your grandmother." Most people enjoy being noticed; Audrey was no exception. And she was a woman one noticed.

I had always thought of her as miscast. Instead of underplaying the role of assistant headmaster's wife she should have married a man placed high in a large corporation, perhaps a cabinet minister, someone for whom an elegant wife would have been a distinct asset. I watched her operate once, at a Haddley graduation. It was the year I met Chris; all those who had lectured the senior class as part of the career counselling program were invited. I had not wished to attend, but Chris had leaned on me and I couldn't refuse. Besides, the guest speaker was a client of mine, a pompous windbag, who was forever trying, unsuccessfully, to get himself elected to Parliament. His theme had been the interdependence of society; we were all "cogs in one giant machine." Then he switched metaphors. "Consider the termite," he began. "The worker termite is just about blind and cannot therefore strike, picket, or stage sit-ins. If only our Canadian workers would follow the sterling example set by the termite workers, then capitalism would live forever." He went on to point out that the warrior termites cannot feed themselves and must depend on the workers for food. "Can you imagine the provincial police or the riot squad totally immobilized while the striking workers feed them Big Macs and Pepsi-Cola?" He waited; the junior school giggled on cue. The rest of us sat in a trance of boredom. It had been a hot June day and the gymnasium was stifling. Not content to leave the termite there, the speaker went on to draw the obvious moral that agents of the law are part of society too. Next came a cautionary word for those who seek power. "The queen remains queen only so long as she does her job, grinding out eggs approximately sixty a minute. As soon as she falls behind production schedules she is devoured by the workers. Power is responsibility." I found myself wondering idly about a society where old queens love to eat workers, enough to pay money and risk beatings.

The ceremony ended, finally. Over tea and punch I watched Audrey, in an understated little nothing black dress (which brought out her hair), carry stage centre around with her as she moved through the crowd. She totally eclipsed the other Haddley wives, who fell roughly into two camps: the dumpy ones who wore silk print suits with a brooch on the lapel or a charm bracelet, and the younger ones who tugged their hair back into an earnest bun and wore flat-heeled shoes. The men on staff cruised Audrey, looking at her in that furtive, unpleasant way that men look at a woman they know they can't have. Several of the fathers were a shade too attentive. But to watch her operate around Chris impressed me. A smile, a handshake, a brief exchange with a parent, all attention for another, laughing at a joke – a laugh more platinum than silver – she knew her role and played it beautifully. I realized she would make a formidable antagonist, even if the excitement had left their marriage. But then it generally does.

What Chris saw in me was the possibility of a little excitement, and illicit excitement at that. I didn't alienate his affection for Audrey, not by a long shot. Like a ripe peach, he was so ready to fall, all I had to do was stand with my hat held upside down under the branch to catch him. An important aspect of the middle-aged male menopause, one that is consistently ignored by advice-to-the-lovelorn columns, is that some men grow tired of screwing not only their wives but women in general. They grow bored with heterosexual sex; they just don't want to plug that hole one more time. Socially approved sex can pall; even threesomes and wife swapping won't fill the bill for everyone. So they strike out: bars, baths, soft drugs. Sometimes they turn a bit kinky and go after little girls or little boys or fatties or geriatrics. For the most part, however, those who are not chasing young and nubile women are chasing young and nubile men.

I think the reason Chris responded to me is that I wasn't young. Private schools teem with adolescents, and Chris looked on anyone under twenty-five with professional distance. Young people were his livelihood, and he treated them with the affectionate detachment a gardener might show for sprouting cabbages. The very proximity of the young gave him immunity. I have sometimes wondered whether dairy farmers ever drink milk or poultry raisers tuck into a bucket of Kentucky Fried Chicken.

My age put me well out of the student category, and I certainly was available. As I said before I am what passes for an attractive man if you happen to like the type. Chris did. He also liked the idea of my being a lawyer. If one is going to break the rules, better with someone of one's own class who has an established profession. Along with their other considerable drawbacks private schools are breeding grounds for snobbery. Snobberies, I should say; neither staff nor pupils are immune. Those students from outside Montreal who cannot boast local family fall back on school vacations at St. Moritz or celebrity houseguests or why they bought Lincoln instead of Cadillac or Pucci, Gucci, Halston, Klein, St. Laurent, de la Renta, and the rest of those who have grown thin catering to moneyed insecurity. Chris was very aware that his father had been a judge and his grandfather a Member of Parliament. Audrey herself came from an established Kingston family. They lived in a house so good-tasty it set one's teeth on edge. Everything from the pale green walls to the beige broadloom to the early and not terribly good Goodridge Roberts over the mantelpiece had that just-so look that exiled ease. The path to the Currier and Ives coaster found itself blocked by the Eskimo carving, a hunter harpooning a seal, around which one had to reach carefully in order to put down the Waterford tumbler, Eileen pattern. It made my own apartment seem positively carefree and slapdash; a pad.

Not that I went to Chris and Audrey's very often, sometimes as extra man at a dinner party, once or twice for bridge, a game I dislike and play badly. Chris had the ability to regard me as nothing more than a friend when I was under his roof. I almost envied the way he could compartmentalize his feelings. When he came to my apartment he came as a lover, as eager and ardent as someone half his age. On the other hand, I could not slide him into ready slots; in his home I felt like an interloper. After a while I stopped going altogether.

My plan being to stow the bag of clothing in a luggage locker, I got off when the bus came to a stop in front of the provincial terminus. As I pushed through the door I happened to notice a woman at the information counter standing in three-quarter profile. God almighty! It was Millicent MacLean. I wondered what the hell she was doing at the bus depot. Without waiting to find out I fled back through the swinging door, almost colliding with a stout woman lugging a carton tied with rope. I scrambled into a waiting taxi and told the driver to take me to Windsor Station. Why not. I was a friend of Windsor Station, having donated a small, tax deductible sum to keep that hideous pile of Victorian architecture from being torn down. I don't much like Windsor Station, but at least it is a known evil, better no doubt than the high-rise instant slum, which would be knocked together in a matter of weeks to replace it. The driver wished me a Happy New Year in French. I returned the wish in a tone which suggested further good wishes or conversation would be unwelcome. He observed that it was warm for this time of year. I agreed. He said I was out early on New Year's Day. I agreed. He confided he had been driving all night. I allowed as how he must be tired. He agreed. I longed to tell him just to keep quiet, but I was beginning to learn the price one pays for having a guilty secret. One does nothing to draw attention to oneself; one plays it in low. Yet ordinarily I might have responded to the simple good will of a tired man wishing me well, but the shopping bag of dead man's clothing on the seat beside me soured the milk of human kindness.

The cab drew up in front of the irregular-shaped grey limestone building. To compensate for my foul mood I overtipped the driver. Then into the vast, deserted concourse, once a temple to trains, now visited by only a devout few, like a gothic cathedral in some obscure foreign city far from the beaten tourist path. I walked over to a bank of lockers, shoved a quarter into the slot, and pushed the bag of clothing into the rectangular hole as far as it would go.

Outside the station I stood for a moment, uncertain. A walk might clear the fumes from my brain. Maybe some breakfast at a greasy spoon. I had to look after myself, at least until I disposed of the various Dale Lawton fragments now congealing in Winnifred's deep freeze.

Dorchester Boulevard at best is bleak. Even the gentle April rain, the soft May breeze, the laughing June sun, cannot metamorphose the street into anything but a long, dull street flanked with tall, expressionless buildings, towering over rows of shoe boxes. With its concrete strip dividing east and west lanes the street has a certain awful symmetry further enhanced by the strophe-antistrophe of construction and demolition, a paradigm of urban ugly. On a cold January morning the non-existent charm is diminished, but it suited my mood as I tramped along, flagellating myself with the recollection of the year before.

Chris and I hadn't even stayed up to see the New Year in. He was exhausted after Christmas in Kingston; keeping up appearances can be tiring. One thing I will say for Audrey and Chris; regardless of what they felt about one another they maintained a flawless façade, brittle as glass perhaps but smooth as enamel. Not even the children suspected their *Better Homes and Gardens* life wasn't made with one hundred per cent pure butter. I am certain that is why your well brought up English Canadian is so curiously non-aggressive; he uses up his aggression just fighting himself. Warlike people are seldom introspective. But the English Canadian is a little like one of those land mines left over from the Second World War, which still turn up from time to time. No trouble if you don't kick it too hard. But like the mine we go with a considerable bang if detonated. Left alone we tick quietly away, submerged and inoffensive.

Chris and I shared a wavelength on stress. Our private radar scanners picked up small signals of tension or impatience, a tilt of the head, an angle of the shoulders, even the way of gripping a glass, which beamed that the day had been less than ideal. Our body language reduced itself to shorthand. The whole cloth we were cut from was tarred with the same brush, as I had once suggested to him. Like most teachers would have he bristled at the mixed metaphor.

"You're doing it again," he said mock ominously.

"You rose to the bait," I replied gleefully. "How about birds of a feather who flock together are tarred with the same brush."

"Speaking of tar and feathers ..."

"Okay, okay. I was just trying to separate the men from the sheep."

God, doesn't it sound childish or dreary or both? But then love is except for the people directly involved. To be a spectator around people in love, especially young people in love, is one of life's more boring situations. All that smiling and cooing and petting and pawing are enough to make one turn Trappist.

Being in love, really in love, is a kind of sickness; and anyone with a shred of self-respect conceals the symptoms. Being sick is bad manners, especially in evergreen North America, land of jogging suits and crunchy granola. People die of heart attacks in the street not because passersby think they are drunk but because their obvious distress is an affront to the rightness of things. People just don't do that sort of thing. One simply does not talk back to one's elders, push peas onto the fork with the thumb, or die in the street. It is bad form. But the young have yet to learn that what we call good manners is an elaborate defence mechanism designed to protect the middle aged and elderly. With few exceptions the young have no awareness of anyone outside themselves; hence they are invulnerable, self-protective like aluminum. And with the possible exception of Romeo and Juliet young lovers are a pain in the ass.

So are middle-aged lovers, I expect, only they are a little more artful at concealing the symptoms. I digress. Maybe it's that I don't want to remember last New Year's Day, on which we arose fresh, rested, and free of the traditional hangover. Chris talked seriously for the first time about our future, his and mine. We were sliding gently into a Bloody Mary after having that particular kind of hard-edged morning sex. I suppose I should say we made love. But we didn't make love; we had sex. There's a lot of difference. Oh, we made love most of the time, hugging and kissing and squeezing and feeling around; foreplay it's called in the manuals. But having sex is clinical and efficient and tidy, as tidy as something as messy as sex can ever be, and not bad at all.

We were sitting quietly and beginning to feel the instant euphoria that only vodka on an empty stomach can induce when Chris announced he planned to go for early retirement, fifty-two, fifty-five at the latest. Once he had quit his job he was going to leave Audrey and come to live with me. By then I would be close to retirement myself. We would cut loose and travel. "You don't have to give me a quick answer since you'll have about ten years to think it over."

"Will you love me in December as you do in May? There'll be a lot more silver threads among the gold."

"I'll still be singing 'Love's Old Sweet Song.' "

"Ten years is a long time. How do I know you won't leave me for an older man?"

"I don't have enough imagination or energy. One marriage; one extra-marital affair – and that one homosexual. I seem to have touched all bases."

"You have killed two birds with one stone, that one rolling stone that gathers no moss."

"Thrown by the hand that rocked the cradle, and which will soon kick the bucket if you don't let up."

"Tell me," I continued, "if you leave your wife to live in sin with me won't it spoil your chances for an honorary doctorate, bestowed by some small northern college? I thought that was one of the perqs of being a retired assistant headmaster. After earning an M.A. in some tough academic discipline, like remedial reading or team teaching in grade seven, you get an honorary Ph.D. so you can be introduced as Doctor So-and-

## EDWARD O. PHILLIPS

So when you get up to read the lesson in church or speak to groups in parish halls. I won't be able to introduce you as my friend, the honorary doctor."

"It's just one of the many small sacrifices you will have to make for the pleasure of my company."

I smiled and fell silent. Why in our moments of deepest feeling do we become suddenly inarticulate, like autistic children. Chris had just told me he loved me, more surely than declarations or marathon lovemaking or extravagant presents could possibly have conveyed. And I said nothing. How I longed to tell him how much I loved him, then and always, how I was touched by his easy confidence that ten years hence we would still be lovers. I overlooked the ready optimism he appeared to have always in reserve, nor did I allow myself to dwell on how unlikely it seemed he would really leave his wife after what would be more than thirty years together. Caught up in the mood of the moment I suspended my better judgment and allowed myself to believe the so-called declining years spent with Chris became suddenly desirable, a time to anticipate rather than accept with resignation, a truly golden age. I longed to tell him his love made me confident; I felt not so much young again as renewed, a tuned-up version of myself. I wanted to tell him, but instead I smiled and said nothing.

As a young child I remember a room in our house Mother called her sewing room, a small bedroom where she turned out crooked seams on a treadle Singer. On the wall above the sewing machine hung an engraving of Hope by George Frederic Watts. In sepia tones a narcoleptic asexual youth, blindfolded and holding a lyre, languished atop a globe I took to be the world. Even as a child I thought hope must be for the stupid and spineless. Then to learn at college from that least hopeful of poets, Alexander Pope, that "Hope springs eternal in the human breast: Man never is, but always to be, blest," convinced me that someone out there was being stingy with the rewards. Dante got it: "Abandon hope all ye who enter here" – a good motto for someone entering the customs house to coax a Christmas present valued at over ten dollars from the *petits fonctionnaires* behind the counter. In short, I set little store on hope.

Yet in spite of Watts, in spite of Pope and Dante, in spite of my own nature, Chris gave me hope. Somehow we would manage to survive our ad hoc meetings, occasional dinners in old Montreal, terse telephone calls made from office to office. We would survive ten years circumscribed by my apartment, the one place where we could meet without restraint. We would survive the daily problems, the increasing demands made on diminishing reserves of energy, which are the heavy price one pays for responsibility. We would survive deteriorating health and the resulting absorption in self. We would survive, to totter hand in gnarled hand into an arthritic sunset.

I knew better. God only knows I knew better. But I felt happy and lighthearted and gay – in the old-fashioned dictionary sense. I loved him, yet I smiled and sat silent. I can only hope he knew. I missed my chance, and now I can't have another.


I FORCED MYSELF TO STOP THINKING about Chris. Although I wasn't hungry, common sense dictated that I eat. Flanked by taciturn taxi drivers in a greasy spoon diner I ate bacon and eggs and somehow managed to keep them all down.

# 5.

ALTHOUGH I LIED TO LARRY about my elaborate New Year's lunch I really had planned to visit Mother at some point during the day. I decided to stop at my apartment for some fresh clothes. I showered again, even though I wasn't dirty and too much washing in winter dries out my skin. I shaved and dressed. The suit I was wearing had to go to the cleaners; I considered throwing it out along with everything else I had been wearing as I had stood on the landing and swung the ash tray. I rolled the clothing to stuff into yet another garbage bag. Union Carbide, who claims to manufacture the bags, must declare a supplementary dividend on the strength of my consumption alone. Should I have the suit cleaned for the Salvation Army or the Turnabout Shop? It was a beautiful suit, lightweight wool in a fine houndstooth pattern, worn maybe half a dozen times.

I knew I was fretting about the suit, about when to visit Mother, to avoid confronting the enormity of what I had done. Yet no amount of tearing my neat grey hair or gnashing my even white teeth was about to magically knit together the semi-frozen fragments of Dale Lawton. I had no lightning rod to channel atmospheric electricity into that one violent life-inducing jolt. No Frankenstein I. Not even the dumb, bumbling, kind, remorseful, natural creature. I was the one corrupted by society, setting a higher value on style than substance, fearing the publicity more than the punishment, the spotlight more than the sin, the glare more than the guilt. I was the true monster. And I showed every symptom of catching an old-fashioned case of bad conscience. An old-fashioned case of an old-fashioned disease, almost eradicated like smallpox or scurvy. Who today has a conscience good or bad, except politicians during a campaign. When I was young every second adult I knew had his appendix taken out. Then the hysterectomy came into vogue, followed by a run on gall bladders. I can't actually pinpoint the excision of conscience, but it seems to have gone the way of other diseased tissue. Better no conscience than a bad one.

"What's done cannot be undone." How comforting it would be to dismiss the events of the past few hours with a bit of Shakespeare. Will I end up like Lady Macbeth, prowling Winnifred's house in my terrycloth judo robe, one size fits all, carrying a flashlight with Duracell batteries, taking frequent showers with Dove so as not to dry my skin, and muttering that all the after shave lotion in Ogilvy's will not sweeten this little hand. Or will I end up like Hamlet, "sickbed o'er with the pale cast of thought," unable to dispose of those plastic parcels in the deep freeze, my one hundred and fifty pounds of flesh. O brave new world that has such bodies in it.

Hold! Enough!

I had to return to Winnifred's to pick up my overcoat and the car.

Consumed by an overwhelming restlessness I started to leave my apartment carrying my plastic bag of clothing. A latter-day rag picker. I paused. Supposing somebody opened the bag; supposing it tore. Why would anyone throw out a perfectly good Hardy Amies suit, Hathaway shirt, Liberty tie, and Florsheim shoes. Why indeed? Was I not being unduly squeamish? If I discarded clothing I wore every time I did something unpleasant I would soon be like the storybook emperor, naked in the street. Was I perhaps in some obscure way trying to buy off fate, discarding the clothes in which I committed the crime and thereby sloughing off some of the blame. I remembered a scene in *The Cherry Orchard* where the impoverished Mme. Raneyvskaia gives her last gold piece to a passing beggar. The gesture does not save the cherry orchard any more than discarding a perfectly good suit was going to change my situation in any way except by possibly arousing suspicion. I tossed the clothing onto the bed. The suit and tie would go to the cleaners, the shirt to the laundry, the shoes into the farthest corner of my closet.

As I rode the elevator down to street level a thought began to nag me, a question for which I could supply no ready answer. Did I feel a genuine sense of guilt for what I had done, or did I feel I ought to feel a sense of guilt? Was my distress intrinsic or imposed, a remorse built of brick and mortar, or was it simply an eye-pleasing afterthought like paint or wallpaper, chosen at random and changed at will. Did I quail from an atavistic belief in the old law of Hammurabi: "If a man destroy the eye of another man, they shall destroy his eye."

Law school had taught me otherwise, law complicated by prosthetics. One no longer extracts a contact lens for a contact lens, a lower bridge for a gold tooth. If one shoplifts with an artificial hand is the mechanical limb to be amputated? Does one perform a lobotomy on someone who steals information from a computer? As a man of education and supposed cultivation I eschewed the superstitious and irrational; I put my faith in the scientist, not the shaman. Still I could not rid myself of the nagging sensation that someone up there was watching. My skin crawled. I wished he would keep his eye, in fact his entire attention, on the sparrow. How could I make myself feel more contrite than I did?

But of one thing I was certain. I must make up my own mind about my guilt. Society through its courts of law was not going to decide for me. I had little faith in the judgment of my peers. I had spent my life too close to due process to trust it. I intended to dispose of the frozen fragments piecemeal. I was playing my game: one player, no rules, loser lose all. I did not intend either to be caught or to confess. No one would ever know but me. My conscience would have to fend for itself.


MOTHER WAS TESTY; she generally is on holidays, which she resents as breaks in her routine. "I thought you were coming to dinner last night," she began before I had my overcoat off. "I was all by myself except for the nurse, and Walter's coming for lunch. Madame made turkey tetrazini, but I wonder if there'll be enough."

"Did she make it with the Christmas turkey?"

"Naturally. There was half a Butterball I didn't want to waste."

"Mother, that turkey is one week old. Do you want us all to begin the New Year with salmonella poisoning?"

"Don't be ridiculous, Geoffry. Of course it's all right. You always did fuss so about your food. Anyhow you can help Walter serve. I have all I can handle with my crutches. I gave Madame the day off. She's gone to her family in Boucherville. Why didn't you bring me a Sunday *Times*?"

"It's Tuesday."

"So it is. But I understood you to say you were coming last night. We had a lovely piece of salt cod out of the deep freeze."

"You know I don't like salt cod." It was true; I didn't like salt cod. I wondered if I was ever again going to eat something that came out of a deep freeze without feeling squeamish.

"Well you should. What with food prices going up and up. It's an excellent source of carbohydrate."

"Don't you mean protein?"

"Perhaps."

"Shall we have a little drink while we wait for Walter?"

"Well, maybe just a little one wouldn't hurt."

I hung up my overcoat; then from the pantry I brought two generous gins on the rocks.

Mother looked frankly seedy. Her fine frizzy hair of no particular colour floated about her face in a wickerwork of wisps. What passes at first glance for high colour is in reality a fine mesh of capillaries expanded from alcohol. She keeps the thermostat of the apartment turned way up, permitting her to slut around in a series of sleazy polyester robes even in the coldest weather. Today she wore cabbage roses exploding across a navy blue background; the Fu Manchu sleeves interfered with her crutches. It looked like a cheap shower curtain. Leftover women who drink a little fall into blowsy fat or else a kind of concentration camp emaciation. Mother had grown painfully thin. And in spite of her being my own mother I think I would have had difficulty in describing her features to one of those police artists who make portraits based on verbal descriptions. Even if had I been looking straight into her face I would have had difficulty translating her features into words: a nose, a mouth, two eyes, blue I think. Eyebrows? Not black, not grey, sort of sand-coloured. Nose? Just a nose. Not long, not short, not broad, not pointed. It was easier to describe Mother's face by what it wasn't than what it was. That went for her personality too.

At least with her ankle in a cast she wasn't after me to chauffeur her around. She used to drive her own car until she caused a head-on collision halfway across a covered bridge in Vermont. Both cars were doing about ten miles an hour; she was barely even shaken up, but the experience unnerved her completely. The impression of being in a tunnel made her feel she was on an amusement park ride that shot out of control. Now she takes taxis. She never uses public transportation fearful lest the metro doors clamp shut just as she is stepping off the train to carry her trapped and screaming onto the next station. She is certain the bus will shoot away just as her foot is about to touch the curb. I have tried to explain that her life is in far greater danger every time she steps into a Montreal taxi; public transportation being one rare instance where safety lies in numbers; but she refuses to be convinced.

"May I take off my blazer?" I asked, overcome by the heat. It was one of our little rituals, like my always standing when Mother comes into the room. It gives her the illusion she has brought me up properly. I hung it in the hall closet beside my overcoat. Over and above the depression and boredom induced by strings of cold, grey days one of my principal reasons for disliking winter is the torture of central heating. Those who supervise public buildings, apartments, and department stores seem never to have heard we face an energy crisis. Hot, dry interiors suck moisture from skin and sinus. Central heating depletes, making one far more cross and irritable than heat waves which blanket the city in July. Mother's apartment was a case in point. Plants, fresh from the greenhouse, burst into bloom, faded, and died in that intense, artificial heat, their life spans measured in hours rather than days.

"Did you see what your sister sent me for New Year's?" asked Mother as I re-entered the room. From the depths of a brocade wing chair, across her leg, which was resting on a needlepoint stool, she handed me a flat box. Whenever she referred to Mildred as "your sister" it was to put me in the wrong. In this instance I had arrived empty-handed on New Year's Day. "I certainly didn't expect anything more; she gave me a lovely present for Christmas," continued Mother, her tone pure mealy-mouth. The meek shall inherit the earth because the only way to deal with them is to kill them and that's against the law. I opened the box.

"It's a lovely Herpes scarf," said Mother.

"I think you mean Hermès," I replied, as the bell rang.

I opened the door to admit Walter Morgan who, under the circumstances, I was glad to see. I have always considered the very act of describing people as elfin is itself elfin, a synonym for tiresome. But Walter Morgan was as close to an elf as I would ever want to get – small, round, and shiny. "Happy New Year, dear boy," he smiled, creasing his old child's face into a mass of wrinkles as he extended a diminutive white hand to shake mine in a surprisingly powerful grip. "As Pocahontas said to John Smith, 'Long time no see.' "

"Do you suppose John Smith gave Pocahontas a poke?"

"I do hope so," he giggled putting a small package on the whatnot beside the door, a hybrid piece Mother picked up at an auction, something between wash-stand and commode.

I took Walter's coat to hang up while he scurried across the room to kiss Mother on both cheeks and thrust the package into her hands. There were tiny explosions of "Constance," "Walter," "Happy New Year!" "How absolutely wonderful to see you." "You're looking so well," and the rest of that ritual cant with which the elderly greet one another. Never was peace pipe smoked, treaty signed, nor three white feathers inclined toward royalty with more formality than two old people greeting one another. For all its seeming spontaneity the transaction is as rigid as a triolet. You are looking well; you haven't changed a bit; we don't see each other nearly as often as we should. These three essential bits of information must be conveyed.

Walter's package held three cakes of English lavender soap. "Oh, Walter, you shouldn't have," Mother beamed.

I knew Walter drank only sherry, Harvey's Bristol Cream if available. "Sorry, Walter, only Shooting today," I said, handing him a glass.

"I'll be a good sport," he replied with a wink.

"Geoffry, I do wish you would go to the liquor commission and stock up properly. I hate to keep asking Madame, and I hate not being a good hostess," but the combination of half a tumbler of gin and the presence of an old friend worked its spell. The plangent whine had left her voice. By chiding me she was in effect apologizing to Walter for not having his brand in the house.

I have always liked Walter, and since he's an old family friend, I have known him, quite literally, all my life. Back when I was a child, when everyone around was taller than I and talked down from a great height, Walter Morgan was the first adult who spoke directly to me as if I were a person, an equal. His tone did not drip with the overripe condescension my parents' other friends adopted when talking to the little man, nor did he ruffle my hair. He never asked me about school. I realize now he flattered me, and no one is immune to flattery which does not degenerate into fulsome.

## EDWARD O. PHILLIPS

My father patronized Walter with the kindly tolerance a hearty yet intelligent heterosexual male feels toward someone who is light on his feet. "I don't care if he is a pansy," I remember Mother saying defensively, "he has never been anything but a perfect gentleman in my house." To me, a pansy was a small, velvety flower. I was puzzled. When I asked Mother why she called Uncle Walter a pansy she hedged and said he was sensitive. Not finding the answer to my satisfaction and possessed of the lethal directness of the young, I asked Walter himself why Mother called him a pansy. The resulting breach took almost three years to heal.

It has become a yawning cliché to describe someone as being born at the wrong time. Walter, however, is to a great extent a casualty of his time. He has energy and imagination and money, the last allowing him to become a kind of intellectual dilettante; he knows a lot of things about a lot of things. He can spot a piece of Spode at twenty paces or tell from across the room if the pine armoire is fake. But he has never managed to tap his full potential, to dig below the surface and become the recognized expert. He could have been anything he wanted, and I look at him today as a kind of wasted resource. When Walter was young, to be what we call a superachiever was considered pushy and in the worst possible taste. At seventy, Walter is only fifteen years older than Larry, but they belong to different epochs. Walter is a member of that vanishing species known as a gentleman. No one could ever accuse Larry of being that; he isn't even a lady. Had Walter been young today there would have been no stopping him. But there have to be those who pave the way. Larry and I had an easier time being ourselves because of men like Walter, just as those men twenty-five years my junior must look on me as going the way of the blue whale or carrier pigeon. Walter has found an outlet of sorts in a kind of baroque sensibility. He looks at the world obliquely, finds it wanting, and laughs. More important he makes me laugh.

I wanted desperately to stay diverted, to have my mind kept away from its central preoccupation. "What's the latest project, Walter?"

"I thought you'd never ask. What would you say to starting a big little magazine aimed at women over sixty. I say a big little magazine because the typeface will be large, large enough so that when the old dears can't find their reading glasses they will still be able to wear the glasses they ordinarily use for bridge. I have a title: *Harpies' Bazaar*. It will be frightfully exclusive; only those above a certain income level will be permitted to subscribe. Questions asked. Sufficient funds. Extravagant wrapper. Also all subscribers must pledge at least fifty dollars to The Society for the Prevention of Carriage Lamps on Town Houses."

"*Harpies' Bazaar*" said Mother from her chair. "Will it be for musicians?"

"Not exclusively, Constance," replied Walter, and quickly turned his attention back to me. "What we won't have," he continued, "are any advertisements to do with feminine hygiene. We will assume our readership has come to terms with down there surgically or otherwise. Nor will there be anything about cooking; women over sixty are sick of the kitchen. Nor will there be ads for cooking aids, not even for Cuisinart. The only kitchen ideas will be for decorating; how to put the kitsch back into kitchen. You know, pussycat oven mitts and an old news kiosk as a bar."

"Will you have restaurant reviews?"

"Quite definitely. But most of our readers will be on diets so our reviews will feature decor, moist banquettes and piquant table cloths."

"Travel section?"

"Absolutely. It will be called 'The Red Spotted Hanky,' and on the facing page there will be an ad for Vuitton luggage. We will run an advertisement for a camera that takes a picture, develops it, then sticks it in an album."

"Oh, Walter, you're being silly," interrupted Mother, but I bought her silence with another gin. I also filled Walter's sherry glass; the conceit was promising.

"Do you intend to nourish the mind?"

"Most certainly. All aspects of the arts will be covered. Books: Report from the Writers' Block. Music: On and Off the Record. 'Last night a performance by the Institute for Contemporary Music of Kodak's *Firebomb Suite* for buffoon, hobo, transsexual flute, and uptight piano, was cancelled when it was discovered the performers outnumbered the audience.' Theatre Reviews: A Peek at the Proscenium. Ballet: Points on View. 'The Colonial Ballet's revival of *Swarm Lake* was a qualified success. Svetlana O'Sullivan danced a lovely queen bee Odile, but her black hornet Odette lacked sting.'"

"When your father was alive," interrupted Mother, who obviously had not been listening, "we always had beefsteak and kidney pie for New Year's Day lunch. Poor Craig."

That kind of remark really slows down a conversation. Walter, however, was quick. "Let's drink a toast – to Craig Chadwick."

"To dear Craig," echoed Mother.

"To Father," I added, uncomfortable. There was a moment of lugubrious silence before I reset the conversation On button. "Will you have an editorial page? Letters to the editor?"

"I'm surprised you even ask. The letters to the editor page will be entitled 'A Dollar for Your Thoughts.' I myself will write the editorial, firm and crisp at the beginning, soft in the middle, gooey at the end. For the first issue I will discuss how Canada is a per capita country. French Canadians drink more soft drinks per capita; Albertans produce more oil per capita. Statistics give one the impression of substance. If all the stewardesses on Air Canada were laid end to end ..."

"... it wouldn't surprise me in the least." Walter and I shared a conspiratorial giggle. I looked at Mother, who reacts like litmus paper to the slightest trace of off-colour; but she sat in a contented haze, sipping and smoking, our voices no more than white noise. Gin, cigarettes, and the presence of people who offered no threat, were all she needed to be happy. A fortunate woman.

"Considering the income level of our readership," Walter continued, "I believe we must include a financial section, but not dry as dust monetary reporting. I have already written to Sir Jodrell Bank and he has agreed to supply a business horoscope: Scorpios sell, Virgos buy, Aquarians sit tight, sort of thing.

"As you can see it will be a general interest magazine. Sports: how a winning jockey broke his leg and was shot; how a well-known sportsman was poaching kudus in Tanzania when something he disagreed with ate him."

"Will you report on our sweaty armpit national sports, hockey and football?" I asked.

"Oh, dear, I suppose we must. But of course we'll call it meterball. Report from the 91.44 meter line. I must confess that for me a grey cup will always mean a dirty brassiere. When we get to the social page I will try to eschew the obvious. For instance, everyone reports on debutante balls."

"I didn't think debs had balls."

"Let me tell you, dear boy, these days they have more balls than their escorts."

"Walter, really." Mother gave a limp giggle.

"Getting back to the social page. I will report on the B'nai Brith dinner dance in the hospital wing; how the Knights of Columbus picnic lunch alfresco was cancelled due to a blizzard; and when a certain lesbian actress finishes drying out in the hospital she will be all set to begin filming *Rowboat*, the life story of Madeleine de Verchères.

"I would like to include a section on home handicrafts: Let's make a baby harp seal out of polyester velvet. Beauty aids: this month we will feature pores and the upper arm ..." The upper arm. Two upper arms. Neatly taped together with masking tape and tidily wrapped in double green plastic garbage bags. At this very moment freezing solid. A package that would just about fit into a plastic shopping bag. The City of Westmount incinerates garbage. Find a large pile of trash put out for disposal, maybe behind a row of shops; conceal the shopping bag as just another item of garbage ...

"... classified ads ... jobs for receptionists. Every older woman dreams of going back to work as a receptionist.

Geoffry – are you there?"

I snapped alert. "Sorry, Walter. I was thinking of something else. You were saying?"

"Finally – and this is where you can be of help – I want to dot the pages with homilies, heavy typeface in little boxes, bits of wisdom that will help one through the day. So far I have: 'Nudity is a luxury few can afford.' 'It's cheaper to be a godmother.' 'Cry over spilled milk.' 'To err is human; to blame the cleaning woman divine.' Any suggestions?"

I thought for a second. "Only talk to strange men; it's the ordinary ones you have to worry about."

"Excellent. Just what we need. Any more?"

"There's nothing wrong with chicken soup a shot of vodka can't fix."

A low rumble from Mother's chair told us she had fallen asleep. It disturbed me to hear her snore. Mothers shouldn't snore, any more than they should burp or sweat or fuck. Mothers are above such things. Mothers can have the curse since the physical aspect is more than cancelled out by the image of a tall, fierce, bearded male figure – Lear or Othello, Verdi's Monterone or Marquis of Posa – hurling imprecations at a cowering female form. The curse was larger than life and negated the menstrual flow and half-empty box of sanitary napkins in the medicine chest, which were not meant to be played with in the bath.

Still, it saddened me to hear her snore, slack in her chair, her mouth half-open, Walter's present still in her lap. She looked so old, almost dead. I wanted to wake her, reassure her, but of what. She was better off asleep, and her afternoon companion was due any minute. I put Walter's box of expensive soap on the table beside her chair and covered her with a slumber rug. Mother would never use that lavender soap any more than she would wear my sister's scarf. The scarf would join the other gift boxes in her closet until moth and rust did their thing. The soap would go into her underwear drawer, to make things smell nice.

Walter and I checked out the turkey tet and decided it

wasn't a very good idea. We blunted our appetites with cheese and crackers, sitting in the kitchen and talking about old movies until the afternoon nurse showed up. Mother woke up and suggested we all have some lunch, but Walter pleaded an engagement. Mother insisted we come back soon: "How about Friday?" Walter accepted; he accepts everything, not because he is a freeloader but because he dreads time unaccounted for. I said, "Why not?" I certainly wasn't going to be leaving town. We said goodbyes, I drove Walter home, and headed back to Winnifred's. If I manage, I thought to myself, to get through the rest of the week, which looms as a tunnel without a glimmer of light at the far end, I must face the fact that in twenty short years I will be Walter's age. Will the mantle of seventy sit more lightly on my shoulders than it does on his? A single man at seventy; checking the daily obituaries to find out who I knew at school is being buried, wondering how much longer I will keep the flat before moving into the residence where I have prudently put my name on the waiting list. Afraid to drive the car at night or to drive on expressways. Afraid of ice on the streets, of falling on the metro, of going out at night. Afraid of being forgotten, passed by, pushed aside; the fear of going out paling beside the fear of not being asked to go out at night. Nor will I acquire a cat.

I can travel, cruise the Caribbean with five widows from Orange City, New Jersey, at my table or else take a slow freighter to Greece with eleven other passengers, only eleven, among whom I may find one who is remotely compatible for mornings spent climbing around ankle twisting ruins under a scorching Mediterranean sun. Spain by bus, luggage outside the hotel room before 7:00 A M. Or a tour of African fauna. Bouncing around the Serengeti Plain in a jeep to stare at state-subsidized wild animals, torpid lions, and half-tame zebras. Bad accommodations and worse food. Don't drink the water; don't put ice in whiskey; don't eat fruit that isn't peeled; don't approach the animals; don't leave the compound at night. Have a good trip.

Nor do I see myself as one of those splendid golden-agers,

who keeps on working right up to the end, dying with his boots on, more likely his orthopedic oxfords. From the boardroom to the box. Died: Chadwick, Geoffry, at the Montreal office of Lyall, Pierce, Chadwick, and Dawson on May 24, 2010. (He even worked holidays.) Beloved brother of Mildred. Not bloody likely. It's bad enough to have spent my life as a liberal lawyer, just another liberal lawyer, without hanging on past respectable retirement age.

Maybe one of the reasons I resent Walter – maybe resent is too strong a word. Regret? – is that in him I see traces of myself, like pentimento. Walter strikes me as having done nothing with his life; by that I mean nothing he can point to as real achievement. He is well-read, well-travelled, steeped in the so-called arts. But, dammit, he should have done something! How many times have I myself closed the file or laid aside the annual report to daydream about books I might have written, pictures I might have painted, sculptures I might have formed. Sometimes I imagine myself singing Tristan, even though with my narrow chest and small head I wouldn't be heard past the prompter's box. My height must forever prevent me from dancing the young man saved by Giselle, while my definitely unheroic speaking voice would be much better suited to Polonius than Hamlet. I wanted to paint, but not on Sundays. Lacking the courage to quit law and paint full time I preferred to look askance at Laurentian snow scenes, chianti bottle with lemons, and views of picturesque Peggy's Cove, which are the preserves of amateur painters. I knew I could never write *The Ambassadors* or "The Waste Land," but a lecture I once gave on tax loopholes was edited and published in an obscure legal journal. I had only enough imagination to realize I did not have enough imagination to do imaginative work. I shun the word creative, that most debased of words. You too can peel potatoes creatively. Look upon shovelling the driveway as an exercise in design. Paint your steps with good taste. Then for the truly desperate there's always macramé.

Like Walter I am not burdened with problems of money.

I could quit the firm tomorrow and live comfortably. Mother is more than self-supporting. But work, even work I don't much like, gives my life a shape. I dread the vacuum, twenty-four hours a day to fill, rapidly depleting my meagre inner resources. The blank page, the empty canvas, the naked armature, the full scotch bottle. Rather than hazard the risk of change I clung to what I knew, the known evil. Yet even the life I held in some contempt seemed suddenly very desirable threatened as it was by the present contents of Winnifred's deep freeze. But hand wringing must now give way to positive action.

I drove through the early January dusk and pulled into Winnifred's garage. I was just about to pour myself a drink when I was interrupted by the cat making enough noise for ten. Then I remembered I had forgotten to feed her. From a tin of something that looked as though it had already been digested I forked a serving into a saucer. While her attention focussed on food I sneaked down to the basement and reached gingerly into the deep freeze to give the top package a tentative pinch. It turned out to be a forearm and rock-solid to boot. I decided to risk my first drop.

Loading the package containing the frozen and severed arms into two shopping bags, one inside the other for added strength, I dressed and left the house. Walking diagonally across the nearby park, deserted except for a couple of people exercising dogs, and the inevitable joggers, I cut down to Sherbrooke Street. The holiday had emptied the usually busy street, punctuated now by only a few sparse pedestrians. I walked briskly, but without undue haste, prompt purpose rather than scared scurry. Whether from lack of sleep or too much gin at lunch I found the normally bland strip of small shops infused with all the angular menace of an expressionist movie. Darkened store fronts glowered ominously; the hard light from street lamps painted innocuous façades with brooding chiaroscuro. I felt certain I was being followed, but under the circumstances who would not? Still ... but by whom? The bogeyman? When had I last even thought of the bogeyman? When Mildred and I were children the bogeyman loomed large in Mother's attempts at discipline. "If you aren't good the bogeyman will get you." The bogeyman worked overtime in our household; he got children who stole candy, told lies, read at night under the covers, played doctor, and didn't wash their hands after doing number two. He was also on standby for ad hoc situations, pushing one's sister off the wharf in her crisp muslin or catching minnows with a sieve and putting them into sherry. Mother invoked the bogeyman so often I think she must have paid him a retainer. Does the bogeyman get you if you commit murder?

But I hadn't cheered myself out of the feeling someone was padding along behind me; for three blocks my radar hummed. I swivelled my head around to catch a glimpse of a male figure about half a block behind. And why not? A public street is for the public. But the sensation of being stalked persisted. At the next corner the light turned red. Not a car approached the intersection but I stood, outwardly the conscientious pedestrian, until the figure drew up beside me. I turned to see a stocky, balding man about my age. He caught my glance and smiled, his teeth ochre under the street lamp. "Warm for January, isn't it?" He giggled; an odd sound, three short barks followed by a fourth, up an interval of a major third. Very strange.

"Yes." The light changed. I started across the street; the stranger fell into step beside me. "Do you live around here?"

"No."

From a pocket of his short fake fur coat he took a package of cigarettes and offered me one. "Smoke?"

"No, thanks."

Still keeping pace he lit his own. In the flame of the cheap lighter I could see his ring, a large, square chunk of black onyx with a diamond in one corner, a convoluted initial in the other. He reeked of Jade East after shave. "I live only a couple of blocks from here. Want to come up for a drink?"

It finally dawned on me that I was being cruised. I had to admit the idea of a drink or two or three sounded good, terribly good-but not good enough to put out for. At least not for someone who smelled of Jade East with its overtones of furniture polish. Bald I didn't mind; overweight I could overlook; but not the Jade East. And I found the shopping bag in my right hand, to say the least, inhibiting.

"Not just now, thanks. I have an engagement."

"Come up for a few minutes. I have movies, good ones." He giggled again, three barks followed by the upward interval.

"I can't watch movies. I'm astigmatic. Please excuse me." I had been around enough drunks in my life to know he had been drinking. I turned up a side street; the man followed persistently.

"Haven't I seen you somewhere around?"

"Quite possibly. I've been around." I continued to walk briskly; the man kept pace.

"My name's Fred. What's yours?"

"Greg."

"Hi, Greg. Say, I'm sure I've seen you around before. Trans-American Baths maybe? The Tropical Paradise? The Jack Boot?"

"Probably at a benefit performance of *Deep Throat*. See you." I crossed the street, Fred padding along like Poor Dog Tray.

"What do you like to do?"

"Supposing I told you I was straight."

"So's a corkscrew." He laughed his flakey little laugh. "What are you – oral? Greek? I'm into discipline myself," he confided, almost shyly. "I have boots that would fit you, gauntlets, a leather jock strap. You can tie me up, anything you like." He licked his lips which gleamed moist in the halflight.

Regardless of circumstances my idea of a good time has never been getting myself up as Use the Gestapo Girl and whipping someone. "You are my slave; I am your master-your mastress!" Role playing at its most extreme, and I was up to my neck in dissimulation as it was. However, there ought to be a severe and summary punishment meted out to men who drench themselves in cheap cologne.

"Look," I said, "I'm on my way to dinner. I'm late as it is. Some other time." I quickened my pace. I was trying to play the whole thing in low. But the situation was becoming grotesque. To be solicited for a little light S and M, while carrying a shopping bag holding two dismembered and frozen arms, taxed my poise to its outer limits.

"I'll walk along with you," he replied. "I've got nothing better to do. We can exchange phone numbers."

My reply was to take off at a full gallop. Although I had not run for years I used to race sprints and hurdles at school. Clutching the bag under my arm I loped along for nearly five panting blocks until a thumping heart and lack of breath forced me to stop. For a couple of gasping seconds I leaned against a lamp post, relieved to see that fat, flakey Fred had not followed me.

I cut back down to Sherbrooke Street. The spontaneous sprint had carried me some distance beyond the Westmount city limits, and I had no idea of how the neighbouring community disposed of its trash. Better stick to Plan A. Back on home ground I passed a row of shops, which backed onto a lane parallel to the main street. I checked carefully to see whether I was being followed. A few people strolled on the opposite side of the street. I ambled into the lane and made for a large mound of garbage bags awaiting removal. "Hey, get out of there!" The voice was male, and angry. "You heard me; I said come here!" There followed a rush of footsteps as an enormous Great Dane galloped past me towards the street carrying what looked like a chicken carcass in his mouth. I flattened myself against a wall as a man appeared in the opening of the lane. "Drop that! Drop it at once! At once! Beowulf! Drop it and sit!" The dog did neither, but took off down the street with the owner in hot pursuit, shouting at him to come back.

Still flat against the wall, my heart knocking against my rib cage, I couldn't help thinking that maybe Beowulf ought to attend obedience school. Stress has always filled my mind with irrelevancies. I edged my way toward the pile of garbage and was just burrowing a hole large enough to hide my shopping bag when I was nearly impaled on a shaft of light, which blazed suddenly from a third-storey sash window across the lane. I froze, hoping desperately I might blend in with my surroundings like a hare in a hay field.

A man's voice became audible. "Hey, Marjorie, close the window, eh?"

"I'm trying to get some fresh air in here."

"Fresh air be damned; there's an oil shortage."

"There's no shortage of cigar smoke."

A man's silhouette appeared in the window, which then closed with a crash. Curtains pulled roughly together killed the square of light playing over a dirty brick wall.

I grabbed my shopping bag, pushed it into the opening I had made, and covered it with several bags of trash. Then I walked briskly out into the street and hailed a cab. As I gave the address of Winnifred's house and sank into the back seat I was aware of two overpowering sensations. One was an almost gasping sense of relief. The other was a feeling of something very like gratitude, to Beowulf and his cross owner, to Marjorie and her cigar-smoking husband, who had all seen fit not to notice me.

# 6.

A BOOKLET ENTITLED *You and Your Freezer* taped carefully by Winnifred to the side of the appliance warned the new owner ominously not to overload the machine with unfrozen items. Even a large commercial freezer would have found the body of a medium-sized male a challenge. It would take Winnifred's machine, even turned up as far as the dial would go toward Colder, a fair time to solidify the larger sections of the body. And it seemed to me somehow that in their frozen state the incriminating segments would be more likely to escape detection as quickly. I chafed with impatience to get rid of everything relating to the episode, but I knew haste could cause that one slip which brings detectives and police to the door just before the final commercial.

I carried my overnight bag down to the kitchen and poured myself a drink. The very ritual of getting out ice and pouring whiskey into a glass can soothe, a western variation of the tea ceremony, only you can keep your shoes on. Sitting at the kitchen table I took out the dead man's wallet and counted the money: three hundred and fifty U S. dollars in big bills, a hundred and fifty Canadian, not a bad little nest egg for someone pleading poverty. What was I going to do with the cash? Should I send it to the address on the driver's licence, attention Mr. Lawton Senior. I could only presume the couple in the photograph to be parents. They looked like parents, drab to the point of anonymity, their aggressive ordinariness heightened by the crude black and white contrasts of the snapshot.

Photographs disturb me, especially those of myself. I keep no albums, no British biscuit tins of snapshots; no studio portraits in tarnished silver frames dot my dresser. The only photo I have of myself is glued firmly into my passport and makes me look like an ageing child molester. People wielding cameras are not welcome at my parties. My sister Mildred is a tireless snapper of shots, to which her Christmas cards bear witness. She interrupts the flow of a gathering to group people into quasi-Victorian tableaux. Then we must wait expectantly for the camera to disgorge the image from its mechanical uterus, an image one can only see by peeling off a moist covering like placenta. Worse still, she mails copies of prints to anyone in the picture. Most people are delighted. I find the whole thing strange. For a culture which fears death as much as ours; which has developed a whole vocabulary – casket, interment, remains, funeral home – to deal with the non-fact of death; for whom making a will becomes an admission of defeat rather than the act of a prudent administrator, this culture rejoices in collecting images of our dying. That is what photographs really are, images of death, of moments gone, frozen into icons of decay. Who today needs a skull as memento mori? We have photographs.

Mr. Lawton Senior, his short-sleeved sports shirt buttoned up to the neck, his arm stiffly around his wife's shoulders, faced the camera as if it were a rifle. Mrs. Lawton, not so much fat as amorphous in her cheap cotton dress, looked up at her husband, affording the camera a profile shot of hair in a bun, no doubt confined by a net. They made a neat, clean, respectable couple, not my kind, God knows; but then few people are. What would they feel, how must they react as days, weeks, months passed in anxious flow with no word from their son? When would they become alarmed? The very presence of the snapshot in the wallet indicated some filial feeling. How would they react should they learn their son made a living by hustling older men. Supposing a totally unexpected envelope arrived bearing a Montreal postmark and stuffed with bills? No message, no return address, just five hundred dollars. Is it from Dale? It must be from Dale. Why hasn't he written, or called. What is he doing up in Canada. When is he coming home?

I did not mean to kill Dale Lawton. I can say that honestly, even to myself. In spite of the rage I felt I did not want to kill. Frighten, hurt, maybe even maim – but kill? No. I did not. But the deed is done. If ever the well-worn words of Donne came to haunt me it was now. I had made my own personal discovery that no man is an island, that my action must reach out to affect the lives of those I didn't even know. How boring it is to be rendered inarticulate by crisis; if not inarticulate, then reduced to time-worn saws and cliches. Why do words let us down just when we need them the most?

Far from being honest and kind I understood that to send the money to the elder Lawtons would be a cruel and irresponsible act. I went to Winnifred's desk and took two envelopes, size eight and size ten white business. Into the size eight I fitted the bills and sealed the bulging envelope. On the larger of the two I printed Salvation Army Headquarters, Notre Dame Street at Guy, Montreal. I put the smaller envelope into the larger and glued several stamps onto the upper right-hand corner. I have always admired the Salvation Army even though the workers make me very nervous, especially when they stand beside department store entrances, ringing handbells with that special bullying meekness that only those wearing a uniform can muster.

I tore the photograph into tiny pieces, which I dropped into the bag for wet garbage. Winnifred has a small garbage bag for wet garbage and a larger one for dry. I was maintaining the status quo. With kitchen scissors I cut the Visa,

## EDWARD O. PHILLIPS

American Express, Master Charge credit cards into narrow strips. The driver's licence and the receipt for shirts I tore and discarded. Finally I thrust the wallet itself deep into coffee grounds mixed with the remains of the daube. I sealed the wet garbage bag and put it into the dry garbage bag which I put outside for pick up.

There remained the watch and the knife. Nothing really connected the watch to Dale, no inscription on the back, no initials. I rubbed it hard back and front to remove any tell-tale prints. It was a handsome watch, one of those big, square, digital, solid state, mini-computers, which counts down the minutes and seconds right before your eyes. It was unsettling to observe. Time moves faster on a digital watch than it does with a sweep second hand. I wonder if Dale ever learned to tell time the old-fashioned way through configurations of hands. Did he learn to tie his shoelaces or did he move from bootees right into boots? Did he learn multiplication and long division or only how to change the battery on a pocket computer? I learned all these skills, reluctantly, and resented each and every child today who did not have to do likewise. I would never dream of wearing the watch, or even of passing it on. Not because it was simply a dead man's watch – I still keep my father's – it was a murdered man's watch, and therefore tainted. Somehow it must bring harm to the wearer like the Hope diamond or the red shoes, which danced their wearer to death, or the robe steeped by Dejanira in the blood of Nessus which killed Hercules. And were I to part with the watch, stuff the belt, boots, and knife into some anonymous trash can, then dispose of the body, nothing would remain to link me with Dale. But in some obscure way, far too visceral for my intellect to formulate, I felt bound to this dead man by an invisible bond, clammy not so much to the touch as to the imagination. I could not even say it reached beyond the grave except metaphorically because a grave, a plot, a stone, Dale must never have.

Either I went through with my plan and got away with it or I got caught in the attempt. There was no going back.

Even if I were to have a change of heart I did not even have a complete corpse to produce for the police. "I'm sorry, officer, I lost a piece." I decided to keep the watch. No one would ever know it wasn't mine, not that anyone would ever see it in a box in my dresser. The object would serve to keep memory green. Just in case my complacency at getting away with killing a man ever dulled my sense of having committed the ultimate misdemeanour, I wanted Dale's watch as a reminder. My own memento mori. And I was just beginning to understand, in my gut, not my head, that snuffing out that vital spark is wrong, quite simply wrong. Had I been flying a plane at stratospheric heights using technology to bomb people whose skins were a different colour from mine and whom I couldn't even see, would I have this same sense of profound wrong? I doubt it. Murder is a personal act, like making love. One has to be directly involved in the process. Hand, ash tray, temple; as tidy as a syllogism.

The drink did not calm me down, not a bit. I was tired, bone tired, but still restless. Going down to the basement, I retrieved the boots and the belt from under the hot-water heater and put them into a small canvas tote bag I found behind some other bags on a shelf in the passageway, then slipped the knife along with the envelope of money into the pocket of my overcoat. This time I turned up the hill towards the top of the so-called mountain.

Walking the streets of Montreal in winter anywhere but along the most heavily travelled thoroughfares reminds me of those punishments in Greek hell, walking but staying forever in the same place. Coarse salt and sand thrown at random from trucks combine with snow to form a heavy, greasy mixture with all the traction of powdered graphite. The foot advances, flexes, bends, only to rotate on its own axis like a well-oiled ball-bearing. The best way to get traction is to take tiny mincing steps, a caricature of the homosexual walk. It's hard to be butch walking in snow just as it's hard to be butch carrying a white cardboard cake box by the string. Of course if the snow lies fresh and deep it's man's country, man. One exchanges the Tom Thumb steps for the seven league boots. "Fee-fi-fo-fum / I smell the blood of a big macho number." It doesn't really rhyme. I used to think boots, Kodiak boots, construction boots, hunting boots, were one of the last strongholds of the truly masculine. That is until I went into a bar one night to find just about every trick wearing construction boots with heavy tractor-tread soles. Whatever happened to the lucite mule? One stoned number, his boots not so much laced as lashed up to the knee, had approached me, conspicuous in my thick-soled oxfords (Ivy league queen), and asked if I gave golden showers. I drew myself up. "Me Jupiter, you Danae-and we'll call the boy Perseus." The young man looked blank. "I don't know where your purse is. I carry a shoulder bag myself." He drifted off.

I continued inching my way up the hill, by now beginning to sweat freely. Even walking in the road was not much easier. On one of the less travelled side streets a long bank of snow, pushed up by the plough parallel to the sidewalk, was surmounted by sandwich boards placed at regular intervals and painted with a large P, circled in red. At some point in the very near future a snowblower must pass, its revolving circular teeth masticating and engorging the snow to spew into trucks following patiently behind. I chose a spot in front of two large houses whose dark windows suggested the owners were out, perhaps even away; but I waited until the woman in a natural mink coat, walking a pair of miniature schnauzers, turned the corner before digging a hole in the snowbank and burying the boots. Chewed up by the snowblower, spat into a waiting truck, dumped into the municipal melter, I believed the boots would be altered to the point of anonymity.

I continued down the opposite side of the hill until I was safely outside the municipality of Westmount and into that of Montreal before I slid the envelope addressed to the Salvation Army into a large red and white letterbox. Just past an intersection I paused only long enough to slip the switchblade knife through the grating of a sewer. As an afterthought I fished in my pocket for the key to the Windsor Station locker;

it followed the knife through the grating.

On my way back up and then down the hill to Winnifred's I passed the semi-detached house where my parents had lived when I was born. Fifty years ago. It didn't seem possible. I stopped and looked at the house, red brick, comfortable, undistinguished. Father had always wanted to streamline the front, to knock off the little balcony forming a sort of *porte-cochère* over the front door; but then we moved to a larger house. I don't remember why. What I do remember, twenty-five years later, is my father. He was in my thoughts as I walked back through the anonymous dark to Winnifred's house.

Father had given me his gold pocket-watch the year before he died, of cancer. I remember being touched by the gesture for I knew how much he loved his watch, big, handsome, easy to read, like my father himself. He was a fine looking man in that firm-jawed, clean-cut, almost comic-book hero way. And along with the comic-book heroes he believed the world could be made a better place. If only we pursued good and fought evil and worked hard our grandchildren or even our children might well enjoy the millennium. I think most of us today tend to forget how profoundly the Depression affected those touched by it.

Father never went to college. As a self-educated man, his learning had been far more eclectic than that of today's students who stick to the reading lists and Cole's notes. But like many men of his generation Father held an unshakable faith in the value of a university education. College provided the open sesame to whatever kinds of success beckoned. And even the most independent adolescent cannot avoid being influenced by parents; I had been no exception. Furthermore, I loved and respected my father; I listened to his opinions. He wanted life to be better, easier, more rewarding for my sister and me than it had been for him. For the first-born son a profession must supply the golden key. Also Father was very human. Most of us have secret urges to do things for which we are not particularly well equipped. I would love to paint or sculpt or sing. Father had a secret hankering for politics, a hankering that fortunately he never indulged except on a minor municipal level.

He belonged to that now dying generation, who hoped to live out their private ambitions vicariously through their children. "I wanted to be a doctor; my son will be a doctor." "I worked hard all my life as a nurse; my daughter will marry well and never have to work." Nowadays, parents seem to spend much more energy worrying about what their children shouldn't be doing than what they should. Are they drinking and driving; are they on drugs; are they breaking the law just for kicks? Is she pregnant? I don't mind about his not being an architect just so long as he stays out of jail. "Do you know where your children are?" flashed ominously onto the television screen. Middle-aged flower children, who have given up communes for causes watch their well-tailored son go to work for an insurance company and wonder where they failed as parents. A Ph.D. in medieval history watches his son choose to become an electrician and earn double his father's salary. Women who marry do so at least twice, the first time for sex, the second for security. Number three may be for sex again. The fourth is generally a tax shelter. Parents grow obsolete faster than appliances. Motherhood self-destructs in twenty years. The old order changeth.

Father had had his heart set on my being a lawyer. Not only was law the profession he regretted never having studied, it opened doors into politics. One of his cornier jokes was that he had studied the law of averages at the school of hard knocks. I remember the mythical slogan that any American shoeshine boy can become President of the United States. By the same token, any liberal lawyer can become Prime Minister. So I went into law on a what-the-hell kind of basis. I gave little thought to the future while at university. I had a car, a generous allowance; I got perfectly adequate marks without too much work. And I was reliving Father's youth for him in a way. He had longed for me to go into politics, to serve the larger cause. He believed to live in Canada was a privilege, to serve the country an honour. He had so much integrity at times it hurt.

I was always a bit of a sour ball, smartass kid. My angle of vision was far more oblique than Father's, clear-eyed and direct. I could always see the wrinkles beneath the pancake makeup, the clean cuffs and dirty fingernails, the pee stains in the crotch. Father took people much as they wanted to be taken. My father warned me against cultivating cynicism. Like the boy in that cautionary tale who made faces until his features froze into a permanent grimace, no doubt the younger brother of the boy who bit his nails until his fingers fell off, I would find my habits of thinking trapped in the quicksand of jaundiced cynicism and be incapable of reacting to that which was honest and upright. I remember replying people were honest when they could afford to be; it was an expensive virtue, and that upright had more to do with an elastic spinal column than wholesome habits of thought. Father chuckled, and with that immensely irritating condescension all adults have on tap would assure me that I would learn as I grew older.

I did learn as I grew older, but what I acquired was information, not attitudes. I seem to have been born with those. So was my sister Mildred, but Father never paid much mind to my sister. He was good to her and loved her and all that sort of thing. But as both daughter and younger child she existed on a lower plane than I. Father was not a deliberate chauvinist, but at certain times certain attitudes hover in the air. Ideas have their fashion just like the bustle or the zoot suit. There was a time when people believed the earth to be the centre of the universe. I doubt they rolled out of bed in the morning and said, "Zounds! the earth is at the centre of the universe, forsooth." But they believed it nevertheless.

By the same token Father believed women had their place.

He did not believe women should be lawyers or mechanics or cab drivers; nor did he believe men should be secretaries or elementary school teachers or hairdressers. He did not approve of women smoking. He frowned on men who did needlepoint. So do I now that I come to think of it.

And so it came to pass that I entered the law faculty at the French university, the plan being to acquire fluent French and a law degree in one package deal. I stepped backward into a time capsule. Once upon a time, long, long ago, a student went to the university. What that student found was a gaggle of other students who made Chaucer's Clerke of Oxenford look like a real swinger. They hid one another's books and gave one another bumps on birthdays, *la bascule*, they called it. They played elaborate jokes on April first, *poissons d'avril*; and went into close little closets to tell celibate priests about their meagre sex lives. They regarded me with a friendly curiosity; when I came into the student lounge it was a close encounter of the third kind, without the special effects. Some were kind and friendly and intelligent; others were hostile and suspicious, and had never read Balzac because he was on the index. I never cracked the code. I remained on the outside looking in. After one year I returned, with an audible sigh of relief, to the university on the English side of the mountain. I graduated, not brilliantly but adequately, married, and went to work.


I DECIDED TO REMAIN AT WINNIFRED'S to sleep, fearful to leave the house unattended until I had cleared the deep freeze. Supposing there was a fire or a furnace failure or any one of a half-dozen household mishaps, which could bring police, fire, or repair departments swarming through the premises. And Richard was arriving the next day. Then there was the cat, whom these stretches of solitude were making increasingly strange. It wouldn't have surprised me in the least if she had begun to speak, like Saki's Tobermory, and blurted out the whole story. Nothing in fact could have surprised me. I was quite literally stunned, a combination of shock and fatigue which slowed down my reactions as though I were moving under water.

# SUNDAY'S CHILD

The word "sleep" loosely describes those hours spent lying in bed with the lights off. I spend little of the night in an actual state of unconsciousness. Once I even had a try at valium, progressing gradually from the whites to the yellows and finally to the blues. I slept all right, right through the day. I had felt as though I were living my life with a pillow case over my head. One day I gave up pills cold turkey; better to be awake part of the night than a zombie for the entire day.

As a child I read volumes by flashlight while the city slept. I wonder if there is any real connection between insomnia and introspection. Do people who sleep unbroken sleep throughout the night and work all day have any time to worry about themselves? Long night watches summon thoughts; and I long ago stopped playing with abstractions or wringing my imaginary hands over ecology, nuclear fallout, and the dismemberment of our country. Maybe I would if I thought something could be done. If only I could wave a wand or intone an incantation or summon a genie and suddenly mercury would evaporate from the rivers and Lake Erie return to its pristine, pre-industrial state. Such is not the case. Even our self-denials are petty gestures, turning off one sixty-watt bulb as banks of lights blaze all night on construction sites, or saving the daily paper for recycling as our forests are decimated.

However, at that moment, I found any public concerns I might have harboured completely swallowed by private ones. I had a few drinks and watched television, without really seeing it, waiting for sleep to come. But even after the late show – Susan Hayward as a highly improbable Basque trying to save a wagon-load of grapevines from a prairie fire somewhere in the southwestern United States – my mind would not stop flickering like a television screen with no program. Largely to avoid dwelling on the body in the basement I found myself remembering the final days with Chris. It was sort of a counter-irritant. When you stub your bare toe you can almost forget that you have just hit the nail squarely on the thumb.

Like most endings it had begun simply enough. A singer,

whom I knew Chris greatly admired, was coming to town for a recital and I volunteered to get tickets. The hitch was that the recital made up part of a series for which I had not subscribed. After numerous telephone calls, much tact, and a promise of lunch at the Ritz, I charmed a pair of tickets from one of the music committee members, a voracious widow who tried to have me for dessert. Bursting with the news, I had telephoned Chris at the school only to be informed Mr. Pratt was not to be disturbed. Any telephone calls made during business hours had to be cryptic, filtered through a school secretary whose hearty arrogance recalled colonial India where her parents had grown up. She had come with the job, a creature of steel wool hair and mismatched teeth for whom cohabitation must ever remain a mystery. She adored Chris and protected him with the ferocity of a doberman pinscher. Audrey hated her.

The second time I called she told me Mr. Pratt was on the telephone. My third call brought the information that Mr. Pratt was busy with a pupil. I replied that I had a client waiting and that I wished to speak with him. She replied that it was most irregular, that Mr. Pratt didn't like to be disturbed when his door was shut. I replied that I would be in meetings all afternoon and unable to call back. She replied that, well, she didn't know. I replied that she had better get off her skinny ass and put Mr. Pratt on the phone.

There was a click and Chris's voice came onto the line. I could tell he was cross. Three boys from the Haddley Middle School, of which Chris took charge, had been caught by the head gardener at the Westmount flower show, which this year featured rabbits in a small enclosure with its own tiny thatched cottage. The boys had climbed the fence, broad-jumped the moat full of goldfish, and tried feeding Mars bars to the astonished animals. Their green blazers and gold-striped ties branded the boys as fish, from Haddock Hall. Tampering with the flower show, its cross of Easter lilies dominating the variegated display in the dank, rambling greenhouse, was like drawing a moustache on the Mona Lisa. They had brought shame onto the Middle School, announced Chris in a dark-brown voice. Not to mention rotting the bunnies teeth I replied, prepared to interject that I had finally wangled tickets for the sold-out concert we both wanted to attend. But Chris was testy; it wasn't the rabbits but the principle of the thing. I replied it wasn't the principal; it was the assistant headmaster who seemed to have left his sense of humour at home. Wasn't he feeling well? Yes, he was feeling quite well, just under pressure. What did I want? Good news about tickets. For what night? Tomorrow night. He couldn't go; opening night for the school play. My own sense of humour began to desert me; those tickets had cost me hours on the phone and an expensive lunch, and I asked why he couldn't go to the second night of the school play. Furthermore, I couldn't think of anything more deadly than an all-male production of *Lady Windermere's Fan*. Chris turned from testy to frosty and suggested I go to Place des Arts alone. A slight click on the line told me the secretary had been listening to our conversation. "And tell that goddamn Gorgon Medusa not to give me so much fucking flak when I call."

"Why don't you call me later," said Chris in a faraway voice.

"I'm going to be tied up all afternoon. Maybe I can change the tickets for the following night." I was trying to be funny.

"Can't make it. I'll be in Toronto."

"Toronto! Why the hell are you going to Toronto?"

"School business," he mumbled.

"Shit!" I said clearly. "Call me when you get back." I hung up and cleared my desk, wondering whether I would give Walter Morgan a call or go alone to the recital with a thirteen-dollar place to put my topcoat.

Two days after my telephone conversation with Chris I had gone to meet a client for lunch, the kind of lunch I don't particularly enjoy: heavy French food preceded by drinks, which meant a long soggy afternoon. But duty called. Waiting in the mirrored foyer of the restaurant, I was handed a note by the *maitre d'* to the effect my guest had been unavoidably detained and would call me at the office. I cancelled the reservation and walked down the street to Murray's for a club sandwich and a cup of coffee. Even though I have always firmly disbelieved in the claptrap of guardian angels and retributive justice I had to admit there was a certain grim humour in the way I was about to learn why Chris had gone to Toronto. I entered Murray's at the peak of lunch hour rush; people stood in line for the counter. I checked tables, all full, when I caught sight of Audrey Pratt, alone at a table for two. At precisely the same instant she looked up, spotted me, and, with a wave, indicated the empty seat. I did not particularly want to sit with Audrey, but there seemed no other choice short of bolting from the restaurant. I nodded and crossed to sit in the empty chair. "Hello, Audrey. I thought you'd be home slinging hash for the kids."

"They're at school for lunch today. How are you, Geoffry? It's been a while." As the starched waitress handed me a menu, Audrey turned her head, giving me a glimpse of the most perfect profile I have perhaps ever seen. A striking woman was Audrey, in that tailored, deliberately understated way. It would be difficult to imagine her smooth, short pageboy mussed, lipstick smeared, or manicure chipped. I could not picture her washing pots or pushing a vacuum cleaner, yet I am sure she did.

I gave my order. "Did you come downtown to shop, or just to look at the grownups?"

She laughed to reveal toothpaste-commercial teeth. "A bit of both, I expect. Although I suppose it's foolish to buy anything until we know whether or not we are going to move."

I snapped alert. "Move? Are you going to sell the house?"

"Didn't Chris tell you?" Audrey knew Chris and I saw one another occasionally but assumed, at least as far as I could tell, that we met on a locker room buddy basis.

"Tell me what? I haven't seen him for a while." Fear lent me guile.

"Well, he seems to feel he has reached a dead end at Haddley. He's tired of being assistant headmaster, and I can't say

I blame him. Chris needs a new challenge. He's forty-five; if he doesn't move now it will soon be too late. Anyhow word is out that Cranbrook Academy – do you know it?"

"Isn't it a boys' school in Toronto?" My voice sounded surprisingly calm.

"That's it. Anyhow word is out the headmaster is leaving and Chris has applied for the position. He's in Toronto now for an interview. It's all come up rather suddenly."

The bottom dropped out of my stomach. "Do you suppose he'll get the job?"

"I think he has as good a chance as anyone. He has good credentials and plenty of experience."

Under no circumstances could I let Audrey see how I really felt. "How do you feel about going?"

"I love Toronto, always have. And none of us speaks French."

"You could learn."

Audrey gave a deprecating shrug. "I suppose we could. But it's not easy to learn a foreign language as an adult."

"But what about your life here, your friends? We'll hate to see you go."

"Toronto isn't the end of the world. I'll come down to visit. Friends will come west to visit us. I hope you'll get up to see us, Geoffry." She looked straight into my eyes.

"Of course I will."

"We don't see nearly enough of you. I certainly don't." She paused. "I don't suppose you're free for dinner tonight?" She threw another eyelock on me across the small table.

"But Chris is in Toronto."

"That's just the point." Through the panic and utter confusion I managed to hear a distant bell. Audrey was coming on strong. Just what I needed. She laughed far back in her throat. "Don't look so shocked. This is 1979." Her face took on a mock serious expression. "I love my husband – and all that. But he isn't around very much these days. And I don't intend to be the kind of mousey little wife who stays at home with the children while her husband runs around. But you still haven't answered my question."

"Question?"

"Will you have dinner with me tonight?"

"I am tied up unfortunately. There's someone ..." I let my voice trail off.

"I'm sure. A man as attractive as you must have a very full dance card. But if you're free one evening give me a call."

"What about Chris?"

"No problem. He's out three or four evenings a week: badminton and swimming and school business, or so he says. I can always get away. And now I must dash – dentist appointment. I'll hear from you?" She picked up her cheque and walked towards the door. She walked tall, back straight, shoulders high; but the movement of buttocks under fitted skirt promised a lot of action in the feathers. For a second I found myself wondering what it might be like making love to my lover's wife, kissing that lacquered mouth, fondling those breasts, entering first with tongue then with cock where Chris had entered, and all the while imagining them together. Or I could imagine the three of us, a sexual ballet playing on my mindscreen like a soft focus, soft core, slow motion, porn flick. The image faded. Although I enjoy most sexual activity short of pain I am not a voyeur.

The waitress stood before me, starched, netted, nasal. "Will that be all, sir?"

Will that be all. In the course of moments I had learned my lover planned to leave town and hadn't even mentioned it to me. Also his wife wanted to make it. Just like afternoon TV. Leaving a tip for the waitress under my untasted sandwich, I headed for the door.

"Don't Ever Leave Me"; "Never Say Goodbye"; "Linger Awhile"; "When Your Lover Has Gone"; "Here's That Rainy Day"-the popular songs get right to the point. The only thing that really matters in a love affair is being there, just being there. The warm, breathing presence. As a *summa cum lade* graduate from the school of long-distance affairs – London, Paris, New York, Quebec City, Toronto – had learned one lesson: long-distance love affairs do not last. Even those that begin with the understanding that meetings will be infrequent start to sag after a while, sometimes only a few weeks. Absence fails to make the heart grow fonder; or if it does grow fonder the *inamorato* is generally someone more easily accessible. More hopeless still are those affairs based on regular meetings which must then face prolonged separations. Love is not for commuters. I knew Chris and I would never survive his moving to Toronto. What frightened me was the realization that we might not even survive his considering Toronto without telling me first. To have learned quite inadvertently from Audrey about the projected move made me angrier the more I thought about it. By the time I finally saw him two days later rage and resentment and wounded pride had cooked up a dandy witches' brew, simmering quietly but steadily away on a back burner.

As Chris sounded the buzzer I opened the door to my apartment and returned to the kitchen, where I was engaged in the disagreeable task of extracting ice from the second tray. The first tray had gone into my first two drinks. I heard Chris close the door; he came to the door of the kitchen to grin boyishly. "Do I laugh with delight when you give me your smile; Or tremble with fear at your frown?"

"Neither, Sweet Alice."

The next thing I knew I was pinned against the refrigerator. "I've decided to forgive you for hanging up on me," he said, zeroing in to kiss me.

"Down boy," I replied, turning my face so his mouth plopped noisily against my cheek. "That's how you catch germs. All I have is scotch."

"Suits me."

"You seem in good spirits." I led the way into the living room. "How did things go in Toronto?"

"Okay, I guess. How was the recital?"

"Good but thin. She took a bow after every song, made an hour's worth of singing seem like an hour and a half. What she sang she sang beautifully, but it was still a con. By the time she finished her encores she had sung what would have been a reasonable program."

"Who did you take?"

"Whom."

"Touché. Whom did you take?"

"Walter Morgan, a family friend from way back. He said her gown looked like an ad for Modess ... because."

"A real jock observation."

"You better believe. What took you to Toronto? You weren't too clear on the phone."

Chris paused just a second before answering. "I went to interview a couple of prospective teachers."

"Isn't it customary for the interviewees to seek out the interviewer?"

"Not necessarily."

"Chris," I put down my glass. "I had lunch with Audrey recently. A chance meeting – we aren't having an affair. She told me you had gone to Toronto to be interviewed for the position of headmaster of Cranbrook Academy. One of you is not telling the truth."

"Well, now," he said and stopped. I was reminded of a wind-up Victrola that has just run down in mid-record. Chris sat staring at the floor and flicking the edge of his highball glass with a fingernail – *ping, ting, zing* – a habit I had not until this moment found annoying. "I guess the cat's out of the bag."

"It is – and it has used up eight of its nine lives."

"Supposing I were to tell you I know what you are thinking but I don't want you to worry?"

"Doesn't help very much."

"I didn't think it would."

"You applied for a job in Toronto. If you don't get it you planned to say nothing. If you do – and only if you do – would you then face me with the news. Is my scenario terribly off-base?"

"No. I can only repeat I didn't want you to worry."

"Supposing, just supposing you did get the job, and

assuming that I still believed in the status quo, how did you propose to go about telling me?"

"That's a bridge I would have to cross."

"Spare me the saws. On second thought perhaps you had better start counting chickens; they seem to have hatched. Put them into detention for breaking their shells. I've known you've had problems with Haddley. Don't we all know that no situation is perfect, that we have to take the rough with the smooth, that the road winds uphill all the way? Don't we all know that? I think we all know that. In fact I'm almost certain we all know that."

"Spare me the irony."

"But I must confess I had no idea you were fed up to the point of leaving, not only Haddley but Montreal as well. What staggers me is why did we never talk it over. You are making a unilateral decision on something that will profoundly affect both our lives. I feel a bit like the shareholder who owns forty-nine per cent of the stock and hasn't been consulted on the takeover."

"Why get all worked up about a hypothetical situation? I don't have the job yet."

"Okay. Just answer me this and answer me straight. I'm putting you in the box. If you are offered the job – sorry, position – will you accept it?"

His pause was only momentary. "Yes."

"Then that song and dance routine about not upsetting me is a pile of expedient bullshit. Maybe it's just as well you didn't present it as a *fait accompli*. I'd have cold-cocked you with a chair."

"Your language appears to be slipping."

"You're fucking right it's slipping. You have deceived me. Doesn't that sound quaint? Pure gothic heroine? Let's use the real word; you lied to me. You lied to me on the telephone, you lied to me a moment ago, and all along you have been lying to me in your mind. I'm no saint, Chris – to coin a phrase – but in the three years I've known you and loved you – yes, loved you – I have treated you straight. You have known my whereabouts at any hour of the day or night. I won't go so far as to say I've never looked at anyone else, but that's as far as it's gone, ever. A look. I have considered you above everyone else. And stop banging your fingernail against that goddamn glass."

Chris decided to play winsome. His smile could always illuminate a room. "Geoffry, you're getting all worked up over nothing. Let's talk it over in bed."

"Let's not!" It is difficult to talk about moral imperatives in the buff. "We are talking about two different things. You reduce the whole problem to simple acceptance or nonacceptance of the Toronto job. Bugger the job. What I want to know is why I had to learn the news inadvertently, from your wife, who furthermore –" I stopped. Telling him about Audrey's play for me would be fighting dirty, and I was pontificating about fairness.

"All right, all right. Have it your way. I honestly could see no point in telling you about my plans until they were certain."

"Why rock the boat? – to coin another phrase."

"Something like that. I knew you would be upset. Hell, I'm upset myself. It's not an easy decision to make. But what real difference is it going to make? We just won't see each other as often that's all."

"Christ, you are beginning the menopause, and instead of wearing menopausal mauve you're making a menopausal move. Let me put something to you. For three years I have respected your family obligations. I didn't enjoy doing so, but there they were, the wife and kids, like varicose veins or haemorrhoids; you can only get rid of them surgically so you have to learn to live with them. I made do with whatever scraps of time you had left over from family and school. Fair enough. My work makes demands on my time too. But I always knew you were a local phone call or a short ride away. If something important came up I could see you or talk to you in any given half hour. But Toronto? On top of a staggering phone bill I'll be lucky to see you once a month. I'll come to

Toronto and stay in a hotel; you'll come to Montreal, if the pressures of a new job will let you get away. We'll compromise on a day in Kingston; meet me outside the penitentiary. Have you ever tried seeing someone regularly in hotel rooms, or a furnished studio apartment? It's pretty bloody dreary, let me assure you. A bottle of scotch and toothbrush glasses and pulling on your trousers to go down the hall to the ice machine. A bad and overpriced sandwich from room service. Overheard conversations from the next room. Here at least we have a reasonable place to meet. It is my home after all. Hotel rooms and service flats are for tricks. We are supposed to be lovers, but if you move we'll be sliding backwards. It won't work, Chris. I'm too old. Twenty years ago I might have given it a try, but no longer."

"But if we really love one another isn't that all that really counts?"

For perhaps the first time Chris fully grasped that we were threatened.

"I'm sorry to say this, Chris, sorrier than perhaps you realize; but love is not enough. Maybe at eighteen, but not at fifty."

"Have you ever thought of moving to Toronto?"

"Not really. Law is not a profession that travels easily outside the Province of Quebec. Even if we open an office in Toronto, and there's talk, I'm the only member of the firm who's fluently bilingual. I have to stay. My mother is here; maybe that's not much but I do feel a certain responsibility-to my father more than to her. Last but not least comes inertia, a powerful force after fifty. *J'y suis, j'y reste.*"

"What you're saying in effect that if I take the Cranbrook appointment it's the end of us."

"Yes."

"I'm going to take the job if it's offered."

There seemed nothing further to say. I ought to have said nothing. But I was stung. I simply could not believe that the past three years could be dismissed, that they could vanish like steam from a kettle.

I was cooking up a zinger when Chris began to quote.

"'Our two souls therefore, which are one; Though I must go, endure not yet; A breach, but an expansion; Like gold to airy thinness beat.'"

It took me a stanza to realize the poem was something by Donne. But I was in no mood to be quoted at. "If you intend to quote poetry I'm going to watch television. Call me when you have finished." I rose to go into the bedroom.

Chris laid a restraining hand on my arm. "Come on, Geoffry. Hear me out." With no attempt to conceal my impatience I sat.

"If they be two, they are two so; As stiff twin compasses are two; Thy soul, the fix'd foot, makes no show; To move, but doth, if the other do...'"

Of course, the compass image. It failed to strike the appropriate responsive chord as geometry was always my downfall in school.

"'And though it in the centre sit; Yet when the other far doth roam; It leans, and hearkens after it; And grows erect, as that comes home.'"

Poetry ought not be recited aloud. I dismiss the oral tradition as belonging to another age. Most poets read their own work badly, in flat monotonous voices which permit the poem to speak for itself if it can. Actors bury the poem under layers of vocal tricks. Chris didn't recite badly, but I was totally unreceptive.

"'Such wilt thou be to me, who must; Like the other foot, obliquely run; Thy firmness makes my circle just; And makes me end where I begun.' It's true you know." He smiled into my eyes.

"Everything is true in poetry. That's why I never read it. I detest fleeting insights and thoughts that lie too deep for tears. Your verses fail to convince me of anything except that you probably got A-minus in your metaphysical poetry course. Take your compasses and stuff them. My soul is insufficiently elastic to stretch down Highway 401. And remember that sensitivity is the last resort of the truly selfish."

Chris laughed. "A tidy little epigram, if ever I heard one. Hey, Geoffry. Cheer up. You're making it bigger than it really is." He put his hand over mine.

I pulled my hand away. "You behave like a sixteen-year-old boy trying to get his hand on his girlfriend's box, convinced once he does she will be unable to say no. But it figures. You are forty-five going on seventeen. What makes you think for a second you won't be shovelling just as much shit at Cranbrook as you do at Haddley?" I chose my words carefully. Like most school teachers Chris disliked profanity and discouraged its use in Haddley's halls.

"Geoffry, there is nothing to be gained by self-conscious vulgarity. It ill becomes a man of your vocabulary to backslide into those locutions." He folded his hands in his lap.

"Backslide my ass. And don't use that high headmaster tone of voice with me. I did not feed candy to the rabbits. I only feed assistant headmasters to the lions." That was my exit line as I barged out to the kitchen to make myself another drink.

Chris rose to follow. "Can I – may I have one too?"

"Why not. After three years of siphoning up my liquor what difference does one more drink make."

My remark drew blood. "That's a rotten crack to make. You make me sound like a really cheap bastard. I had no idea you were going to behave like such a son of a bitch."

"Christopher, there is absolutely nothing to be gained by using those nasty words. Rummage around in your rich vocabulary and see if you can't come up with something better."

"I've never seen you like this before."

"I've never been like this before. After all it's not every day I discover the person who has figured most prominently in my life is hoping to leave the city, and without having the simple grace to tell me first. Shall I consult my *Etiquette in Canada*?" I pulled a book from the shelf behind the couch. "Let's see how Gertrude Pringle would deal with our particular situation. Do you suppose I should look under 'The Well-Bred Man' or 'Etiquette in Towns and Villages.' How about

'Deaths and Funerals'?"

"Geoffry, what is it you really want?"

"That's very simple. I want you to forget you ever heard of Cranbrook. What's so goddamn great about being a headmaster? Finish out your tenure at Haddley, and live with me after retirement. Nothing more than our previous plan." I knew even as I heard myself saying the words that I had lost. I was talking not of a plan but an illusion.

"But now that you know I'm dissatisfied with Haddley don't you feel you're being just a bit selfish?"

The appeal was so outrageous that I could almost have laughed. "Of course I'm being selfish, and furthermore I don't care. If you think for one small second you're going to lay a guilt trip on me save your breath."

"I see. You would prefer to see me unfulfilled at Haddley than contented at Cranbrook."

"Unfulfilled? Unfulfilled! Shit! You sound like some bride at Niagara Falls whose husband suffers from premature ejaculation." I rose and crossed to the window. At least once during an emotional scene one of the protagonists must cross to the window. About to observe that nowhere in the Haddley-Cranbrook debate was the pleasure of my company a determining factor, I discovered, to my surprise, a reserve of vanity I did not think I possessed. I would not toss myself onto the scales to be weighed off against some other consideration. Pride aside, I was not about to turn the emotional thumbscrews, to manipulate Chris into staying. I loved him. I loved him all right. But not enough to sell myself short.

And hadn't I always known it was a January-May romance? Chris was my last love affair; I was his first. Five chronological years could not begin to describe the gulf of experience and attitudes that widened steadily between us. He did not know, as I knew with absolute certainty, how his move would erode our love for one another. The easy optimism that believed a new job must lead to improvement failed to appreciate the corrosive effect of infrequent and transient meetings. Oddly enough his incorruptible optimism was one of the qualities I had truly admired, little thinking how it would one day cause him to seek out those proverbial greener pastures. I knew the grass to be no greener on the Ontario side of the fence. And if Chris did not already know I could not convince him. Nor was I about to try.

I turned back from the window. "Maybe you're right, Chris. You'll never know about Cranbrook unless you give it a try. We'll work it out somehow." It was my way of saying goodbye.

"I have only one question," said Chris. "Wherever did you get that copy of Gertrude Pringle?"

"I found it at Mother's house, when we were moving her to the apartment. I read it daily."

Suddenly Chris and I began to talk of other things. Bright, brittle, self-conscious, our conversation piled up non-sequiturs like someone cording wood: the Eaton Centre, people seen at the recital, a new restaurant in Yorkville, a refurbished one in Old Montreal, *Swan Lake* at the O'Keefe Centre, Astaire and Rogers on PBS. We sounded like two people who had just been introduced at a clever party. When our too-animated chatter began to flag we went to bed. It was like making love to someone I had known long ago, sex with an old lover back in town after a long absence. The clock threatened; he had to go.

Chris and I continued to see each other for a while, but something hovered between us. A sheet of mylar, transparent, impenetrable, kept us from touching. Our meetings were reflections of past encounters, echoes of earlier times. Without future we found ourselves without even a present, and the past turned out to be too insubstantial to sustain us. We met less and less frequently. One day he called; I said I was busy. I was busy the second time. He called a third time; I said I was busy. He understood the code. He did not call again.

BY NOW I WAS TIRED ENOUGH that turning out lights and locking Winnifred's front door seemed a huge effort. I hauled myself up the stairs, unbuttoning my shirt as I went. Dropping my clothes over a chair I fell into bed and prayed for sleep.

# 7.

AT 5:00 A.M. I ROLLED MY LEGS over the side of the bed and levered myself into a sitting position. My back gave a couple of creaks, but I guess I can't really complain. Most people my age seem to have back problems, anything from lumbago to spinal fusions. They form a club whose dues are measured in pain and inconvenience. You can tell them by the way they head for the straight-backed chairs at parties. They never volunteer when the hostess suggests moving the sofa to make more room, nor do they push stuck cars out of snow drifts. We pay our price for being upright primates; animals seldom if ever have bad backs.

I put coffee on to perc in an electric percolator I'm sure the Smithsonian would kill for. The appliance was old when Winnifred bought it years ago at a garage sale. Then I went reluctantly down to the basement and opened the freezer to give one of the packages containing a leg an experimental poke. It felt hard to the touch. My plan was to drive the package somewhere out of the way and dump it. Then I hesitated. Supposing I had an accident? I am a careful driver, so defensive, in fact, I often leave the car in the garage and take cabs. My insurance record lies unblemished in some computer or other. But I still did not want to risk being rammed or side-swiped by some driver less defensive than myself while I had bits and pieces of Dale in my trunk, my car being towed away to a centrally-heated garage while the package slowly thawed.

I wasn't thinking clearly. The likelihood of an accident remained slight and I would put the package into a suitcase. Thus resolved, I settled down with a day-old newspaper. I flipped to the business section, which I always read because I feel I ought to. Some stocks were up; some down; the dollar was poorly; we were going to run out of oil in about three weeks. Same old shit. The editorial page reported a speech by a prominent American windbag who assured to whom it may concern that with the world in crisis at this point in time the United States of America was not going to stand idly by watching tensions escalate without making interventions, peaceful or otherwise. I turned to the entertainment section which I always save until last and best. The Institute for Twentieth Century Music had given a concert and one of the composers, piqued by the negative reaction of the press, had published a rebuttal. I began to read: "The composition of Percussive Trio was essentially a matter of rendering an image of motion-not yet definable through any of the sensory manifestations-into sound, by a process of increasingly specific ramifications. Each compositional level possesses its own integrity, so that each successive layer derives from the previous one as an entirety, specifically that no literal association can survive unaltered from one to the next."

I turned the page. My eye fell on an item about a tragedy in the east end of the city. Accidental death in the papers is always a tragedy. No more does tragedy deal with the fall of those in high places or the fatal flaw. Nowadays anyone who accidentally stops breathing becomes, courtesy of Rigor Mortis, a tragic figure. In this instance I'm sure it was very sad for the parents whose children playing hide and seek hid and sought themselves into old refrigerators abandoned in lanes. The latch caught; two children suffocated. To prevent a repetition of the tragedy the city was launching a clean-up campaign to rid back lanes and vacant lots of abandoned refrigerators. And if one or two of them held fragments of Dale Lawton would anyone be the wiser?

I dressed and drove down the hill to my apartment building, where I let myself into the garage. At the end of the parking area through a door lay the extra storage lockers for each apartment. Among other miscellaneous items, mine held a large Samsonite suitcase given to me for Christmas some years ago by a lover who should have known better. Standing empty it almost takes two hands to lift; full of clothing and shoes it would be about as portable as a stove. However one finds strength in moments of crisis. Do we not have the Incredible Hulk as living proof? Those who fail to catch his large green presence on the screen can find him in the comics. He is the Jolly Green Giant without the jolly. And he is considerably less chic; his rags and tatters cannot compete with the Giant's natty tunic made of leaves which just manages to cover his jolly green cock. Imagine a double date with the Jolly Green Giant and the Incredible Hulk as escorts. Either we get the best table at Regine's or Studio 54 or there won't be any Régine's or Studio 54.

I drove the suitcase back to Winnifred's. The package of one truncated leg just fit. I wondered how a mere leg could weigh so much. The living do not appreciate the dead weight of the dead. I lugged the suitcase out to the trunk of my car. Fortunately my car is ordinary to the square of five. Whatever my self-image it is not defined by my automobile, one of the middle-income models from Detroit in a sombre shade. Not long ago I saw a cashier from the local supermarket arrive for work in his car. A spotty youth trying desperately to grow a bushy moustache, he drives a low, sleek, silver two-seater. He wears a matching silver windbreaker and gauntlets. He sheds the car in the employees' parking lot, the windbreaker and gauntlets in the locker room. In apron and maroon clip-on tie he spends the day punching items through express cash before climbing back into his fantasy for the trip home. Even as a younger man I didn't much care about a car; just so long as it went. And I have always disliked sex in a back seat.

I drove down to St. Catherine Street and headed east. Traffic flowed easily as I preceded the rush hour congestion. Across St. Lawrence Boulevard to St. Denis. If you are turned on a wheel of spikes in Alexandria or find yourself roasted to death on a grill in Rome or have the misfortune to be beheaded in Montmartre, Montreal names a street after you. I would prefer to die peacefully in my bed without even the immortality of a dead-end lane in my name. I turned right at Sherbrooke Street and proceeded still further east. Turning onto a side street I began to cruise slowly past rows of darkened houses, their outside staircases describing graceful arabesques against sombre, grey façades. Who would have thought that an architectural shortcut, the outside staircase tacked on to eliminate the interior stairwell, would have become as much a Montreal logo as its whale-shaped mountain or the immense dome and truncated transepts of Brother André's basilica? The street slept. Day-shift workers were recharging themselves for another day's labour; night-shift workers had not yet begun to straggle home. It is a street of families, families whose children lack playgrounds. They play hockey in the street and hide in lanes, sometimes in abandoned refrigerators carted outside to make way for the gleaming new appliance won in a raffle or bought on credit. It is a safe street, silent, secure, and, above all, deserted.

I drove slowly, pausing to squint up dark lanes peopled by stealthy, secretive city rats and battle-scarred, street-wise tomcats. From an alley to my left a gleam of dull white beckoned. Straining through the gloom I could make out the rectangular shape of a refrigerator, propped at a rakish angle against the side of the building. I pulled my car over to the curb, taking care not to block the entrance, then opened my trunk, hoping any casual passerby might think me a travelling salesman, *un commis-voyaguer*, reaching for my sample case, while in fact I was unscrewing my licence plate.

Nonchalantly, I examined the refrigerator, an old-fashioned model with metal catch instead of vinyl seal. So old was the machine that the round cooling mechanism sat on top like a hatbox. I opened the door. "Jesus Christ!" I said under my breath at the sight that greeted me. A calico cat, her eyes glazed, lay on her side with five kittens in nursing position. I was appalled. Not to want five kittens is understandable; but to shut them along with the mother into a refrigerator to die of gradual suffocation or starvation struck me as horrifying. At that moment the mother cat stirred weakly, revived no doubt by the sudden rush of fresh air. The kittens awoke and attempted to nurse, their movements hardly visible. Common sense told me to get out, to let someone else find them. This kind of thing happens all the time. I actually turned away and started walking back toward my car. But life, any life, seemed suddenly very important. I simply could not leave her behind. I called myself a sap, a fool, a patsy, and worse; but I turned back to the refrigerator.

The lane was littered with trash, including a pile of empty cartons. I chose a dry one, which once held beans in tomato sauce, and lined it with an old beach towel I found in the trunk of my car. Then I placed the mother and her five feeble kittens into the carton, which I put into the back seat of the car. Almost as an afterthought, I opened the suitcase, lifted out the green plastic package, carried it to the refrigerator, and put it in the empty rectangular space, closing the door. Back at the car, I snapped the suitcase shut, slammed down the trunk hood.

I drove north two blocks before turning back toward St. Denis, at which point I pulled over to the curb just long enough to nip out and replace my licence plate. Okay, Mr. Bleeding Heart, what now? *"Blute nur, du liebes Herz!"* I couldn't take the cats back to Winnifred's. Her own cat would object strenuously to the uninvited presence of a townie and her brood. And God only knows what kinds of fleas, distemper, rhinotracheitis, worms, and worse, had infected these stray street cats. But if I was going to play Hercules wrestling with death for the life of Alcestis I had to see it through. I wondered how many of its nine lives the mother cat still had on credit. The box was ominously quiet. I knew the SPCA would be closed at this hour as would all the animal hospitals. Quo Vadis? Glumly I drove back to my apartment building and turned into the garage. I lifted the box of cats from the back seat and carried it up to my apartment. The animals lay supine, but I was determined to put one over on Rigor Mortis.

"Well, well, Geoffry Chadwick, let me give you a hand. I'm good with pets."

"Get lost, Rigor Mortis. I'm about to do my heavy Florence Nightingale number."

I put the box onto the kitchen floor. From a cupboard I took a can of condensed milk and poured it into a saucepan on the stove. As it warmed I added a shot of brandy. I poured the mixture into a Royal Doulton soup plate, which I placed on the floor beside the box. Then I lifted the mother out and held her, nose pointed at the dish. She could barely stand. I tried to be patient. There was no point in worrying about the kittens; if I didn't get the free lunch counter back into business again it was curtains all around anyway. Gradually she began to lap, tentatively at first, then with more and more interest. Between the warmth and the milk and the brandy I could see her beginning to revive.

I knelt holding her. It was 6:30 A.M. I hadn't had any sleep. I had a body to dispose of. I was supposed to get up to Toronto to find an office apartment for my firm. I was ruining the crease in my trousers. I ought to have been up at Winnifred's keeping the lid on, figuratively and literally. Instead I was coaxing a half-dead stray cat to drink brandy and milk in my kitchen. I wasn't humane; I was goddamn crazy. Still I held her while she drank. After she emptied the bowl I lifted her back into the box. I poured the rest of the condensed milk into the bowl and in another bowl I mashed a tin of sardines with a fork. The bowl had belonged briefly to my daughter Allison, one of the few things that remained to remind me of her. On the bottom was a picture of a tabby cat, tucked comfortably into bed, that used to be the logo for Pullman cars.

The mother cat was painfully thin; she didn't look as though there was much in her to void. But I took the bottom section of my grill pan and filled it with torn newspapers hoping she might have the sense to use it. I was frankly dubious. Cats really aren't very bright. Even though those gleaming eyes and pointed ears and brisk whiskers combine to make them look intelligent, they aren't. I put down a dish of water, closed both doors leading into the kitchen, and turned off the lights. If the mother survived the next few hours I would take her to the vet for examination and boarding while I decided what to do.

Suddenly exhausted I decided I could not face even the short drive back to Winnifred's. My joints felt as though they were made of styrofoam. I could scarcely remove my clothes before falling into bed only to discover I had passed beyond sleep. Not for me the snug, trouble-free, wake-me-when-it's-over slumber typified by the Pullman cat on the bottom of the baby's bowl. I couldn't seem to get myself comfortable. Susan had bought that bowl herself before the baby was born. She was determined to have all kinds of pets so the baby would grow up to love animals: dogs, cats, hampsters, gerbils, fish, budgies. I pointed out that the hampsters, gerbils, goldfish, budgies wouldn't last long if we had a cat; nor would the cat be around long if the dog were feisty. Did I have a better suggestion? Yes; how about a condor in a cage, a tank of piranhas, and a mammal of some sort, maybe an armadillo which could run around free without fear of the dogcatcher. But were armadillos good around children? Perhaps we should consider a boa constrictor, or a pterodactyl. Hard to come by, I countered, and impossible to house train. Perhaps a grizzly. In an apartment? Susan and I had turned the whole thing into a running joke. What would make the ideal pet? A kiwi? A unicorn? A sphinx would ask too many questions and gobble up the neighbours. Zebras were surly and gnus unpredictable. Why was I remembering all this nonsense? A baby's bowl, with a sleeping cat on the bottom … .

I had met my wife Susan at a debutante ball. Only by

chance did I go to the ball in the first place, having been pressed into service as last ditch escort for a cousin whose slated escort had broken his leg on the parallel bars two days before the event. It was my particular bad luck to have tails hanging in my closet. Mother believed every young man ought to have a complete set of evening clothes, tails and a dinner jacket, double-breasted, naturally. I wanted a single-breasted tuxedo but Mother wouldn't hear of it. As she was paying the bills she had the deciding vote. Also included were white flannels and a lightweight blazer, also double-breasted, for summer occasions. I expect Mother had seen one too many 1930s zany comedies where everyone dresses for dinner, and a brain surgeon down on his luck turns up as the butler and girls in afternoon dresses to the floor scurry about giggling, shrieking, and solving murders. Mother believed firmly that clothes make the man.

So it came to pass that wearing my tails along with Father's mother-of-pearl and platinum studs and new white kid gloves just like a waiter I rang the doorbell and handed my cousin Beverly a wrist corsage of three gardenias on a little plastic bracelet. Beverly was pretty in a damp sort of way. Her brown hair hung in a lank pageboy and long, white gloves made her long, thin arms look longer and thinner. She wore a halter-necked slipper satin gown with lots of fabric gathered over the bust to conceal the fact she had little to conceal. We were part of a larger group organized to meet at our reserved table in the ballroom at the Windsor Hotel.

I can still remember my first impression of Susan was that she seemed so much more alive than the others at the table. Not that she was pretty, not in the least. Her small blue eyes sat close together over a pug nose above a mouth wide enough to park a jeep. Good teeth, though. I have always been a bit of a tooth freak. If you don't have good teeth get caps. As Susan was not a debutante but only along for the ride she wore pale orange chiffon. I have always loved the colour orange and I have always loved chiffon, that most feminine of fabrics. Female impersonators never wear chiffon.

# SUNDAY'S CHILD

They come out in lame and sequins, chain mail, and armour. They wear exaggerated helmet wigs in improbable metallic shades, basilisk makeup, and gauds of jewellery. They are so pathetically old fashioned, anchored in a concept of 1940s movie glamour that was itself artifice pushed into androgyny. I went to a drag party once, glaringly conspicuous in a grey pin-striped suit. The other men were all dressed like movie extras about to attend a meeting of the PTA. I won't be patronizing and say it was sad just because I did not have a good time. Everyone else did. Only I thought a drag party would be a little like a masquerade party, everyone whooping and hollering and milking their assumed identities for all they were worth. Instead everyone played it so small-town-respectable you could have cut the decorum with a butter knife. Even the bitchery was muted. As Winnifred might have said: "It was a real drag." If I ever wanted to trick myself out in female attire the first thing I would do is buy *Vogue* or some other fashion magazine and get myself up in style. The layered look would suit me, tall and thin as I am; but with a jacket over a vest over a tie over a shirt what else have I been wearing all my life?

It soon became evident to everyone at the table that Susan was at odds with her escort, the kind of youth who used to be called a lummox. He drank much and badly, meaning his intoxication showed. He went off to have a drink in some other party's suite (renting a suite in the hotel for the night of the dance was the in thing to do), and passed out cold on one of the beds. We never heard from him again. Straight down the Memory Hole. All of which left me in a curious position. I was attached to the Beverly/Susan group; deb dances are tribal affairs, and although I was officially Beverly's escort, a warm body helping her on and off with her coat, I certainly was not her date. We weren't screwing as were most of the other couples on the floor. But I was a good dancer. After manoeuvring Beverly around the floor a few times – she was totally unrhythmical and talked nonstop – I asked Susan if she would care to dance. Would she ever. So she put her gloved hand into my glove; And we danced together – and fell in love, to paraphrase that painfully sentimental Second World War poem Mother used to play on the gramophone in a perfect orgy of red eyes and sniffles.

We did, though; we fell in love. In love in that way one can for a certain brief charmed period of youth, before one has learned to question and before the spirit has grown inelastic along with the muscles. It is a time when sensibility and sensuality and sentimentality fuse and become indistinguishable. Chronic sexual desire changes from an itch in the groin to affirmation that love will last forever. We were too young to understand Mother Nature's plan for perpetuating the species. All we knew was that we wanted to get married so we could set up shop and stop screwing on the sly.

And screw we did. If we thought we were going to be alone for five minutes we were hard at it. In the basement, in the garage, on the living room floor, while parents napped, behind the shelves of jurisprudence in the law library. We went on picnics and forgot to eat the sandwiches. On the ground (lumpy), in a car (constricted), in a rowboat (tippy). When it turned cold we checked into motels. Once in a moment of sheer extravagance we checked into a downtown hotel only to find Father's closest friend shacked up with some young woman in the next room (inhibiting).

For the first time in my life I found myself actually wanting to be faithful to one person. It was a whole new trip, although that word had a different meaning then. Before I had met Susan my sex life was pretty much catch-as-catch-can; girls I could persuade to put out, the occasional divorcée. I had a few fucking buddies, guys my own age who thought the same way I did. We'd meet from time to time, have a few beers, get it on with each other. No sweat. And when the outlets grew scarce I could always tryst privately with my own right hand.

But with Susan I had my first intimations of permanence. I think now I may have liked the idea of a lasting relationship almost as much as I liked Susan herself. And that was the factor that tipped the scales. I loved her, and I liked her too.

When we announced our desire to get married neither set of parents was anything but pleased. Father thought it time I settled down and suggested only that we wait until I had passed my bar exams. I bought Susan one of those really Westmount engagement rings, a ruby with a diamond on either side, set in platinum claws, an old lady's ring; but Susan loved it. Father scheduled the ring on his insurance policy. It had, after all, real as well as symbolic value.

The June wedding was considered a lovely affair. I wore a morning coat; yes, I had one of those too, hanging in the bag beside the tails. Susan turned out to be an extremely organized young woman with loads of tact. She manipulated all the parents beautifully and spared me much. All I really had to do was show up at the church. I put my foot down on two things: no flower girls, no stag party. As far back as I can remember I have disliked jocks, male bonding, and the smelly locker room camaraderie enjoyed by that dreariest of creatures, the slightly insecure heterosexual male.

Susan and I had spent the night before the ceremony in the wedding suite, which she had seen fit to reserve a couple of days in advance. I think that may have been the night she got pregnant. She came down the nave in white *peau de soie*, wearing a coronet to secure the veil, but I still prefer to think of her in the orange chiffon. Anyway the wedding was just like any other except that I was on stage. Tears, telegrams, toasts. Champagne, cake, confetti. Speeches, sandwiches, sincerity. Wedding presents, waves goodbye, wet hankies. The works. Mother even managed to catch the bride's bouquet.

With new clothes and new luggage and our new status writ large, we drove downtown to our suite. The following day we flew to Bermuda on a plane full of newlyweds. It's easy to spot newlyweds; they all have new shoes and luggage. And they change from going away outfits into Bermuda shorts. Bermuda itself is about the dullest place I have ever been, dull and dangerous. Narrow roads, erratic drivers, and swarms of visitors out of control on motorized bicycles.

## EDWARD O. PHILLIPS

The beach was beautiful; food edible. I didn't play golf but we walked on the links. We went into Hamilton where Susan bought teacups and sweater sets. After five of our projected ten days we both admitted that outside of sex there was precious little to do. I suggested we head for New York where we spent five of the most nearly perfect days I have ever enjoyed.

New York is a very romantic city. I don't mean romantic from the movie viewpoint of love and sex. New York is romantic in the medieval fairy tale sense, beautiful and dangerous. Between the castles of Empire State and Chrysler stretch enchanted concrete forests filled with dragons and basilisks, manticores and chimeras, damsels in distress and loathly ladies side by side with knights and wizards and sorceresses. New York has them all. Mind you, at times the knights look very like policemen in navy blue instead of chain mail, the sorceress may turn out to be a hard blonde in blue sequins playing cigarette-scarred piano and singing in a husky contralto about the men who got away. A basilisk may snatch your purse and the wizard dwindle into a doorman getting you a cab on a rainy night. Details. The spirit of New York crackles with romance. In another time there stood a city ... .

To be young and in love is pretty good, but to be young and in love and in New York City is twice as good. Even the Metropolitan Museum seemed a house of wonders rather than an endurance test. The Staten Island ferry became our own private galleon; we were both absolutely certain the Statue of Liberty held her torch aloft just for us. We stood on top of the world, or so we felt, as we strolled the observation deck on the Empire State Building. Susan's cup ran over when she discovered sweater sets cost more at Saks Fifth Avenue than in Bermuda. We stayed at the Plaza and felt like Scott and Zelda Fitzgerald although we behaved better. We had drinks in the Oak Room before dashing to the opera to watch Aida sacrifice everything for love; we found her behaviour perfectly rational. Over late supper at Luchow's we talked about what a good idea it had been to come to New York, what a good idea it had been to get married, how clever we were to be us. Love, especially young love, is not without fatuity.

Susan had boundless energy and enthusiasm along with a liberal conscience nurtured in the better private schools and colleges. As a girl she worked in summer camps for underprivileged children and came home with lice in her hair. As a student she took arms against a sea of troubles and worked for a slightly left-wing political party. She insisted we visit the Bowery so she could beat herself with her own good fortune. I have never enjoyed the spectacle of human misery, neither for therapy, guilt, or compassion. A certain number of any given group must lose out. Certain children will be mongoloid, autistic, retarded. Some will develop polio or cystic fibrosis. Some will be hit by cars. The same holds true for adults, a set number of whom will end up as drunks and bums. I have no wish to scrutinize them. Susan accused me of being hardhearted. I called her a limousine liberal; she called me a cast concrete conservative. We nearly had a spat. Instead we compromised by walking around Greenwich Village and looking at the bohemians and homosexuals and dope addicts and lesbians who gravitated toward that delicious cesspool of human aberration. It was not the last time in my life that I was to visit the Village.

After five packed days we were just about ready to leave. We took the overnight train north to Montreal.

Down the platform of Windsor Station we walked, Susan carrying her makeup case, me the box of teacups. Into a cab we climbed and set off to our new apartment to begin playing house in earnest.

We were still dithering over whether to exchange the second wedding-present toaster for a percolator or a large wooden salad bowl, whether to go teak or traditional in the den, when Susan discovered she was pregnant. Not that she started throwing up mornings or craving asparagus; she turned out to be a marvellous pregnant person to be around, healthy and delighted with the whole idea. She had missed a couple of periods and thought she had better check.

## EDWARD O. PHILLIPS

We revised plans for decorating the den. Instead of raw sienna with one wall of modular bookcases the room became off-white with one wall papered in flying Dumbos, cross Donald Ducks, and pompous Mickey Mice. We bought an old pine crib for decor and an ugly but solid one from Eaton's for the baby. The tidings were glad; all the inlaws rejoiced greatly. Mother took to knitting with her customary lack of expertise. Her needles were too large for the tiny garments, which came out loose and shapeless. Uncertain of whether to use pink or blue wool she chose white and hard blue-green. I'm sure that deep down she believed that if you put a pink sweater on a baby boy he would grow up to be a pansy.

"Just Molly and me; And baby makes three." The insidious and very much to be guarded against reality of sentimental cliches is that they zap you when your guard is down. Susan and I were quite frankly ecstatic over the baby, the missing prop from our domestic scenario. She was thrilled at the news, and I found myself caught up in her excitement. The day we got the positive report we discussed over dinner, always soup or *hors d'oeuvres*, always wine, whether the big city Harvard/Radclifife environment was more enriching than the smaller Amherst/Mount Holyoke campus life. I did not intend to inflict the McGill/University of Montreal parochial experience on the foetus. Over coffee – I ground the beans myself by hand – we tried to decide which private schools we would approach the second we learned the sex of the child.

It was a strange time. I rode through the following months on a crest of euphoria. I guess Susan and I talked endlessly about the baby. I'm not sure. Perhaps I talked about what happened at the office. To be a practising professional was still shiny and new; I basked in my own importance. I suppose I did. I don't really remember now. It all happened so long ago, and to someone else. I was someone else then; I had plans and ambitions, a few illusions. Even the novelty of going to work, winning the bread and bearing home the bacon, blinded me to the fact I had chosen a profession for which I had aptitude but no enthusiasm. Still I was buoyed up by discovery, new wife, new job, new apartment, new baby on the way. It was a time when the socially acceptable still had the charm of novelty. As we age, as the approved begins to pall, we seek increasingly more experimental methods of rubbing the tarnish of boredom from our lives.

It is difficult to talk about happiness. Like virtue it becomes its own reward; also like virtue happiness seems bland to the point of boredom whenever one attempts to describe it. "I was happy," elicits a so-what kind of response. "I was miserable," rivets attention. But I can still remember, even so very long ago, a feeling that all was right with the world. The year was not at the spring; the hillside was not dew-pearled; if the lark was on the wing it was surely in a warmer clime than ours. Nevertheless like Pippa I looked at the world and found it in order.

Susan gave birth to a baby girl in one of those deliveries that might have come straight from a medical textbook. When the pains started at regular intervals I took her to the hospital, pausing only to snap shut the already packed overnight bag. After brief labour she produced a six-pound baby girl who howled when slapped like any sensible baby would.

We were nearly buried under an avalanche of baby presents, seven rattles, a veritable zoo of adorable stuffed toys, and enough hand-knitted bootees that walking from here to Vancouver the baby could not wear them all out. We could have opened a boutique. When Susan arrived home from the hospital she had in effect two children to deal with. I was absolutely certain the child would not live through the week. If she burped I thought she must have an ulcer, if she kicked she was having an epileptic seizure, and if she cried whatever she had must surely be terminal. Susan spent almost as much time coddling me as she did the baby. I was starring in my own sitcom, life-sized and natural colour. I did not hand out smelly, phallic cigars.

Each morning I called Susan from the office just to make certain they were both still breathing. One morning she told me to call her mother's house instead where she was taking the baby to spend the day. She had her own small car, a wedding present from her father. She bundled up the baby in a cocoon of shawls, and took the car keys from the desk. The key chain held a lucky rabbit's foot. I suggested once the chain had proved very unlucky for the rabbit; Susan laughed and said I was stuffy. I was still shaving that morning when she left; she kissed me on the forehead because I was covered in shaving soap. The water was running and I did not hear the door close.

Police conjectured later that she had just been turning onto Cote des Neiges when the cement mixer, its brakes having given out up past the hospital, struck her with all the momentum built up during that long rush down the hill. Susan, the baby, and the driver of the truck all died on impact. Little remained of the car. Susan's father insisted the coffin be shut, and my father insisted I not try to see her. She had been identified; that was enough. I simply failed for a while to register that both Susan and the baby had been killed. They were simply absent, not dead. I sat stunned at the undertaker's; people came up and in self-conscious murmurs – why must sympathy for the dead, more precisely the living, always be inaudible? – muttered the platitudes of grief. Then they withdrew to converse in stage whispers which carried into the street. It was generally agreed that I was behaving wonderfully.

It's odd; when someone you really love dies, do you stop loving that person? Does the end of the person, physical and legal, terminate the emotion except as a memory? I don't think so. Somewhere beneath the scar tissue of many loveless love affairs and the barnacles of endless promiscuities there is something in me that still loves Susan, or the memory of Susan, as she was, still alive. Memory is highly untrustworthy, as anyone who has spent five minutes cross-examining a witness learns fast; but often it is all we have. I do not keep photographs, but once at Mother's, when we were moving her out of the house, I came across my wedding pictures, snaps of Susan and the baby, our studio engagement photograph. The young woman in the pictures was almost a stranger, someone I had once known but almost forgotten. Yet the Susan I remember, the girl in the orange chiffon dress, is still vivid.

After her death I grieved for Susan. Then I began to grieve less. Youth is resilient. After a while I began to realize how little residue remained. We fell in love, married, set up housekeeping, had a baby; all commonplace experiences. We had no real fights, no serious problems, not even any extraordinary celebrations. I discovered that I had practically nothing to hang on to, nothing to keep memory keen. Not that I wanted to dwell on the past or savour my unhappiness like old port. But I felt cheated. Everything had gone so smoothly, so according to blueprint, that once Susan was dead, once grief began to abate, I found the whole experience slipping through my fingers like fine white sand. Of all those tiny particles there was not one I could clench in my fist and say, "Here is my marriage. This proves it all really happened." I think it was just about this time I discovered how photographs block memory. I studied the freeze frames of my brief time with Susan. They recorded seconds; I wanted to grasp the whole. Finally I put the photographs away; one day I burned them in the kitchen sink. It always comes as a relief to finally let go.

It was only after the death of Susan that I began to see men on a more or less regular basis. From the perspective of fifty years old, the reason seems abundantly clear; I was sexually attracted to members of my own sex. However, unlike middle-aged people, who are honest with themselves and lie to others, the young are what they consider honest with others, yet they lie to themselves. In my youth, two teenaged men who enjoyed one another's bodies had to find an alibi. "God, weren't we drunk last night!" The beer or the rye became the villain of the piece, not our own sexual drives. "All cats are grey in the dark," was another oft-quoted homily, suggesting we were in the grip of a biological drive that demanded satisfaction, however indiscriminate. One needed to explain away moments of passion, all the more passionate because forbidden. Always we worried more about what others would think of us than what we thought of ourselves. If there was one thing worse than going to bed with a live man it was, just possibly, being found in bed with a dead woman. The humiliation would be well-nigh unendurable; how could one ever live it down. Yet the risk added zest to the first fumbling adolescent attempts at homosexual activity on the daybed-sofa in the basement rumpus room. Mutual masturbation ("Don't squeeze it so hard"); fellatio ("Watch out for your teeth!"); *soixante-neuf* ("Could you move your knee? It's in my eye"); sodomy ("Ouch!"–"Relax."–"It hurts!"–"Give it time"). In the messy aftermath of Kleenex and averted glances, of one thing could both parties be sure; the guilty secret would go with them to the grave. Of course, I'm talking about myself at sixteen. By the time I turned twenty-one, I realized most people couldn't have cared less about my sex life.

It is easy to chuckle about the whole thing now, but my reason was no less specious. I almost managed to convince myself that I was somehow being less unfaithful to the memory of Susan by having it on with dudes rather than stupping wenches. I subscribed to a variation of the all-cats-are-grey-in-the-dark school of pious promiscuity. As a young man, I needed sex – one had only to read Kinsey – yet sex with my own sex, which could never lead to marriage, did not constitute a betrayal of my marriage which sleeping with women would. Even someone with a minus I.Q and no legal training could shoot that argument full of holes. As if my reasoning process did not already merit lashes and days in solitary I did sleep with women. Not right away mind you. I allowed a decent period of homosexual mourning to elapse before I returned to the arena where women confront men.

It began with an affair with a Jewish graduate student in linguistics. I met her at a party full of young professionals with a sprinkling of graduate students, like wedges of tomato in a salad, for contrast. Gloria was pretty in that full-figured way, which meant she could soon be fat. She had fabulous luxuriant dark hair. After she suggested I drive her home she asked me in for a cognac. There were no etchings but I did not have to strain to read the writing on the wall. She was warm and soft and comfortable. Unfortunately she took the whole thing dreadfully seriously, retiring to the tiny bathroom to insert her diaphragm with the high sanctity of a vestal virgin tending the sacred flame. When we actually got down to business she kept repeating, "It's so good, it's so good," in a tone suggesting she was in extreme pain. She called out to God. When she came it was a religious experience.

At first I found her humourless intensity sexually arousing. I could even overlook the lectures on phonemes and morphemes and what languages belonged to the Indo-European family and wasn't it fascinating about Finnish and Hungarian being related. That was before she got onto the subject of her family. Gloria had exactly the same problems that anyone else has with a family, only the members of her family appeared to begin every sentence with the direct object. A linguist you want to be? And the piano? All the piano lessons you took. A Steinway we bought. It was obvious her family believed less in morphemes than in dotted quarter notes. Gloria was in full dress rebellion against her family. Having an affair with a goy was one manifestation. Foreskin the bell tolls.

Trying to run a kosher apartment was another.

It has always struck me that the Jewish dietary laws made perfect sense when one considers searing Mediterranean heat, no glass or stainless steel utensils, no refrigeration, no government standards of sanitation. There are things to be said for living in the twentieth century. But in Old Testament times, so lovingly chronicled by Cecil B. DeMille, those who were careless about food died. However, with the sanitation facilities now available, with gleaming germ-free kitchens and bi-weekly garbage collection, to run a kosher house strikes me as excessive, like going to mass every day or giving up innocent pleasures for lent.

But Gloria was determined with a two-burner stove and tiny sink to turn back the clock. A further complication arose from her being obliged to do the dishes in the bathtub situated across the main passageway in its own tiny room complete with forty-watt bulb. One night, she had me for dinner, borsht, all-beef wieners, salad. On top of everything else she was dieting, so for dessert we shared an apple. And I loathe sweet red wine. Next time was somewhat better: good vegetable soup, gefilte fish (Jewish quennelles), and a scratch cake, no mean feat considering the size of the kitchen. After eating we prepared solemnly for the ritual of love, which had her lying on the bed moaning softly before I had even touched her.

One day I suggested making a meal myself to bring along. I dabbled in cooking in those days and could turn out a handful of quick, palatable meals. Arriving at Gloria's with a flourish I heated and stirred and served up. "Oh, it's so good!" she exclaimed, tucking in with the voracious hunger of one who has been too long dieting. "What is it?"

"Beef stroganoff."

"Is the recipe a secret?"

"Not at all. Beef, naturally, mushrooms, sour cream –"

"Sour cream!" Her voice registered shock. She plunked down her fork. "Ohmygod. You've ruined my dishes."

"What do you mean I've 'ruined your dishes'?" I considered the stroganoff a success and was miffed at her reaction.

"Don't you see? Milk and meat in the same dish?"

"You mean all that kosher nonsense? Forget it."

But Gloria would not forget it. Her dishes were contaminated. A simple washing would not suffice; a little water would not clear them of this deed. The dishes must be buried, in earth, for at least twenty-four hours. I pointed out that in mid-February burying anything in earth was a frank impossibility. However were she to bury the dishes in a snow bank the spirit if not the letter of the law would be observed. Gloria looked dubious, but short of buying new dishes and pans she had little choice. I helped her to bury the plates, knives, forks, lovely old Coalport serving dish she had from an aunt, ladle, and stainless steel double boiler. The only snow bank outside her converted row house had been pushed up along the sidewalk by a snow plough on one of its infrequent visits to her little travelled dead-end crescent.

We made love and fell asleep.

During the night the snowblower passed. I seem to remember hearing it dimly through half-slumber. It was only in the morning when I looked out the window onto a bare street that I realized the plates, cutlery, double boiler, and Coalport tureen had been chewed up and spewed into a truck for transport to a distant dump. I began to laugh silently. Gloria noticed my shaking shoulders and came to stand beside me at the window. She was not amused. The angrier she grew the harder I laughed.

Why dwell on the rest. The episode made a breach that subsequent meetings could never heal. The last I saw of Gloria was her engagement picture in the newspaper. She was shortly to marry a toothsome medical student and she wore an engagement solitaire the size of a lima bean. *Sic transit* Gloria.

There were other women, other affairs; some brief, some briefer. The intervals between them grew longer and longer. In the meantime, I continued busy on the bar circuit, especially those catering to the white-collar alternate lifestyle, where I met a series of doctors, engineers, salesmen. Whenever you pick up a trick who says, "I'll bet you can't guess what I do," you know he's a hairdresser. The turnover was high. I had turned thirty when one day I realized over a year had passed since I had last slept with a woman. That was my own personal Rubicon. Whatever the term: pansy, homosexual, queer, gay, practising the alternate lifestyle, or whatever, I had passed into a phase of my life where women were either relatives or business associates or dinner partners. On any other kinds of involvements I closed the file.

I MUST HAVE DOZED OFF at some point, for I awoke with a jolt to the strange familiarity of my own bedroom. With extreme apprehension I made my way to the kitchen and opened the door just wide enough to let myself through. I peered into the box to see the mother busily grooming one of the kittens. The others nursed greedily. Most of the milk and all of the mashed sardines were gone. I opened a small tin of sockeye salmon – that cat never had it so good – then showered and dressed.

I covered the box with a large bath towel, as having pets in the building was in violation of my lease, and drove the family to the local animal hospital where I related a heavily edited version of how I came by the cats. The young woman in a white smock assured me they would do everything possible, shots, flea bath, worming, to put the adult animal back into smooth running order. The kittens barely had their eyes open; it would be some time before they could leave the mother. What the hell, I thought as I climbed back into my car. Out of sight, out of mind.

I had to drive back to Winnifred's house and see to her freezer, and my nephew Richard was due to arrive some time later that day. Not that I thought he would head straight for the deep freeze and begin poking about. Somebody else's deep freeze is oddly inviolate, like a desk or a night table. I wondered what kind of sound, pompous, avuncular advice I could possibly utter to my nephew, while the body of a man scarcely older than he lay congealed in the basement. The mere fact of Richard's presence loomed as one more item on an already overcrowded agenda.

I had no idea of when he was due to arrive, or even how; and I was too nervous to stay around the house all day waiting for him to show up. At least another fifteen hours must pass before I could attempt my next disposal; I was more comfortable in the dark. Locating an extra house key, I placed it under the mat at the front door, hoping Richard might have the wit to look for it there, should he arrive before I got back. Leaving my car in Winnifred's garage, I took the metro downtown, where I thought I would kill a couple of hours, maybe go to a movie. After some breakfast at a delicatessen, small steak and toasted bagel, I was now faced with the problem of how to spend the rest of the day. Giving in to an overpowering yawn, I stretched my arms high over my head. Every muscle felt sore, perhaps not so much sore as clenched. And it was too early to start drinking, even for me. What I needed was a massage, not a movie, or heat – something to help me unwind. It was then I was struck with the novel, for me at least, idea of going to a steam bath for the sole purpose of using the facilities. I had been to plenty of steam baths or health clubs or fitness centres in my time. As often as not I never went near the steam room or sauna, preoccupied as I was with having as much sex as I could find in the private cubicles. There was a so-called sauna in my apartment building, a claustrophobic little closet with an electric heater that never gets the room really hot.

I hailed a cab and gave the name of an older steam bath, one to which only about fifty per cent of the clientele went for the sole purpose of making out. I paid my entrance fee, was handed a sheet, a towel, and a wafer of soap, then I pushed my way through the door. I had never been to a steam bath in the morning before. Uncertain of what to expect I looked around. A handful of men wrapped in sheets lay sprawled on lounges, looking and sounding like beached sea lions. I found my room and undressed and, wrapping myself in the scanty towel, I shut the door and headed for the shower.

I don't know whether I should have turned left instead of right, but I found myself heading down a different passageway from the one through which I entered. A door to one of the rooms stood open; I could not resist a look inside. Reclining on a bed lay a young man looking every bit like Goya's *Naked Maja*. He was bathed in a tarty red glow from the bare bulb jutting from the wall over which he had carefully draped a pair of red bikini briefs. Catching sight of me he smiled. It wasn't exactly a smile; he drooped his lids and sucked in his cheeks, like someone doing a bad imitation of Joan Crawford.

Amused and surprised by the sight of this unexpected oasis of pleasure in an otherwise drab establishment I must have slowed my step. The young man raised a languid hand. "Before you come in I must warn you – I am a male companion."

"That makes you either a hustler or an orderly. I'm not in the market for either, thanks."

By way of answer he tossed his head.

"Careful of whiplash," I said as I headed for the door leading down to the showers, and went from there into the steam room, which stood empty.

I sat, enveloped in moist heat, feeling tension slowly ooze out. After a while I went across the passageway into the dry heat room, which looked like something out of a Fellini movie. Two old men, their stomachs hanging in collapsing folds like rolls of pastry dough, sat conversing in some language I couldn't even recognize. They were not speaking Portuguese, which sounds like drunken Spanish, nor did they utter the soft gutturals of Russian. Whatever they spoke was almost drowned out by the snores of another man, flat on his back, whose contour reminded me of that of the Island of Montreal: a flat alluvial plane rising steadily to the high curve of Mount Royal before falling off to plane once more. Under the hard ceiling light my own January skin looked blue-white and faintly luminous. A dwarf came in, reeking of sweat. Catching sight of me he began playing with himself under his towel. I withdrew to the steam room.

Through the swirling grey vapour I could distinguish the outline of an older man sitting stolidly on the lower bench. I climbed to the top bench and sat crosslegged, letting my head fall forward. The door opened and a figure came in. Even though steam rolled thickly around the room I could tell the man was young, the silhouette crisp and erect. He climbed up and sat down beside me. Almost immediately I began to pick up vibes; he was one of that fifty per cent. I turned to look at him and through the mist caught the gleam of a smile. Getting blown in a steam room has never been my idea of a meaningful relationship, but I had to admit there were certain therapeutic possibilities. I had come here to unwind after all. At that moment the older man rose heavily to his feet and shuffled slowly out. As he pushed open the heavy door some of the steam undulating around the dimly lit room followed him into the passageway. The second the door closed the younger man reached out and put his hand on my knee. "Oh my God!" I exclaimed out loud. Stretching from wrist to elbow a tattooed dragon coiled up his arm.

Unfolding myself like a bent pipe cleaner I clutched my towel around me and fled from the room. Without even pausing to shower I hurried to my cubicle. Drying myself as best I could with the threadbare towel and the sheet I tugged my clothes onto my clammy body and left the steam bath.

Hailing the first passing cab, I went back to Winnifred's house. Peeling the damp clothes from my still moist body I stepped into the shower, turning the water as hot as my skin would allow. I have no idea how long I stood there, but gradually the water began to run a little less hot, then less. Finally when the hot-water tap alone ran tepid I turned it off and towelled myself dry. Crawling into bed, I fell into a sleep so profound as to be almost drugged.

# 8.

FROM FAR, FAR AWAY I HEARD a ring and another ring, then another; the ubiquitous telephone pulled me back to consciousness. I cranked myself out of bed and shuffled like C3PO into Winnifred's bedroom where a princess phone glowed softly on the night table. "Yes," I grunted.

"Uncle Geoffry," said a man's voice. "It's Richard. Mother said I was to give you a call."

"Welcome to Montreal, Richard," I said with hollow heartiness. "Where are you?"

He named a downtown location; I gave him directions and rang off. I scrambled back into my clothes. While waiting for Richard, I made coffee. Then I listened to the news and scanned the papers, both English and French, to learn whether any stray bits of body had turned up unexpectedly. A man had been found shot to death in the trunk of his car in the north end of the city, gangland slaying suspected. An old woman had been beaten to death and robbed in her east-end apartment; police had arrested a suspect. A woman crossing against the light on a busy intersection had been done in by a bus. A south shore fire had claimed lives; the highways, as always, lay strewn with bodies. Of my own disposals, nothing.

Along with the enormous sense of relief I could not be entirely certain I did not feel just a tiny bit cheated, that after all my sleepless anxiety I did not even merit a few lines on the back page. Was I really prepared to court discovery so that people I didn't even know might enjoy a tiny thrill of shock as they read of an arm turning up in a municipal dump, an abandoned refrigerator bursting open to spill its disagreeable contents, a mangled pair of boots surfacing in a snow-removal truck?

No sooner had I finished checking the plants to see if they needed a drink than the doorbell rang for the first time since Larry returned just before midnight on New Year's Eve. The tall young man standing on the doorstep shivering looked so unlike my nephew as I remembered him I thought there must be some mistake. "Uncle Geoffry," he said holding out his hand to shake. The grip was firm, a good sign. I remember my father being adamant on the subject of a firm handshake; he hated to shake, as he put it, a dead fish. As he looked directly at me, the clear candid gaze so much a part of the handshake ritual, I could see with something very like a pang that he had my father's eyes, wide set, clear blue, with a tiny line of white visible around the iris.

He wore a denim jacket, inadequate for the temperature, jeans, boots. God, how conservative are the young. In one gloveless hand he carried a package which obviously held records, in the other a packsack. Naturally he was hatless; no one under forty wears a hat. I stood aside to let him enter. He put down the pack on the floor beside the hall bench and carefully laid his records on the seat. Slipping off his jacket he folded it neatly to lay on top of the records. Having freed his hands he stepped back into the entranceway and pulled off his boots. So far so good. But then I knew Mildred's children had good manners; she was a real whip cracker.

"Your room is at the end of the hall upstairs – posters of Honfleur Harbour and the cathedral at Rouen. Would you like anything, coffee, a beer?"

"Could I have some tea please, sir,"

"I only have the kind you can drink."

"That will do nicely, thank you," he replied without a shred of smile. His tone was precise, verging on precious. Uncertain of what to do he followed me into the kitchen to hover in the doorway while I plugged in the electric kettle.

"Bag or leaf?"

"Leaf, please."

Tea leaves were a nuisance to dispose of, especially as Winnifred never got around to putting in a toilet on the ground floor. A watched kettle boils, eventually. I spooned leaves into a pot and poured in the boiling water.

"You don't scald the pot first," stated my nephew.

"Not as a rule," I replied. "I seldom make tea."

"Heat that should go into drawing the leaves goes into warming the pot," he explained carefully as though I were twelve years old.

"Is that right," I replied swallowing the rude retort that sprang to mind. The visit was getting off to a poor start. Being taken to task over steeping tea did not augur well for our little talk. I decided to forgo tea and poured myself a highball. "Would you like one of these instead of that?"

"No, thank you, sir. I never drink in the afternoon."

"Late afternoon in Toronto is early evening in Montreal. Shall we withdraw to the withdrawing room?"

Richard followed me down the passageway to sit stiffly in the rocker but only after he paused to straighten the mat covering the seat. Was it only two days ago that Larry and I, in these same seats in this same room, sat getting bombed on dry martinis? Richard seemed ill at ease. So, in fact, was I. I am seldom at ease with the young and I dislike seeing them comfortable around me.

As I noticed earlier Richard reminded me of my own father around the eyes. For the rest he took after his mother. Mildred is considered by many to be a handsome woman. I have always thought she had a face like a correctional institution, but then a brother's loving heart can be unreliable. Along with the family looks Richard had one of those lean, lithe bodies which are a hallmark of the young. As one ages, contours change. Even if weight remains more or less constant, gravity pulls at skin under eyes, at chins; chest slips towards stomach. Nor do I take comfort from realizing it happens to others my age. One sags alone.

Another feature for which I handed my nephew credit was the absence of writing on his T-shirt. A plain dark-blue shirt, it did not advertise a province, a bit of folk wisdom, nor did it hint archly at the wearer's sexual tastes. Age plus the territorial advantage dictated I begin the conversation. "What records did you buy? Rock? Disco? Jazz?"

"I never listen to that kind of music," he replied in a voice indicating I ought to have known better. "No, I bought the Flagstad *Isolde*, the Callas *Norma*, and the Beecham *Don Giovanni*."

"Featuring Wagner, Donizetti, and Mozart in cameo roles?"

"Bellini wrote *Norma*."

"So he did."

He sipped his tea. "Do you like opera?"

"Yes and no. I have always liked the human voice raised in song. But opera has always struck me as overripe, a dinner made up entirely of dessert. And the singers all have double-barrelled or totally unpronounceable names: Lauri-Volpi, Schumann-Heink, Galli-Curci."

"You're going back a long way."

"I go back a long way." Somehow uttering the unpleasant truth did not make it more palatable. "And women who sing are always photographed wearing fur. Do you suppose prima donnas are cold all the time?"

"I've never really thought about it."

"I need another drink." I made my way to the kitchen aware that the evening stretched ahead. Maybe if I took him out to dinner things would improve. As I re-entered the front room Richard stood. I admired the well-drilled courtesy which brings the younger man to his feet in deference to the older but resented the yawning generation gap implied by the gesture. And if the young man had not stood? Of course I would have resented his familiarity, his ignoring the inequality between us. Surprisingly enough I am what passes at the office for a rational man.

"What brings you to Montreal, Richard? Christmas week is a poor time of year to visit anywhere."

"I've come to see about buying a harpsichord."

"Oh." I replied nonplussed. "Why?"

"Because I've decided to switch from piano to harpsichord and organ. Did you know I was taking music at University of Toronto? Actually I'm doing a double degree, performance and musicology."

"That's an ambitious program. But why would you want to give up a civilized instrument like the piano for something as dreary as the harpsichord? Ping, ping, ping. And the organ sounds like an asthmatic piano, all very well in ye olde quainte baroque Bavarian church; but they're in short supply in Canada."

Richard set down his teacup with determination. I could see I had struck a nerve. "I disagree with you entirely. The harpsichord is far more civilized than the piano. Not that I have anything against the piano; it's fine for ensemble work, and accompanying the voice. Even for jazz. But as a solo instrument it is coarse and self-indulgent."

"You'll never get a job playing honky-tonk harpsichord in a whore house."

"I wouldn't want one."

"I don't suppose you would. Oh, well, it's got to be your decision. What do you parents think?"

"They're not too happy. Father wants me to be a professor, an academic rather than a performer; and Mother wants me to continue with the piano. She would really prefer me to play the violin."

"Don't you have to be Jewish to play the violin?"

"Not necessarily. But you do have to start at five years old. I came to music late, possibly too late to be a performer. That remains to be seen."

"What if you don't make it as a performer?"

"I'll teach. May I have some more tea please?"

"Help yourself. Would you like a drink instead?"

"Well – perhaps."

Having ascertained he preferred gin I poured a good belt into a tumbler and disguised the amount with tonic water. Maybe he would loosen up.

As I handed him his drink he spoke. "This seems like as good a time as any for you to talk some sense into me. I'm sure Mother warned you I was behaving oddly. She probably asked you to talk to me, man to man." He almost shuddered at the words.

"She did. She must think I carry a crystal ball around in my briefcase. I warned her I was bad at advising the young. Even clients who pay for my advice often don't take it. Mildred would like you to make a lot of money; it's one of her criteria of success. But unless I am very much mistaken you will have only yourself to support. So I guess it boils down to how many cars or microwave ovens you want in your life."

Richard put down his drink and with quick, precise gestures began to pick up leaves dropped by the fern onto the floor. Another of those punishments in Greek hell, picking up leaves from an eternally shedding fern. "You're right, Uncle Geoffry; it is my choice. But why are you so certain I will have only myself to support?"

"I don't think you will get married; that's all."

"Why not?"

"Do I have to spell it out?" I looked directly at my nephew. His look met mine, wavered for a moment, then dropped.

"You mean because I'm gay?"

"Exactly. And in answer to the unspoken question I know because I am gay myself."

Up to now I thought that only in Regency romances did people blush to the roots of their hair. But Richard did exactly that. Whether it was my correct guess or my own admission I couldn't tell; however the end result was a becoming pink flush beginning at the silver anchor chain around his throat and rising to the hairline of his dark blow-dried hair. I went to the kitchen for another cube of ice; by the time I returned his colour had faded from spanked baby pink to mild sunburn.

As I reseated myself, I was struck by my own absence of tact. To confront my nephew, whom I scarcely knew, with the nature of his sexuality and then with mine was more than direct; it was crude. Ordinarily I would have skirted the subject, dropping just enough hints to show I understood what was what. But I was preoccupied with something far more serious than social niceties. I had not wanted Richard to visit me in the first place, and I was not about to waste time shadowboxing. I changed the subject back to Richard's career.

"As a single man you can pretty well write your own ticket. Should you decide against music there are a few professions you should avoid, politics for instance – unless you want to marry a camouflage wife and have a couple of decoy children. Nor would I urge you to teach at a boy's boarding school. Don't join the RCMP. They always get their man, but not quite in that way. I wouldn't become a monk, if I were you, nor would I join the armed forces. You may get to be captain but you shouldn't make the lieutenant. For the rest, your sexual orientation, if intelligently handled, shouldn't matter too much."

For the first time since we sat I permitted myself to smile. Richard looked at me, his expression solemn, almost shocked, as if the gravity of our fallen state did not permit levity. Suddenly, almost in spite of himself, he allowed a smile to reshape the wide, well-formed mouth he had from my sister. The atmosphere thawed; we had made contact. Also I had regained the upper hand, even if I didn't scald the teapot. No longer was I just the older brother of a mother speaking in tongues across a void. I became one man talking to another some years his junior but a member of the same club. If I had some constructive advice to offer, now seemed as good a time as any. "Richard," I began, "you had better brace yourself because I am about to play the heavy uncle proffering nuggets of wisdom. It has been observed that the things a man knows at forty he didn't know at twenty can't be taught. The observation has a kind of specious ring that helps disguise the fact it isn't true. You stand to learn much from my mistakes and those of my generation. When I was your age it simply would not have been possible for me to admit to an older man that I was homosexual. The word 'gay' meant something different then. Lavender was still a colour; Blue Boy meant Gainsborough. But even if this hypothetical older man had been sympathetic his attitude would have been, 'You are sick; go to a psychiatrist and be made well.' To be made well meant being recast in a heterosexual mould. We know more today, about a lot of things. And only idiots have to relive the whole cycle of human history, making every single mistake before they become true adults, generally around eighty years old.

"I shall begin with the dont's. Don't, I repeat, do not tell your parents you are gay. Things unspoken can be ignored, and I know my sister simply isn't up to coping with the truth; which is to say she'll be terribly upset along the lines of 'Where did I go wrong?' Parents tend to look askance at their children's sexuality, especially mothers of sons, fathers of daughters. Let me ask you this. Do you resent your mother or blame her for your – orientation?"

The young man thought a moment. "Not really. She's inclined to nag, but I don't blame her. If there's anything about her I really resent it's her inability to accept my doing what I really want to do."

"Good. Then shut up about your sex life. It is my firm conviction that young men, or young women for that matter, who are quote-unquote 'honest' with their parents are just laying a colossal guilt trip on them instead. 'I am gay; you are to blame.' You've probably heard the old joke: 'My mother made me a homosexual.' 'If I bought her the wool would she make me one too?'

"Remember I've known Mildred – my sister the mother – a lot longer than you. She's tiresome but she's straight. I know she has been a conscientious mother and has brought you all up to the best of her albeit limited ability. I am well aware that one should not criticize parents to their own children, but I speak to you as a fellow adult. My father used to quote a bit of folk wisdom which applies in this instance: Least said; soonest mended. Don't feel compelled to confess. Confession is for lurid murder trials, also for catholics. You are neither a murderer nor a catholic. Furthermore you must pay the price for being brought up in the austere protestant tradition. Deny yourself the indulgence of telling all. Are you with me?" I took a deep swallow. Scotch helps me to give advice.

"Yes, sir."

"Good. A second don't. Choose any profession you wish, music, teaching, whatever; but don't turn into a professional gay. By that I mean don't let your sexual orientation take over your life. How much time does one spend fucking anyway – in relation to all the other things we do during the course of a lifetime? Have a sex life by all means. But don't become shrill and strident and political. Don't spend your time fiddling in the kitchen – little brunches for the girls. Don't make quiche. Don't fart around with precious decorating schemes or turn into a telephone queen, punching those buttons to tell A, B, C, and D that E just had it on with the postman. Don't move to San Francisco. Don't take up knitting or needlepoint. If you have a sewing machine keep it hidden. Don't turn into a woman baiter, quick to notice the wrong shade of lipstick or the no-longer-in-fashion shoes. Roughly half the people in the world are women. If you cut yourself off remember you will be the loser.

"The gay community is above all else visual – physical beauty, clothing, decorating, appearances, externals. Don't be misled into mistaking the package for the product. The gay community does judge a book by its cover. Tell me, do you anticipate piercing one of your ears?"

"No, sir."

"Good. Ear piercing is for girls, queens, and aborigines. Under no circumstances get yourself tattooed. Get drunk, yes; smoke a little grass, yes; score some coke, yes – if you can afford it. But stay away from the tattoo parlour. No 'Mother and Dad' entwined in a heart; no 'Born to raise hell' around a devil's head; no – dragons. In a world drowning in a sea of permissiveness the last stronghold of the socially unacceptable remains the tattoo.

"Now for the do's. I want to end the lecture on a positive note. Whatever you decide to do, do it well. If you really want to play the harpsichord play it as well as you possibly can. You are in the charmed position of having choice. Don't let others pressure you into doing something you don't want to do. Nor am I advocating a kind of gee-whiz, born-again, ain't-life-wonderful, woolly-minded optimism. I despise moral uplift. Just develop a sense of your own worth.

"If I sound like Polonius giving advice to Laertes I apologize. All older men say essentially the same thing to younger men. Live your life better than I lived mine. You probably won't, but I've said it. Rest in peace, Mildred. And now I will take you to dinner at a restaurant of your choice after which you will be free to do as you please. One last point. I do not relish the prospect of being called Uncle Geoffry or sir by my dinner companion. We are both grown men. Please call me Geoffry. That's what my friends call me. I shall continue to call you Richard. Let tricks call you Dick. And when you fall in love, I mean something that lasts over a week, make sure your lover calls you Richard. It's the small formalities that ease the strain of intimacy.

"Let's have another drink at the restaurant."


I TOOK RICHARD TO A SMALL Italian restaurant, having insisted he wear the parka hanging in the passageway, and borrow a pair of my gloves. It amused me to be telling a twenty-year-old man to dress warmly.

Much can be learned about people from their behaviour at table. Faced with something as basic as food and liquor one sees both the best and the base in dinner companions. Often I learn more about a client over lunch than I do during a conference. As a result I watched my nephew, who was turning out to be a tireless tidier. First he straightened the cutlery; then he put back two paper packets of sugar, which had fallen from their bowl; next he placed the wine list so its spine lay parallel to the edge of the table. People who tidy are in effect laying claim to the space they temporarily inhabit. And Richard seemed very much in control of himself and his immediate area.

He was possessed of a hefty post-adolescent appetite although his manipulation of knife and fork could not be faulted. Mildred believed good table manners put one among the elect. I watched Richard inhale the rolls, so when the waiter took our order I insisted he take a full portion of the house cannelloni; good manners dictated he take only the half-portion. My sister Mildred believed that true character was forged on the anvil of small denials.

It is difficult to converse while devouring two main dishes plus salad, more rolls, and dessert, particularly if one obeys the dictum of not talking with one's mouth full. I did however learn two things: Richard was dying to leave home; also he did not have a scrap of what was known in my childhood as a sense of humour. What young person today worries about not having a sense of humour? Yet to be humourless, in my youth, branded one with an indelible stigma.

His desire to leave home struck me as as natural as breathing. Who wouldn't want to get away from my sister with her middle-of-the-road moralities and easy axioms on right and wrong? Who wouldn't want to escape from a point of view that was exclusively white, protestant, anglo-saxon, heterosexual, progressive conservative, and other directed? Of course Richard wanted to move out. Happily he was being aided quite unwittingly by his mother. Mildred had apparently announced that her house was not big enough for both a piano and a harpsichord and that she did not intend to get rid of the piano. Richard suggested a studio apartment for the harpsichord; Mildred thought it an excellent suggestion.

Mellowed by food, wine, coffee, and a large brandy, Richard brushed the crumbs missed by the waiter onto the floor.

"Uncle – I mean Geoffry," he began with direct and humourless precision, "how did you know I was gay, so quickly I mean? It's not something I'm ashamed of; neither do I wish to be obvious. I am curious to learn how you picked up on me so fast." His tone was that of someone seeking a commonplace bit of information.

I shrugged. "Just sort of a sixth sense I guess."

"A sixth sense is usually a result of developing the other five. You're begging the question."

I saw I was not to be let off the hook. How indeed did I know? Several decades of observation and experience had gone into developing my sixth sense. One puts in time; one learns. How do I know that the demure young woman sitting almost primly by herself in the lobby of the Ritz Hotel is a hooker, more politely a call girl? Her tailored grey flannel skirt, blue blazer, and demure bow at the neck of her white blouse suggest the convent girl rather than the courtesan. Then I notice the shoes, feats of engineering where three straps anchor a sole and perilously high heel to the foot. The hands crossed in her lap, over a black envelope bag resting on knees pressed tightly together, have long nails lacquered a fashionable ugly red, matching the colour on her toes. Makeup is both carefully and lavishly applied, the mouth a touch too shiny, the lids a shade too green. Her old gold hair has the slightly gummy look resulting from conditioner over colour rinse. For just a moment her eyes flicker over me like radar scanners, then return to the floor. Either she has a prior engagement or she has decided I have little potential as a John.

One learns to read the signs. I dismiss your obvious faggot, as easy to decipher as the sidewalk whore. I speak of those men of taste and cultivation who have opted for the alternate lifestyle, the kind of man I hoped Richard would become. He showed promise. The hair, oh so beautifully cut, oh so carefully blow dried. The genetic combination which produces a face which although masculine still seems almost otherworldly in its smooth perfection. For such a face did the wall of thorns part granting access to the Sleeping Beauty.

The look is truly otherworldly, for it promises an infinity of tenderness, an incandescence of passion, intelligence, intuition – everything, in fact, that anyone who has ever harboured a romantic daydream secretly longs to find. And homosexuals tend to confuse physical and moral beauty. That, not rejection by society, but the predilection to seek intelligence in a smooth pectoral, generosity in a flat abdomen, kindness in a muscular thigh, and forever in a large cock, this capacity to confound muscle with mind is a main cause of dissatisfaction.

Poor Richard. He will go through life exciting love and admiration in people he won't even know. How he learns to cope will prove the touchstone of his maturity. I cannot advise him on that. Were I to tell him he was beautiful and his beauty would get him into any amount of hot water I would appear fulsome and arch, the older man paying extravagant compliments to the younger. I might even sound as if I were on the make, which I certainly was not. And even if I were I wouldn't be the first uncle in history who flattered himself into his nephew's pants, or his niece's for that matter. Maybe being all fucked out is the beginning of wisdom.

Instead of giving Richard an answer I shrugged and looked at my watch. "Do you have plans for the evening, Richard?"

"Not really." He thought for a minute. "Do you know anything about St. Luke the Apostle?"

"It's a church."

"No, I mean do you know anything about the music program?"

"It's terrible. I used to date the music director and he's a nerd. Why?"

"They're doing *Messiah* tonight. I thought I might go. You wouldn't like to come?"

"No thanks. I already know that my Redeemer liveth, and when the trumpet shall sound I would prefer it be in someone else's ear. The last time I went to *Messiah* I fell asleep and was apparently the only member of the audience who didn't stand during the Hallelujah Chorus. But there's plenty else to do. Nix to Handel. The night is young."

I was amused to see that beneath the seeming poise that beauty bestows – the profile, the lashes, the cleft chin – Richard was still a twenty-year-old man.

When I suggested leaving him downtown he seemed oddly reluctant. At his age I would have paused only long enough to gulp dessert before high-stepping down Sherbrooke Street. But young men today do not think the way I used to. At my present age the prospect of tramping from one gay disco bar to another, deafened by the noise, elbowing for a drink, trying to figure out sexual preferences from the rainbow variety of pocket handkerchiefs and bunches of keys hanging from back pockets struck me as tiresome. I wanted my beans and bacon in peace. I wondered whether Richard felt the same way. Did a rundown block of seedy bars hold few blandishments? Did he at twenty feel the way I did at fifty? Was he uneasy or simply smart? And wouldn't that be a laugh. The man of twenty knowing what I did at fifty. The child is father to the man. And what do you want to do with your life, Uncle Geoffry?

I paid the bill, under-tipping a waiter who had obviously thought Richard was my date and spent the meal trying to make him. In the street I asked Richard if he would like to split. I almost added I intended to go home and crash but realized it would sound as phony as it felt.

"If you wish to get rid of me I'll go to a movie, or I can just go to my room and read. Downtown at night, here or in Toronto, really doesn't interest me very much."

"I wasn't trying to unload you. I just thought at your age you would sooner be on your own."

"Not at all. This is the first time in twenty years we have ever talked. Couldn't I buy you a drink somewhere?"

"Save your money. At most of the bars around here you will be taken for my trick, not my nephew. There's plenty to drink at Winnifred's." To my surprise I found myself flattered by Richard's preference for my company, having always worked on the assumption that the young must find me as tiresome as I find them. Over and above the kinship I had to admit Richard was an original, at least in terms of my own experience. How many twenty-year-old, compulsively tidy harpsichord students did I know? None before this afternoon. I hailed a cab.

The scenario seemed very *déjà vu*, heading back to Winnifred's with a young man beside me in the taxi. I am convinced we all have about a dozen scenarios in our lives which we play out with different characters: dinner party, marriage, lunch with mother, laundromat, sex, supermarket, telephone conversations where the other party won't get off the line, and office. I was playing out the older-younger man for the second time in days, a scenario which I ordinarily never play, and the last time I played it out things worked out badly.

Although I was beginning to like my nephew I did not relish the thought of rapping until 4:00 A M. Furthermore I was the wrong person for Richard; having come to terms with my own narrow perimeters I had little to offer him except a jaundiced ear.

A bottle of Spanish brandy, dusty and unopened, sat at the back of Winnifred's liquor shelf behind odds of sherry and ends of vermouth. Spanish brandy usually tastes of caramel, but this bottle, named after some long-dead monarch, looked promising. I carried the bottle and two snifters into the front room and put them on the desk. "Do me a favour, Richard, and tell your mother we had a long, meaningful talk. She thinks I've been a punk uncle, and I suppose I have. I could use the points. Help yourself to some brandy."

"Thanks – Geoffry." As he poured for both of us, and carefully replaced the cork, I could tell he was pondering something. He drank, then put down his snifter with deliberation. "Geoffry, do you have a lover?"

The question caught me off guard, causing me to gulp down most of my brandy in one swallow. My immediate reaction was along the lines of mind your own goddamned business. Like Pavlov's dogs salivating at the sound of a bell the merest intimation of a personal question brings a conditioned response. Still I did not want to turn my nephew off after having reached a state which went beyond mere detente. Nor could I accuse him of mere idle or prurient curiosity. He asked a serious, straightforward question, no doubt hoping to enlarge his own experience indirectly through mine. As if sensing my hesitation he gave a half-smile, apologetic, not amused.

"Perhaps I had no business asking that. I did not mean to be impertinent."

"I didn't imagine for a moment you were. But don't you think I'm perhaps a bit old for that kind of nonsense?"

"You're being coy. It doesn't suit you. If I'm only half as pulled together at fifty as you are I'll be more than contented. You've always been kind of an ideal to me. You were always so cool, so self-possessed. It didn't take a genius to figure out you didn't like children, but the more you kept your distance the more I wanted to get close. This is the first time you have ever really spoken to me as though I were in the same room, and I confess I'm flattered."

"You flatter me. And I really didn't mean to be coy. Sure, I have the physical capacity for love or sex or whatever, but mentally I feel very shopworn." There was a brief pause. "Oh, Richard, Richard," I thought to myself, "if only you knew about the last few days, the body in the deep freeze, the mental and moral morass in which I flounder, would you still think me such a worthy model?"

Instead I said, "You did ask me a question. No, I don't have a lover but up until recently I did." I had answered the question; need I elaborate? At a time when people push one another out of the way to get in front of a television camera so they can tell all, when in-depth interviews chronicle sexual tastes, when intimate details of love affairs are graphically described in chapter three, when two drinks after the first introduction your dinner companion is telling all about her abortions, to be reticent about one's private life seems odd, almost perverse. Nor was I reluctant to discuss Chris because he was a man; I would have felt the same reticence about discussing Susan. Did Richard stand to learn anything constructive from hearing about my time with Chris, about two men working things out – for a while anyway. Is there life after coming out? And, considering my real secret, the big one, any revelation I might make about myself and Chris seemed trivial.

Uncertain of how to continue, or even begin for that matter, I poured myself another brandy, ignoring the austere Spanish face on the label, which reminded me I would rue tomorrow. "It is difficult for me to talk about Chris. To begin with I never have; also it is totally impossible to be objective about something as personal as love. Have you been in love yet?"

Taken aback Richard shook his head. "I don't really know."

"Then you haven't. If you had you would know. It's like hitting your funny bone or having the soles of your feet tickled; it's not like anything else. Mind you, I'm not talking about love but the state of being in love. Unfortunately the word love itself has joined the other good four-letter words in a limbo of pejoration. Used promiscuously and carelessly these words have lost their true meaning. Entertainers love their audience. Women at parties love one another's clothes. Children love their goldfish. During the course of any given day you will hear the word applied indiscriminately to Big Macs, El Greco, hydrangeas, lobster, English sheep dogs, and Puccini. To say you love something nowadays carries about as much impact as saying it is nice. I, however, was in love with Christopher. Being in love is an innocuous little phrase when one considers the chaotic emotion it describes."

I paused for a moment. Being in love is not nearly so boring as my lecture was making it sound. Pedantically I pressed on. "If one is fortunate one can love or, better still, like the person with whom one is in love. That is why some marriages last, some relationships. Love changes to enduring affection. Many people, however, fall in love with people they only partially like, sometimes not at all.

"I was taken so completely by surprise when I fell in love with Chris that I never stopped to ask myself whether I liked him or not. I was so busy listening to waves crash against the rocks while bolts of lightning sheared the sky and howling winds bent the old oak tree nearly to the ground; I was so caught up in the emotional *mise-en-scène* that I failed to register how dissimilar we really were. To begin with, he was married. We had two things in common: we both spoke English; we were both the same sex.

"Christopher was a simple man with straightforward priorities. He wouldn't leave his wife simply because he loved me. I wonder even now how I could have loved someone for whom beating the other private schools at football was a consummation devoutly to be wished. He read prayers at weekly assembly with a straight face. He rose like a champion to the challenge of fire drill. He managed to convey the idea to dissatisfied parents that if their son wasn't doing well at school it might be because of something amiss at home, too much television perhaps, sibling rivalry? Too many sweets? He was dotty on diet. You'd think he invented brown rice and bean sprouts. I suppose it all adds up to being a good assistant headmaster, but the constant mediation. Soothing everybody. Easing friction between a fractious student and the old closet queen who teaches Latin. Saying "There, there, dear" to a menopausal secretary furious because examination stencils are late. Then home to a make-believe marriage. At times I found myself wondering if under the firm façade there was any real core, or if he was soft all the way through, like cheap chocolates.

"As I talk to you at this very moment I wonder what it is about him that I loved. I'm far too old to be starry-eyed about sex, although I like it. Did he complement me in some way? Did he respond to some need, other than that we all have for a warm, breathing presence. Here I am trying to come up with a rational explanation for the least rational of conditions.

"Hell. Who knows. Maybe I was turning back the clock. I have never been coy about my age. I don't like it, nor do I lie about it. I don't dye my hair or use make up or contemplate cosmetic surgery, what used to be called a face lift. But none of us is totally immune to wishing occasionally for an earlier and supposedly better time. As you are probably aware nostalgia is very fashionable today. People pay money for tin cigarette boxes and old Mason jars which look just like new Mason jars. Art deco is exorbitant. I do not hanker after an authentic Star wood stove with the chrome still intact or a complete set of Evening in Paris bottles. Yet I wonder if perhaps my particular nostalgia was for someone with a simplistic set of values, someone who believed no problem existed that couldn't be solved, moreover through words. Chris took arms against a sea of troubles. He believed in summit conferences and UNESCO. He believed in knowing where your children are and supervising TV. He paid his taxes on time and swam forty laps three times a week. He read in that deadly serious way anyone with an English or history degree reads, correcting every editorial for style and organization. He beat the thickets of journalism for the dangling modifier or the faulty antecedent. He believed in the law with a belief no practising lawyer could match; his conviction anchored itself in the Ten Commandments. To Moses from God. Now that must have been an interview. Eat your heart out, NBC."

The long-bearded face on the brandy bottle looked at me quizzically. "I seem to be digressing. What more is there to tell? Like most affairs it ended. He left me. I was the one who formally broke off, but he left me nonetheless." Suddenly I had a desperate, overpowering urge to weep; but I have never worn my heart on my well-tailored sleeve. I managed to stem the flow; in the process I realized I was really quite drunk.

I finished my brandy in one swallow. "So much for my rambling. This Spanish brandy packs more of a wallop than I realized. I think I'll turn in. Watch television if you like. Turn off a few lights when you come up. I'm an early riser so I'll make coffee and breakfast if you want it. Goodnight, Richard."

"Goodnight, Geoffry." The young man rose to his feet as I

walked with the unsteady dignity of the drunk out the door and aimed myself at the stairs.

The face on the brandy bottle had been right. On the stroke of 3:00 A M., my eyes flicked open like those of a Sleepy Time Jane doll placed upright. Eyes open, heart pounding, pulse racing, I knew from experience I would face several hours of acute insomnia. Small wonder brandy is given to people who faint; it certainly gets things cranking away. I swung my feet out of bed and pulled on my robe, whose label bore the name of a prominent couturier. Even purchased on sale the sleazy garment was overpriced. The label itself doubled as tab so the robe itself could be hung from a hook; however the stitching had given way at one end and only a couple of threads held the scrap of fabric at the other. It hung limp from the collar of the garment in a state of designer detumescence. And I draw the line at sewing.

On my way downstairs for a glass of milk I really didn't want I paused at the door of Richard's room. It stood slightly ajar, and I could hear regular breathing coming from the bed. I pushed the door open, causing a shaft of light from the hall fixture to fall across the face of the sleeping man. One thing I will say for the young; they look attractive when asleep. They do not snore; their mouths do not fall open; the colour does not drain from their faces. They look asleep, not dead. Richard slept easily, his face turned three-quarters away from me, the cat curled up at his shoulder. I confess that for a minute, perhaps only half, I allowed myself to wonder how things would have turned out had he been my son, my very own son; were he to call me Father instead of Uncle Geoffry. As he was now, tall, talented, twenty, I would gladly acknowledge him as mine. I was not too certain, however, I would have wanted to put in those intervening twenty years. Mildred had seen him through the teething, the measles, the first haircut. She had listened to the hours of practising and had put meals onto the table. Parents pay their dues; they deserve whatever rewards must be forthcoming. Had Susan lived we might have had a son; we had planned to have three children, the nuclear family plus one. No doubt I would have risen to the challenge of fatherhood. One can do almost anything when one has to.

It was odd how suddenly my middle-aged life had been invaded by youth. A New Year's Eve to remember. First the wedding invitation to a wedding at which my own daughter might well have been a bridesmaid. Then the telephone call from my sister asking me to undertake my nephew. Then Dale, a man young enough to have been my son. Just like Richard. I could only hope my nephew would never learn that the older man who advised him on how to live his life with such easy authority was a murderer, or a killer, one who had committed manslaughter. Murder, manslaughter, accidental death: the words come and go; the body remains. It would be comforting to argue that I owed it to Richard, to his trust in me, not to be found out. But even I could not subscribe to that specious moralizing. I owed it to my instinct for survival.

As I went down to the kitchen, humming a bit of *The Mikado* under my breath, I took comfort from the thought that not only do I dislike Gilbert and Sullivan, I generally dislike the other people who like Gilbert and Sullivan.

I poured a glass of milk from one of the cartons clogging the top shelf of the refrigerator. Every other day a diligent milkman, unaware of Winnifred's absence, leaves a quart of two per cent on the doorstep. Winnifred believes whole milk coats the arteries with cholesterol; skim milk tastes like chalk and water. The cat won't go near milk, eating only high-priced bits of beef in gravy and pure brown tuna along with expensive little *bouchcées* wrapped in heavy foil and tiny biscuits which look like cocktail appetizers yclept Meow Mix – "Tastes so good cats ask for it by name." That cat eats better than at least two-thirds of the world's population.

The first swallow of milk went down with difficulty; it always does. Nor was I in any mood for the large, round, happy face on the side of the tumbler, which had once held peanut butter. More than the brandy had me agitated. I was putting in time before making the next drop, and talking about Chris had muddied the spring. Fragments of memory eddied about like bits of silt and bracken, refusing to settle. Fragmented recollections of fragmented moments together. Fragments, nothing but fragments. An hour or so after school and before dinner, when he was supposedly playing badminton. Occasional evenings always with an eye on the clock. Lunch-hour trysts: out of the suit, into the sack, into the shower, into the suit. A hard-boiled egg or a piece of cheese on the run and back to the office for an afternoon yawning ahead until six. "Ah, cannot we / as well as cocks and lions jocund be / after such pleasures."

Yet before I began to wallow in self pity I had to admit that for someone like me the relationship had advantages which a more permanent arrangement did not. No demands were made that I was not perfectly willing to meet; no sticky stretches of boredom when sexual desire, conversation, and scotch all run out at the same time; no illness – the vomiting and diarrhoea of flu audible through the bathroom door. No flat tires or furnace breakdowns. No arguing whose turn it is to stay home because the plumber is coming to plug a leak. No shovelling snow or putting out the garbage. No dirty laundry, old razor blades, used Kleenex. I did not have to endure his friends, his television programs, his food fads. And even if he did squeeze the toothpaste from the top of the tube and leave water in the soap dish so the cake of soap turned into sludge he did not perform these misdemeanours day after infuriating day.

We did not fight. A good fight must never be hurried; it must ripen gradually, like choice Stilton. A good fight must start slowly like an historical novel, build like a Rossini overture, move from highs to lows like the Dow-Jones index, and taper off fitfully like a tropical storm. A good fight is as formal as a *pas de deux* and like a *pas de deux* it cannot be hurried. Chris and I never had time to fight. We had words occasionally, but words are to a real fight what a skirmish is to an epic battle.

Only by formalizing our aggression can we contain it. Unfortunately uncontrolled aggression threatens to swallow us whole. Insults pass for wit on television. Whatever happened to the slap stick or Punch and Judy. Professional sports bring to mind the games of Imperial Rome; we throw Christians to hockey teams. On screen the twenty-minute car chase, where the good-bad guy tries to head off the bad-good guy, demolishing a score of automobiles en route, has already become a cliché. Alcohol which provokes violence is readily available; marijuana which does not remains illegal. Divorce lawyers thrive; singles bars proliferate. People longing for the detente of a relationship find instead the abrasion of intimacy. Love is not the shortest distance between two hearts, as contemporary greetings cards would have it, but the longest and bumpiest road to eventual acceptance.

If Chris and I shared nothing more than fragments at least we did not waste them. Middle-aged adulteries do not unfold to soft lights and music but to the ticking of the clock and the hard glare of noon. With the unspoken awareness that this was all we had, we could not afford the time-wasting indulgences of those who live together.

I forced myself then to stop thinking about Chris. The large white clock on the kitchen wall read 3:30, and a good part of the city slept. I went quietly up the stairs and looked into Richard's room. His deep, regular breathing told of unbroken sleep. Back in my own room I dressed quickly and crept down to the basement.

From the deep freeze I lifted the second package of solidly frozen leg into the Samsonite suitcase, which I carried out through the side door to the trunk of my car parked in the garage. I had to fumble for the lock as the light in the garage had burned out and I didn't know where to look for extra bulbs. Fortunately Richard's room lay at the opposite end of the house. I drove down to Sherbrooke Street and turned east, moving easily through the meagre traffic to within blocks of my last drop. Driving slowly around a block chosen at random I spotted the dull gleam of an old refrigerator about twenty-five feet down a garbage-strewn lane. Beside the mouth of the lane stood a street lamp, whose light almost managed to penetrate the funnel of darkness. I pulled over to the sidewalk and opened my trunk, unbolting the licence plate. I lifted out the suitcase and walked quickly down the lane hoping that nothing unpleasant lurked inside this refrigerator. To my relief the door of the abandoned appliance stood slightly ajar and I could see nothing inside but the metal racks. These I removed and stacked neatly on the ground.

I bent to open the suitcase but the catch was jammed. "Goddamn it," I said under my breath as I caught and tore a fingernail.

I did not even hear them approach, but as I knelt, shaking my sore finger, I caught sight of two pairs of heavy black boots criss-crossed with straps, two pairs of legs clad in jeans.

I got slowly to my feet, my eyes moving past two identical black leather windbreakers, gleaming with rings and studs and zippers, to rest on the blank faces of two men in their mid-twenties, their eyes shadowed by the visors of identical caps, black leather travesties of the Greek fisherman's cap. Tweedledum and Tweedledee, only these two carried switchblades.

"*Ton argent*" said the taller of the two. Obediently I reached into my trouser pocket and handed him the sandwich of bills. He took the folded bills to tuck into one of the diagonal zippered pockets bisecting the front of his jacket. The two of them were creatures from another planet with their matching leather gear and sallow, pockmarked faces. Why do hoods never seem to have good complexions, especially in the movies, where moral worth relates directly to the size of one's pores?

My stomach seemed to fold in on itself, like an accordion. "*Bonsoir*," I said, bending over to pick up the suitcase and taking a couple of steps toward the street. But the shorter of the two stepped in my way.

"*Maudit anglais*," he hissed not precisely through his teeth as several of the front ones were missing. Retracting his knife he tucked it into the top of his boot while from a jacket pocket he took a metal device with four holes, which he slid onto the fingers of his right hand. Brass knuckles. I had seen a pair only once before in a police station.

It didn't take a genius to figure out I was in big trouble. Not content merely to rip me off, these leather punks were going to work me over. Protected as I was by my overcoat they would aim for my face. Down a dim alley feeding onto a deserted street, I was stranded up shit creek. And I was frightened. But somewhere behind the fear, around it, beside it, simmered rage, the same rage I had felt at the sight of the smashed Mexican figure. I could overlook the money; God knows, I had more than this pair of losers. But they wanted to smash up my face for no other reason than I was what I was.

The urge to survive runs deep. And anyone who has watched junk television as much as I have must have learned two things: one is never without a weapon; one must do the unexpected. The shorter punk, wearing the brass knuckles, flexed his shoulders a couple of times, like a pitcher warming up at the plate, while he rubbed his right fist lightly against the open palm of his left hand. Of the two I feared the knife more than the knuckles. Taking two steps backward I grasped the handle of the suitcase in two hands and swung, like a Scottish athlete throwing the hammer. The hard edge of the Samsonite suitcase weighted with the leg of Dale Lawton hit the taller one holding the knife squarely in the mouth. With a cry he dropped the knife and began coughing blood and teeth onto the ground. At the same moment brass knuckles hurled himself at me, but I pushed the suitcase at him, catching him in the chest and causing him to stumble backwards. Dropping the suitcase, I made a v with two of my fingers, and I lunged at his eyes. He screamed as my fingers drove into the soft jelly. Howls of rage and pain splintered my ears as I dashed to my car and locked myself inside. The ignition key was in my overcoat pocket. I fumbled it into the ignition and turned. Nothing. Again nothing. I looked up to see the taller hood, the one with the damaged mouth, grab the door handle as he pounded on the window with his fist. I knew he wanted to kill me. A third turn of the key and the motor caught just as the punk jumped onto the back of the car. I tore off down the street; miraculously he hung on. There was no room on the narrow road to make a U-turn. Bracing myself, I jammed on the brake so suddenly I was thrown painfully against the steering wheel. In my rear-view mirror I could see my unwelcome passenger thrown onto the road; he lay stunned. In a scream of tires I raced off, slowing down only at a red light indicating a main intersection.

The suitcase holding the leg lay where it had fallen, but there was no going back. It was brand new; someone would salvage it. And then? I couldn't worry about that now. It took every ounce of concentration I could muster to control the steering wheel; my fingers were Jello. I drove back to Winnifred's at about fifteen miles an hour and let myself in through the basement door. Climbing the stairs to the kitchen I walked to the table and absently drank the half-full glass of now warm milk. As soon as the liquid hit my stomach I knew I was going to be sick. Hand pressed to mouth I hurried back down the basement stairs past the deep freeze to the toilet bowl beside the wash tubs. Kneeling on the floor with great wrenching heaves I vomited my rage and fear and disgust into the pristine whiteness of the toilet bowl.

# 9.

WHENEVER I THROW UP I REALLY FEEL as though I am going to die. I climbed the basement stairs one more time and leaned over the kitchen sink to splash cold water on my face and rinse my mouth. The doorbell rang; its ding-dong echoing from a box on the wall directly above my head caused me to jump. Not considering who it might be, and hoping the sound had not wakened Richard, I hurried into the entrance porch and peered through one of the steam-covered panes. A coatless Larry danced a samba step on the stoop to keep warm. He carried a small overnight bag. I pulled back the latch. "Larry, what the hell are you doing here? It's after five A.M.!"

"What does Garbo have that I don't have twice as much of? Don't act so glad to see me."

"I always receive callers in the wee small hours. That's why I'm fully dressed. Come inside."

"Can you lend me money to pay my cab?"

I fished my last ten-dollar bill from the watch-pocket of my trousers and Larry slithered down the icy walk on leather soles. "My wallet is gone," he began, as he came back inside. "Stolen or lost during the scuffle."

"Scuffle?"

"In my hotel room. Two Puerto Ricans I picked up in a bar had an argument. One of them cut himself on a knife the other happened to be holding. They were both wearing doubleknit. Did you know or even suspect people still wore doubleknit? Anyway the hotel asked me to leave. The detectives were there, the manager. Doors kept opening and closing up and down the hallway. The whole bit. I was going to the Y but then I realized I had no money. So naturally I thought of my dear old chum."

"Naturally." Anger would have been useless. I was resigned. "Do you want anything to eat or drink?"

"Not now. Just a cot if you can spare one. Does my credit extend to bus fare back to Toronto, if I promise to go quietly?"

"Cheap at the price. I'll put you in the bedroom next to mine. Keep your voice down. My nephew is asleep."

Upstairs I gave Larry a towel and pointed him at a bedroom. I knew he was drunk, but how much I couldn't tell. I closed Richard's door, then my own. I heard Larry begin to snore almost immediately, a chain saw snore audible through the wall. I slid into a phantasmagorical kind of half-slumber.

In spite of the hour I finally fell asleep, I was awake before Richard came down, glowing with that particular freshness only the young can muster in the morning. He disappeared behind the paper while I cooked bacon and eggs, one of the few dishes I cook well. He cleaned the plate along with several pieces of toast launched onto the counter by Winnifred's energetic pop-up toaster. I gave him a key and he prepared to leave on his tour of harpsichord builders. I was just giving him directions on how to get to his grandmother's apartment when Larry shuffled into the kitchen wearing my bathrobe. "Hail, Mary," he began before realizing there was a third person in the room. "Lawrence Townsend, I'd like you to meet my nephew, Richard Carter." Although Larry was older, Richard was still the official guest.

If Richard felt surprise at seeing another person he did not let it show. "How do you do, Mr. Townsend," he said, proffering his hand. Larry looked frankly astonished. Tall, slim, handsome, dressed in various shades of blue, Richard could have quickened a pulse far more discriminating than Larry's.

"Hi, Rick," grinned Larry with a too easy familiarity.

"My name is Richard," replied the young man. "I'll be on my way now, Geoffry. By the way, if a Mr. Gendron calls, would you please tell him I'll call back. I tried to reach him when I arrived yesterday before I came to the house but he was out. He's a harpsichord builder. See you later." He inclined his head ever so slightly in Larry's direction. "Mr. Townsend."

"Well, get her!" exploded Larry as the front door closed.

"His name is Richard," I replied pouring Larry a cup of coffee. "I don't think he really goes for that Rick-trick stuff."

"That girl could be had."

"Perhaps. But not by you, and certainly not here."

"May I say that's a kicky looking dildo in the shower."

"It's not a dildo, dearest; it's a loofah. You use it to wash your back."

"Is that all?"

"That's all."

"By the way, Chadwick – gotcha!"

"What do you mean, 'gotcha'?"

"I mean if your nephew arrived yesterday, as I just heard him say, then whose parka did I find on New Year's Eve?" By now duplicity was becoming more natural than truth. My hesitation was no more than momentary. "If you must know, he was a passing acquaintance I picked up downtown. He must have been drinking more than I realized. When I brought him back here he asked for scotch with a beer chaser, and after one gulp of scotch he passed out. I had just managed to get him upstairs when you arrived. Satisfied?"

"Quite. It's not every day that Caesar's wife turns into Potiphar's wife before my very eyes. Didn't you even get a peek at it?"

"No, I didn't." For some totally irrational reason I was furious at having to lie to Larry. On top of his unwelcome presence here I had been made to look like a fool. I should have counted myself lucky not to have been found out; instead I could barely conceal my impatience. "Now listen," I began, "I will write you a cheque, which you can cash on your way to the bus depot or station. There's a train some time around noon. As you seem to have lost your overcoat wear the parka hanging in the passageway. Please send it back; it doesn't belong to me. I am leaving now for my apartment. Make sure the front door is firmly shut when you leave. I have work to do." With which I left the house.

Although officially out of town as far as the office was concerned, I still had projects to complete. Moreover, I realized I could accomplish nothing if I stayed at Winnifred's, not until the deep freeze had been emptied. White, rectangular, the box lurked in the basement but its presence filled the house to overflowing. While I slept it was there; while I shaved it was there; while I cooked breakfast for my nephew it crouched, only feet below me, the pressure tangible beneath the soles of my feet.

Another important reason led me back to my apartment on this particular morning. That night, if at all possible, I intended to dispose of the body, the headless, armless, legless trunk of Dale Lawton. The sheer bulk of the body would prove a problem, a problem further complicated by my own sense of warped decency. Perhaps I was being foolish, naive in the worst sense of the word, but I was trying to get rid of the body in such a way that no one would be faced with the unpleasant fact of finding the pieces. I don't suppose the more philosophical among us have ever seriously considered the ethical way to dispose of a dismembered body. Still I did not wish anyone to know. It was more than a simple fear of being caught. Who could possibly trace a decomposing torso found in the ditch of an obscure secondary road after spring thaw to a prosperous lawyer? Supposing I packed and shipped the body to a distant destination, bringing the package to the train station or express depot wearing dark glasses and a paste-on moustache under a fedora. Sooner or later some totally innocent stranger must make the discovery. Two police officers, soon to head home to wives and children after a day of traffic violations and disorderly drunks, must routinely investigate a slightly gamey box sitting unclaimed in a luggage depot. Police are human too; even I could not contemplate how vile and shocking the experience must be.

Still, I had a plan of sorts, simple, crude, and dangerous; but a plan nevertheless. Stuff the body into a bag, weigh it down, and drop it off one of the bridges which join Montreal to the rest of Canada. I pulled into the garage of my apartment building and parked the car. I was just walking away when I happened to notice my licence plate was missing. It was still in the trunk where I had put it before being mugged early that morning. What luck I hadn't been stopped on the way down from Winnifred's or earlier that morning. After screwing it back into place I went into the storage area. This time what I wanted was packed in the rear corner of my locker. First, a large duffel bag, the kind used by servicemen during the Second World War, and bought one day on impulse at an army surplus store. I put it into the trunk of my car. Then, stacked in the farthest corner of the locker lay four cement blocks purchased from a construction supplier and used one summer on my balcony patio to support a sheet of arborite. The whole had made a perfectly adequate table, but I had stubbed my bare toe just one too many times on the concrete blocks. Instead of throwing them out in the fall I retired them to my locker. I knew perfectly well they would be of no further use to me, but they had cost me so much effort to grunt and sweat up to my apartment that I decided to keep them. Maybe there lurks a moral, but I am not prepared to draw it. Emptying enough from the locker to give me access to the blocks, I struggled them one at a time into the trunk of my car. Then I piled the rest of the books, which I would never reread, the golf clubs I intended to give away, the broken chair, always to go to the cabinetmaker next week, back into the locker.

I took the garage exit to the street, and a short walk brought me to a bank, then a hardware store. There I purchased a length of chain, a padlock, and one hundred feet of nylon clothesline. I took the purchases back to my car, then took the elevator up to my apartment.

Checking the mail and answering tape took only minutes; nothing that wouldn't keep; and I went into the kitchen to make coffee. A place that is not lived in goes stale. Even though the air filtered daily through a giant circulating machine, one of those real energy burners, it still tasted flat, like water left standing in a tumbler. My latest Maria had obviously been in to clean; everything lay so gleamingly in place the whole apartment looked like a theatre set. Geoffry Chadwick enters stage left and crosses to sink. The jar of instant coffee on the counter, and the spoon, leaving a pale brown stain on the spotless formica, began to reclaim the space, to stake it out in my name. I realized, perhaps for the first time, how much I had taken for granted the casual comfort of Winnifred's house. For all its lack of decorator pretension the house reached out to envelop the visitor. Chairs sagged from being sat in; piles of magazines lay at hand to be read, not stacked in a neat pyramid – *New York Times* to law journals – on the end table. Even the unpredictable cat skittering into the hall at the sound of the front door pushed back the emptiness of unused rooms. And were I to emerge from this sordid adventure undetected I could never again enter my aunt's house with the low-keyed but nonetheless certain anticipation of a warm welcome and a pleasant time. The staircase, the deep freeze, the ash tray, the tools carefully returned to the workbench would haunt me, so many mute Eumenides, until Winnifred decided to sell the house and move. How often had I read that sexual knowledge marks the end of innocence. Totally untrue. Innocence ends when one realizes one can live, more precisely one must live, with the consequences of a deed which can never be undone. Bankruptcies can be paid off, abandoned children decently educated, criminals rehabilitated. Many wrong acts are capable of redress, compensation can be forthcoming, accommodations made. The blindfolded figure can be persuaded to hold the scales in equilibrium. But what can compensate for taking a life?

And supposing, just supposing, I am driven to confess? The urge to confess is primitive, sharing the burden of guilt with another, as primitive as stoning the scapegoat-king and thereby sloughing off one's sins. I mistrust the primitive; it undermines centuries of civilization. I do not believe confession lightens responsibility. Were I to confess to killing Dale Lawton; were I tried and sent to prison or given a suspended sentence and put on parole; were I to appeal and win acquittal I must still accept that my brain sent the signal to my hand to swing the ash tray that struck the man who fell backward down the stairs and died. This is the house that Jack built. This is the cat who lived in the house that Jack built. This is the rat, and so forth. It all comes back to Jack. The buck lands on Jack's desk. It was I who swung the ash tray, and hit that little sonofabitch who was trying to rip me off, that street hustler who turned me on and then said I was old enough to be his father. Would I do it again?

In conclusion, it's best to keep one's mouth shut.

Such speculation, however, was not going to plug the loopholes in a company takeover I was helping to prepare. One immense conglomerate hunted another to devour and absorb. The killer whale stalked the great white shark, only instead of fathomless grey water the arena was the broadloom of boardroom.

I sat at my desk in front of the bedroom window, which commands a superb view of a parking lot, now almost filled with the cars of shoppers seeking January bargains, half-priced Christmas cards and cut rate blown glass ornaments. I could almost envy the optimism of those who buy next year's cards even before Epiphany, the easy certainty they will be around next Christmas and in condition to address envelopes.

Since the episode on the staircase New Year's Eve, I had developed a bad case of inertia. It took me a day to get through an hour, a week to get through a day. I managed somehow to make some progress in my work, and at about 4:00, decided to pack it in and go back to Winnifred's. I had to make some effort toward feeding Richard, and I could finish reviewing the files there. A small leg of lamb sat thawing in the refrigerator, one of the frozen items tossed out of the freezer to make room for the corpse; but I wouldn't tell Richard that. I could open a tin of something or other, and he certainly wasn't going to die without his leafy green vegetable.

I pulled into the garage. The side door to the basement was closer than the front. I switched on the basement light and kicked off my rubbers. Lurking on the far side of the basement the deep freeze appeared to swell. Over three times its normal size it jammed its way into my sight. Taking the steps two at a time I discovered lights burning in the front hall and the front room. Richard's boots sat neatly together in the front porch. I hung up my overcoat on a hanger beside Richard's jean jacket. Something caught my eye, amiss yet not wrong, until I realized the old parka still hung on its hook, the one I suggested Larry borrow. Either he had left without taking it, or he had not left. The front room sat empty and the kitchen lay dark. I mounted the stairs to the second floor. Directly across from the head of the stairwell the door to the room Larry had used stood shut. Faint but unmistakable sounds of sex came through the closed door, moist sounds of suction, as when a cock is being sucked, accompanied by low moans and sighs of pleasure as when the suckee is enjoying himself immensely. My temper shot up. How dare Larry be so tacky as to put the make on my nephew in my aunt's house? How dare Richard be so tasteless as to let himself be made. About to fling open the door, I paused. Whoever lay beyond that door was occupied to the point of oblivion. I pulled my hand slowly back from the door handle.

Winter dusk had fallen. Now was a perfect time to get the body out of the deep freeze and into the trunk of my car. I stole on silent feet down to the basement and out to the garage. From my car I took the duffel bag, the length of chain, and the padlock. Dropping them on the floor beside the deep freeze I lifted the lid and tried to get purchase on the heavy, hard, slippery object in its double plastic wrapper. With a dull thud it slid from my grasp and hit the bottom of the deep freeze. Again I lifted. A third try brought the body over the edge and onto the floor to lie large, inert, and heavier than I could have imagined. In a matter of seconds I dropped the open end of the duffel bag over the thing and pushed it deftly inside. Threading the chain in and out through the eyelets dotting the open end of the bag I tied it closed and fastened the knotted chain with the padlock. Then I began to drag the bag with its ghastly contents across the basement floor.

"Would you like some help with that, Geoffry?" said Richard's voice from the top of the stairs.

His voice hit me like a kick in the groin. Steady, Geoffry, steady. "No thank you, Richard. I can manage quite well by myself." Never apologize; never explain. You can commit murder if you wear a shirt and tie. I forced myself to look at him. "I thought you were out."

"I was, but I came back. Then I went to visit Grandmother. Geoffry," the young man came halfway down the stairs. I stood easily, my weight on one foot, as if dragging a heavy duffel bag across the basement floor was the most natural thing in the world. "Geoffry, I don't wish to be rude to you or your friend, but this afternoon there was a – misunderstanding." By now I had figured out whoever Larry had upstairs wasn't Richard.

"Yes?"

"I came back here about two o'clock. I had to pick up a jar of green tomato pickle Mother sent down for Grandmother."

"Green tomato pickle, for Chrissake."

"Mother makes it every year. She sent a jar down for you too. Mr. Townsend was here, and well – I think he had been drinking. Then ..."

"He tried to put the make on you and you said no dice, baby."

"Not quite like that, but you have the idea in essence."

"Who's he got up there now?"

"I think he's a cab driver." I recalled having seen a cab

parked across the street as I drove up to Winnifred's, but I assumed it was making a pickup at another house.

"Do something for me, Richard. On the bottom shelf of the fridge you'll find a leg of lamb. Put it in a roasting pan – there's got to be one somewhere – and put it in the oven at three-fifty. And hang out in the kitchen until I join you. Oh, and put your mind at rest. I'd have been cross if you had put out for him. Now let's get dinner on the road."

He smiled. "Thanks, Geoffry. Sure I can't help you with that bag? It looks heavy."

"No, no. Just some Superior Court cases I've been storing here. I made room for them at my office. I can manage easily."

I waited until Richard's steps grew faint down the passageway. That was close, too close for comfort, too close even for discomfort, close enough to get rattled and panic. Let's hope my good luck wasn't running out. A sudden burst of adrenalin helped me to half-drag, half-lift the duffel bag across the remaining space to the steps leading up to the side door. A few more suppressed grunts; always remember to lift with the knees; and the duffel bag with its contents lay in the trunk of my car.

Pausing only to note the company and licence number of the taxi parked across the street I re-entered the house and took the stairs two at a time to the second floor. Flinging open the bedroom door I was confronted not by the beast with two backs but a curious creature composed of one body and four legs. "I have an announcement: Veteran Taxi licence number T-20743 is blocking a driveway. Will the driver please move his vehicle at once. *Le taxi Vétéran numéro T-20743 est stationé devant line entrée. Veuillez l'enlever tout de suite.*" The driver's astonished face peered up at me from between Larry's legs. "Get dressed and get out!"

"Jesus Christ, Chadwick," began Larry.

"Shut up." I said in a voice that precluded discussion. A sorting out of arms and legs brought the driver to his feet; I was afforded the spectacle of watching him try to jam his large and very tumescent organ into bikini briefs over which he had to zip up a pair of skin-tight jeans. He dressed in record time. Wordless, I stood aside to let him pass. Seconds later the front door shut. By this time Larry had pulled up the sheet, which he held clutched to his chest like the dowager duchess surprised by a prowler. "Listen, Geoffry, I can explain everything. I – I have a note from my mother."

"Okay. Explain how you came to be kicked out of your hotel. Explain why you showed up here at 5:30 A.M. Explain why you are not on that goddamn train to Toronto. Explain why you tried to put the make on my nephew in my aunt's house. And then explain how you did put the make on that cab driver-again in my aunt's house. While you are preparing your answers let me give you my rebuttal." I crossed to the bed and slapped Larry across the cheek so hard his head snapped sideways. My backhand caught him on the rebound.

"Chadwick, you crazy bastard –"

My third blow cut him off in mid-sentence. "I am not going to hit you any more, Lawrence Townsend the Second; you will probably start to enjoy it. I will, however, say this. If you are not dressed and out of the house in ten minutes you will be spending six weeks in traction." I walked into my own room and closed the door.

Suddenly I was shaking so hard I had to sit on the edge of the bed. High moral indignation is ugly, and I had just beaten Larry for what I had already done myself, only the cab driver didn't end up dead. Our own faults and inadequacies seen in others appear grotesque and distorted, like reflections in the house of mirrors at an amusement park. What was intrinsically so wrong with bedding down a cab driver? I myself have quickened more than one taxi driver's pulse when business was slow, bringing them into my building through the garage so we wouldn't be seen by the doorman. What was so dreadful about trying to put the make on a beautiful twenty-year-old? There has been open season on twenty-year-old men and women ever since Eve bit the apple. Why was Winnifred's house so sacred, especially when she was out of the country? Pecker tracks on the sheets? A little water clears us of this deed. Were I truly civilized I would apologize to Larry and offer to drive him to the station. Hitting him for turning a trick was like hitting the cat for catching a bird. No. The analogy was false. A fifty-five-year-old man ought to have some sense of decorum. An old-fashioned word; an old-fashioned concept. My nephew had it. Embarrassed because a besotted old buck had come on strong, he had rejected the proposal and then worried about being thought rude. Maybe the time had come to shed Larry, the Larrys in my life. He was an old friend, whatever that is. Shared experience is not necessarily shared sentiment. Because I had known Larry a long time I never seriously asked myself whether or not I liked him. Did I like him? No. Did I respect him? No. Did I feel that if he ceased to be my friend my life would be in some way diminished? No.

While I was carrying on my silent debate I heard Larry's door open and his footsteps on the stairs. The front door shut. From my window I could see Larry, his gloveless hands in the pockets of the borrowed parka, his leather soles struggling for purchase on snow and ice, make his way down the street. I watched until he turned the corner out of sight. I knew I would probably never see him again.

I have no idea how much Richard heard; not that it mattered. Uncle Geoffry's friend was in bed with a taxi driver. Uncle Geoffry went upstairs. The taxi driver left the house in a hurry. Then Uncle Geoffry's friend left the house in a hurry. Uncle Geoffry came downstairs and poured a lot of scotch into a glass. He didn't add water. He was very quiet.

I was indeed very quiet as I sat at the kitchen table watching Richard methodically lift each canister and wipe under it. He looked up at the clock. "Geoffry, would you mind if I watched television for a while? There's a program taped in Tanglewood coming in on PBS I would very much like to see."

"By all means. I haven't had a chance to read the paper. Do you have plans for the evening?"

"I may go to a harpsichord recital – unless you have

something in mind."

"No, nothing."

"Would you like to come?"

"Not unless you're prepared to leave at intermission. Perhaps you'd better go alone."

He rinsed the dish cloth in hot water, folded it neatly, and hung it on the long-necked faucet to dry. A real Mr. Clean. Not a bad quality in a house guest. As a matter of fact, Richard was racking up quite a few points. Tidy, polite, self-sufficient, he didn't crowd me. He did not breathe up all the air, nor did he sit heavily around waiting for me to make suggestions like a cheery camp counsellor. He was a little farty; and anyone who wants to study harpsichord is beyond precious – but I liked him. Had he not been my nephew I would still have liked him. And whether he acted by accident or design I was grateful for his leaving me alone to drink and brood.

We ate the lamb in silence, not exactly companionable, but not hostile. Neither of us felt uncomfortable at not speaking. Silently he cleared the table and loaded the dishwasher. I could easily have driven Richard to the concert, but I did not want him in the same car with the body. Not for me to drive down Sherbrooke Street with the quick and the dead in the front and back of my car. I salved my conscience by giving him cab fare for the ride home.

After Richard left I spent the evening trying to complete what I had been unable to finish during the day. My concentration had to fight my intense nervousness over tonight's projected drop. I sat struggling with the files before me until I figured it was about time for Richard to get home. Going up to my bedroom I shut the door and put a pillow against the bottom to block light from giving away my wakefulness. "Playing possum," an expression of my father's. "Geoff," he would say sticking his head through my bedroom door, "I know you're playing possum under the covers. Put away the flashlight and the book and go to sleep like a good man. Now do as I say or I'll send in your mother." "Okay, Dad." Anything to avoid Mother with her moist reproach and ineffectual threats of the bogeyman.

So I hung out in the spare bedroom, playing possum so that Richard might think I was asleep, sneaking out once in the dark for a pee before lying down fully dressed on the bed. I switched off the light and pulled my eyes shut like blinds. Sleep was out of the question, but I thought a little yoga might help me to relax. I could not empty my mind; I knew no mantras, and I could not bring myself to recite "Om" over and over. Om is a small town in Oz where the Wicked Witch of the East lived before Dorothy's house landed on her. How would the Great and Powerful Oz have disposed of the body? Would the ruby slippers help? Tap your heels together three times and the deep freeze will disappear. A few of those flying monkeys would sure come in handy.

I must have dozed off. I awoke to sit bolt upright before looking at my watch; light filtering in the window allowed me to read the dial: 3:00. Cautiously I opened my bedroom door. Richard's door stood wide open. I peered in to see the bed empty. Nor was he on the ground floor, so I dressed to go out and sneaked into the garage. Starting the engine so it could warm up I opened the trunk. Cutting the nylon rope into three equal lengths I secured the end of each piece to one of the cement blocks using one of the two slip-proof knots I had learned to tie during my brief tenure as a Boy Scout. Cold made the nylon rope stiff and unwieldy; I swore under my breath. I passed the other three ends through the chain holding the bag closed and knotted them. By this time the engine hummed quietly. I eased out of the driveway and headed south toward the Victoria Bridge, a low, dumpy bridge, appropriately named. Unlike the Jacques Cartier or Mercier Bridges, soaring, graceful structures spanning the river in defiance of gravity, the Victoria Bridge, with its concrete pylons and heavy steel girders, stands as a monument to all that was ugly about the industrial revolution. It was, however, the closest bridge to Winnifred's house. Just before I reached the ramp leading to the bridge I pulled over and stopped. Not wanting to take any chances, I quickly unscrewed the licence plate and tossed it onto the front passenger seat.

Not a car in sight. Halfway across the bridge I pulled to a stop. Jumping out of the driver's seat I hurried to fling open the lid of the trunk. I gave a tremendous heave and one cement block crashed over the railing of the bridge. Number two followed. Block number three hit the other two with a grinding thud. The sound sent an echo reverberating through my memory of another crunching thud, glass against bone, as a young man fell backwards down a flight of stairs.

With the counter weights hanging over the railing into a void it took surprisingly little effort to lift the duffel bag itself over the railing to plummet down into the rushing black water of the St. Lawrence River, a hundred feet below. For a second I peered into the abyss; pale light danced across the surface of loose ice floating downriver toward the sea. So preoccupied was I that only when I turned to close the trunk did I see a police car pulling up ahead of mine. The door opened and a plump officer climbed out.

"Hey, mister, you all right?" Almost to my surprise I realized he was English.

"Perfectly all right thank you, officer," I replied. "I just paused for a minute to admire this splendid view." I waved my hand airily upstream. "The sombre ice-cloaked waters of the mighty St. Lawrence are a sight to thrill even the most world-weary."

"Have you been drinking?"

"Indeed not. I never drink. Liquor poisons the body and destroys perception. Nor do I contaminate my lungs with nicotine. We live in a world bursting with wonder and I do not wish my awareness to be for one instant clouded. Why even now, at this very moment, we are poised above liquid history. Whatever do you suppose Jacques Cartier would say if he could see us now?"

The officer shook his head. "You're not supposed to stop on the bridge."

"I do apologize. I thought perhaps at this hour; it's not often one gets the opportunity to observe the shifting panorama of city and sky in all its starry splendour."

"Well, don't do it again." He turned back toward his car. Suddenly he stopped. "Where is your licence plate?"

"My licence plate? It's on the front seat of my car," I replied as though that were the most obvious place in the world. "One of the bolts fell off and I was afraid I might lose it – and it's so dirty I thought I would clean it up before putting it back."

The officer gave me a quizzical look. "Maybe you'd better come down to the station. Follow my car. We'll go around the circle at the other end of the bridge, then back across." He heaved his portly frame into the police car, where a second officer waited; I had no choice but to follow. We continued across the bridge, a cortège of two, while I imagined myself confronting a roomful of blue uniforms (Alice blue gowns, as Larry would have called them). Each and every one of them would know I was guilty. How would they know? They would simply know; it was their job to know. Why the hell was I paying taxes to support a police force who couldn't spot a guilty man when he tramped right into the station? Like Hester Prynne I wore a big scarlet letter, only my A stood for assassin, not adulteress. Then again what about Chris? Did sleeping with some woman's husband make me an adulterer, or just a damn fool?

The officer in the passenger seat turned around to make sure I was still following. Good profile. Not bad, not bad at all. One of those humpy Franco-Italian types with big bedroom eyes, sort of like a cocker spaniel. It had been years since I last dated a cop. They're hard work. Even when they're in bed they're still wearing that uniform in their heads. Firemen are far more relaxed about the whole thing. I must remember to tell Richard about lunch tomorrow.

Our two cars reached the end of the bridge. The police cruiser then began to circumscribe the large traffic circle which fed into the other side of the bridge leading back into the city. I slowed down allowing the distance between our two cars to widen. Around the circle we went, a motorized merry-go-round, until the police cruiser headed safely up the ramp onto the bridge with no opportunity to turn. Without undue haste, I eased my own car into the very last turn off before the ramp and headed back toward the protective cover of the next community.

Did I panic? I don't think so, at least not in the sense of flying wildly out of control. But I certainly did not want to follow that police car back to any station. Pulling off the traffic circle had been a sudden impulse, and a dumb one. Far better to have followed the cruiser back to its station to be booked for impaired driving, no licence plate – something involving a fine and a reprimand. Instead I found myself heading into a community laid out like a grid, each house a clone of the one beside it. Those bare, bleak, treeless streets offered no camouflage should the police decide to search me out. Then I remembered that police cars have radios that put them in instant contact with other police cars. In fact, a South Shore police cruiser could be on the lookout for me this very minute. A medium-grey Pontiac with no licence plate would not be difficult to spot on streets almost bare of traffic. And I did not dare stop to replace the plate. I cruised fearfully past cookie-cutter houses when suddenly a pair of headlights flashed into my rear-view mirror. It had to be the police. Without increasing speed I drove to the next intersection, then turned right. At once I pulled over to the curb, killed the lights, and lay flat on the seat below the sight line of the windows. I held my breath; why I don't know. I wasn't hiding in the closet of a deserted mansion while a killer stalked the halls. But I was trying to be very, very small. The ominous car turned onto my street; its lights blazed into my darkened windows. "Here it comes," I thought. The car drove past me and stopped. I could hear doors open and shut. Voices. Then came a sound like a sectional garage door being rolled up. The car pulled off the road; the garage door shut. Then silence. I waited a few seconds before cautiously raising my head to peer through the windshield. The street stood empty.

Far from feeling relief at what seemed to be a fortunate escape, I grew all the more certain that somewhere out there – around a corner, on the next block, just turning off the highway – a police car, maybe even unmarked, prowled in pursuit. In my mind's eye I could see it cruising up and down deserted streets, like a killer fish in a sea movie. I had to get away, but how? I couldn't be too careful. My best plan was to get right off the street if possible, but I knew no one even remotely close by. Even if I had it was far too late to drop in without arousing suspicion. The row of houses, bland as butter in daylight, brooded dark and inhospitable behind snow-covered lawns. Taking a deep breath I started my car and drove slowly around the block, twitchingly alert, certain that out of nowhere a giant claw would descend to yank me off to my noxious nemesis. I didn't know where I was going, and getting there was certainly not half the fun.

Making a left turn onto a side street I spied a house on whose ground floor lights still burned. I pulled into the driveway as though it were my own. Climbing nimbly from my car I paused just long enough to replace the incriminating licence plate before hurrying up the front steps to ring the doorbell. Light from the outside fixture threw me into sharp relief; not another soul moved on the street.

The door opened on a safety chain to reveal a middle-aged woman upholstered in quilted pink nylon, her hair clamped tightly into rollers. "What is it?"

"I've come to pick up my daughter Kimberly-Ann. She babysat for you tonight. Sorry it's so late, but my wife and I fell asleep."

"She's not here."

"Not here. Are you sure?"

By this time the woman's husband, a maroon checked bathrobe under jowls and over flannelette pyjamas had joined her through the crack in the door. "Quite sure."

"Oh, dear, I must have made a mistake. I don't suppose I could use your telephone."

The woman looked over her padded shoulder at her husband. The jowls moved up and down. "He looks all right to me. Let him in."

The woman closed the door to release the chain. There are times when seconds do not seem like years; they are years. The door opened to admit me and I stepped briskly inside. "This is extremely kind of you – at this late hour." I was playing for time. The longer I could manage to stay inside the better.

"Phone's in the kitchen."

I kicked off my overshoes and made my way across an expanse of royal blue shag carpet into a kitchen, which stepped right from the pages of *Good Housekeeping*. I plucked a sand-coloured receiver from the cradle and surreptitiously held my left forefinger over the six small holes in the earphone to block out the busy signal. Then I dialled the number on the telephone dial and waited for five make-believe rings. "Gillian, thank goodness you haven't gone back to bed. Look; I can't find Kimberly-Ann. I'm at the wrong house. The people have kindly let me use the telephone." I turned to smile an ingratiating smile in the general direction of my hosts. "Okay, let me have it again." With my right hand I took a notebook and pen from my inside breast pocket and wrote some gibberish. "Got it ... What's that? ... It won't start? Well, call the service department; they have twenty-four-hour service. I thought the house felt cold when I left ... Of course I don't know the number; look it up. And put the electric heater in the baby's room in the meantime ... Don't worry. I'll pick up Kimberly-Ann and come straight home ... No, I don't want anything to eat – just some hot ovaltine." I rang off. "Right street; wrong community," I said brightly to my captive hosts who stood heavy, inert, unfriendly. "We're trying to teach my daughter to be responsible by encouraging her to take babysitting jobs. She's such a madcap. Last week she baked an angel food cake and frosted it with shaving foam." I laughed a brittle little laugh.

"If she ain't responsible she shouldn't be lookin' after no kids," said the woman, her face an icon of unwelcome.

"Well, yes, perhaps." Their unyielding presence compelled me toward the door. "What a handsome lamp!" I exclaimed, indicating a confection of ruby glass, supported by cherubs holding tear-drop pendants, whose white and gold fluted shade, still swathed in cellophane, effectively blocked the picture window.

"Thank you."

"Well, I must be running along. The furnace has gone off in our house and the baby is sick." I pulled on my overshoes. "Thank you both so very much again. I'm sorry to have been a nuisance." Intractable, immutable, their mass pushed me inexorably through the door into the street. With quaking nonchalance I walked to my car and slid in behind the wheel. From either side of the ruby lamp in the window a face watched sullenly while I made as if to consult my jotted address one last time before starting the car and backing slowly into the street. I had only a remote idea of where I was, and the police cruiser could well be lurking around the next corner.

There are times when one must simply trust to luck, and mine had so far not let me down. I eased onto Route 20, skirting the lower bank of the river, until I reached the Champlain Bridge. Back onto the island and to Winnifred's without so much as a glimpse of the police.

As I climbed the stairs to the spare room I could see that the door to Richard's room was still open. He had not come in. Under normal circumstances I might have worried. It's 5:00 a.m. Do you know where your nephew is? But these were not normal circumstances. I crawled into bed and lay looking through darkness at the ceiling and thinking there was much to be said for the celibate life.

I awoke around 9:00, late for me. Looking across the room at an unfamiliar mirror over the dresser, tucked full of snapshots, I wondered for a terrified moment where I was. The cat scratched and mewed outside the closed door; through the window I heard the sanitation department banging garbage cans. Reality shifted into focus, at least the reality of place. The first thing I noticed on opening my door was that light still burned in the hallway. Richard's bedroom sat empty. I slid on my robe and went down to make coffee. The effort of lifting all that heavy weight last night made itself felt through a small but nagging pain in my lower back.

Having read the paper, with an unsuccessful try at completing the crossword puzzle, and not feeling up to facing the briefcase, I took a pack of limp playing cards from a kitchen drawer. They turned into parentheses as I shuffled them. Halfway through a game of Canfield solitaire: one, two, three, four, five, six, seven; two, three, four, five, six, seven; six, seven; seven; just about the point where I was sorely tempted to cheat – why shouldn't I cover a blank space with a queen? – I heard the front door open and Richard walked in. "Hail the conquering hero. Coffee?"

"Thanks, Geoffry. I hope you weren't worried."

"Not really. I knew the yellow brick road would bring you back here eventually."

"I went backstage after the recital to speak with the performer. We ended up going out for a drink."

"You must have been very thirsty. It's ten A.M."

Richard gave a small, self-conscious laugh. "You know how it is. One thing led to another."

"Never apologize; never explain – and there's nothing like sleeping with the right people in the right places."

"Oh, it wasn't like that."

"Perhaps not. Just remember to put one brick on top of another and one day you'll have a house. Use your assets, and at your age ass is an asset."

"You make me sound like a hustler."

"Not in the least. All I'm saying is it's a rusty old world. You can watch the coloured lights just as nicely with someone who might give your career a hand as with someone who won't. How did he play? Too much loud pedal?"

Finally Richard broke down and laughed out loud. "He hardly used the pedals at all. As a matter of fact he played beautifully; it was a splendid concert. The instrument was really great. He's given me an introduction to the builder, in

New York. I'm going to fly down this afternoon to see if the man will build me one."

"That's just what I was talking about. Make a friend; get an introduction. See America first. Getting there is half the fun. Seriously, though, you may as well get the best instrument you can. It would seem to me you have gone beyond a build-it-yourself harpsichord kit from *Popular Mechanics*. In the meantime maybe you'd like to shower and shave and put on clean underwear. We're expected at your grandmother's for lunch and then I'll take you to the airport. Unless of course you're having lunch with Mr. Keyboard."

"No, he leaves this morning for Boston."

"I see. Just another story of harpsichords that pass in the night."

"Not quite. He's coming to Toronto in a month."

"That means you'll have to sit through another recital; it's a heavy price to pay for a date. Now would you like some breakfast?"

"Not if we're having lunch quite soon."

"I wouldn't count on anything too terrific. If I were you – and you're not a picky eater – I'd have something first; believe me. Why don't you go upstairs and get your act together and I'll have some breakfast ready when you come down.

# 10.

MOTHER LOOKED SURPRISINGLY WELL for Mother. Madame, the housekeeper, must have wheeled her downstairs to the concourse level of the apartment to have her hair done. It looked freeze dried, but it was neat. She wore a burgundy velvet robe, which draped gracefully over the cast while the other foot was clad in one of those Bermuda length pantyhose and shod in a matching burgundy flat-heeled slipper. She wore her pearls, three luminous graduated strands with a large ruby set into the clasp. They were scheduled on her insurance policy, just in case. On the fourth finger of her left hand rings competed for attention: a platinum wedding band; a matching guard ring set with tiny diamonds; her own engagement ring, three diamonds in a row set in platinum filagree; her mother's engagement ring, three diamonds in a row set in platinum claws; the engagement ring I had given Susan, a ruby flanked by two diamonds. Mother had kept the ring all these years with the understanding that whenever I decided to marry again the woman of my choice would get the ring. Mother still wore it.

"You look well today, dear," I said bending down to give her the ritual peck on the cheek.

"I wanted to look my best for my handsome grandson," she replied looking right past me at Richard, who stood uncertainly in the doorway. "How are you today, Dicky?"

" 'Dicky!' Don't tell me you call that great hulk 'Dicky.' "

"Tall though he is I will always remember the day he took his first step. It was in the living room of the big house. I do wish we hadn't sold the house. This apartment gives me cabin fever."

"Some cabin, Mother." I looked down the spacious living room across the Sheraton desk, which sat beneath a window commanding a mouth-watering view of the Montreal skyline. "We should all be so underprivileged."

"I know, dear, but the room looks a fright. The Brymners are on loan to the museum for some kind of travelling show and the settée is out being reupholstered. I feel as if I'm living in a stadium."

Whether the last remark was true or not, Mother was never entirely comfortable surrounded by the handsome pieces she and Father had acquired through inheritance and auction during their years together. She would have preferred a living room set. The gleaming mahogany and marble surfaces, almost liquid in their lustre, troubled her. She attempted to demystify them with little touches, cut flowers in a ginger pot, a pair of Lalique birds, even a folded newspaper. The furniture fought back and gave the room a strongly masculine feel, redolent of my father.

Having kissed his grandmother Richard sat in a wing chair facing her. "Are we going to celebrate the occasion with a little drink, Mrs. Chadwick?" I suggested.

"Perhaps one wouldn't hurt."

"Richard?"

"Nothing for me thank you, Geoffry."

"Geoffry!" echoed Mother. "Doesn't he call you Uncle Geoffry?"

"My name is Geoffry. I was not christened Uncle Geoffry but Geoffry. He in turn was christened Richard, not Dicky. The time has come for you to drop that cutsey-pie cognomen and call him by his real name."

"Geoffry, at times you sound distressingly like a lawyer."

"I am a lawyer. Will you have the usual?"

Mother bridled ever so slightly. " 'My nose myself I painted white; because you see I'm always right.' "

"But I am always right, Mother. Now do you want a drink?"

"Yes, please."

"Sure you won't change your mind, Richard. How about a glass of white wine?" I asked.

Richard nodded.

"There's sherry," Mother piped in. "Walter is joining us for lunch."

As if answering a summons the doorbell rang. I crossed to open it. There stood a beaming Walter, looking like a hobbit. It wouldn't surprise me a bit if he had fur on his toes. He held a bunch of cut flowers wrapped in paper upside down as though he had just shot them. When he entered the room I watched with amusement as he did a double take at the sight of my nephew. "So this is the grandson and heir," he said after he and Mother had erupted into greetings. "You remind me of your grandfather. Indeed, you're a dead ringer for Craig." The observation made me wince.

"He even has Craig's dimples." A hint of accusation clouded Mother's voice, almost as if Richard were indeed robbing the dead. The young man looked frankly uncomfortable.

"Give me a hand, Walter," I said guiding him into the pantry.

Walter gave me a broad wink. "Do you suppose he might?"

"I know for a fact he has." I poured a glass of sherry, one of white wine, and two gins on the rocks, which I put on a tray. Walter put his cut flowers into water. All I could find in the cupboard suitable for long-stemmed carnations was a silver-plated cocktail shaker, which needed polishing. "I'll carry the drinks; you be Tosca," I said, preceding Walter into the living room.

Richard was talking. "I have decided to switch from piano to harpsichord, Gran."

## EDWARD O. PHILLIPS

"I wish I had a harpsichord in the apartment. I'd love to hear you tickle the ivories, a bit of Chopin, or Brahms," said Mother, reaching for her glass.

I admired Richard's tact. Instead of correcting her as I would have done – "You never play those composers on the harpsichord" – he deflected. "I haven't been working on Chopin or Brahms yet, Gran. Right now I'm concentrating on Bach and Vivaldi."

"Is your sister Elizabeth still singing?"

"Yes, she is. In fact she is singing one of the leading roles in her school production of *The Gondoliers*. She's playing one of the gondoliers; I don't know which one."

"Your grandfather and I used to go to Gilbert and Sullivan. There were several companies who performed locally. I remember the last opera we saw was called *Ruddy Gore*. I have always thought it was a dreadful name for an opera. Can you imagine? *Ruddy Gore*."

"The opera is called *Ruddigore*; it's the name of a castle, Mother," I said from behind my gin. Immediately I was sorry. Mother fought back by wilting. To correct her was to crush her. As a child I am sure she must have pouted; but she had learned to refine the process, a geriatric little match girl. Her air of wistful resignation irritated me like a hair in the mouth.

Walter, however, could read the emotional barometer of a room more accurately than anyone else I know. "Well," he began raising his glass, "here's to Epiphany. In two days we are rid of the Christmas-New Year frazzle for another year. Aside from the pace it's become so hideously expensive. Even token presents do mount up so. On my way over the cab driver had his radio on; some choir was singing that interminable carol about all the totally useless things my true love gave me for Christmas. Can you imagine the cost today? Even Nieman-Marcus would quail. And while we are on the subject of quail, where would you find a partridge at this time of year? One sees the occasional pheasant on the mountain, but it's a bird of a different colour. And even if we arranged to have a partridge trapped how could we persuade it to sit in a pear tree. Pear trees, any deciduous trees, in the middle of winter are not very attractive, leafless and covered in snow. Who would want to sit in one? To the cost of trapping a partridge and exhuming a pear tree we have to pay out to locate two turtle doves – not indigenous to North America I might add – three French hens and four calling birds."

"We could get four finches or canaries from a pet shop," I suggested. "And surely some farmer from, say, Ste. Anne de la Pocatière would sell us three French hens."

"Tut, tut, Geoffry; that's cheating. Simple francophone hens won't do. They must be French, hatched on French soil."

"Couldn't we have three sent in from St. Pierre and Miquelon. Certainly cheaper than having them shipped air cargo from Toulouse."

"Good thinking. A franc saved is a franc earned. But now we come to five gold rings. With the price of gold climbing daily we have ourselves a pricey little item."

"I don't suppose we could substitute five brass curtain rings."

"I'm surprised you would even ask. Gold, and twenty-four carat at that."

"Speaking of carrots," said Mother, "Millicent MacLean dropped in this week. She brought me a carrot cake which she had baked herself. Delicious. Too much frosting though. I dislike sweets." Having captured our attention she drained her glass. It was her way of asking for a refill, preferring to go thirsty than ask outright. I made the trip to the pantry, topping up my own drink at the same time. "Which brings us to six geese," I said, re-entering the living room. "Do you suppose they have to be alive? They're noisy bastards, and dirty."

Walter laughed. "Six geese a-laying? I'm afraid six dead geese would be out of place in the carol. They must be alive and hissing. Have you any idea how much one must pay for a goose?"

"Some people pay all their lives," I replied. Richard stifled a laugh.

"I'm sure they cost more than turkeys," added Mother

after a swallow. "Even frozen. And they're so greasy to cook."

"We're talking about live geese, Mother. However, there's nothing in the carol to suggest they can't be local. How about trapping six Canada geese, or would that be too wildly ethnic?"

"Geese are geese," replied Walter. "And apparently some island just off the Toronto shoreline is infested with them. They refuse to go South; they must have heard Florida is full of Canadians. Still, by the time you send a goose catcher to Toronto and put him up at the Royal York plus expenses it does mount up."

"It'll be peanuts compared to tracking down seven swans a-swimming. Back to Europe one more time. And they're even meaner than geese. A mother swan will break your arm with a peck."

"There are swans in Ottawa, believe it or not," said Richard. "They were a present from the Queen during Centennial Year. I remember our teacher made a big thing of it in school. They swim on the Rideau Canal."

"Our problem is solved," exclaimed Walter, clapping his hands.

"Not completely," continued Richard. "The carol calls for seven swans a-swimming. Adult swans mate for life. How do we come up with an odd number?"

"Are there no – bachelor swans?" Walter raised one eyebrow. I used to think raising one eyebrow was the pinnacle of sophistication.

"Wouldn't a spinster swan do just as well?" replied Richard looking directly at Walter, who giggled.

"Got it," I said. "Seven cygnets. Pre-pubertal. Most aquatic fowl swim from birth."

"Speaking of signets," said Mother from her chair, "whatever happened to Craig's gold signet ring. I know you have the watch, Geoffry; but I have no idea what happened to the ring."

"Mother has it, Gran," said Richard. "She plans to give it to me on my twenty-first birthday."

"That's nice, dear. I thought perhaps I'd lost it." There followed a short pause, but the ring issue seemed to be settled.

At that moment Madame, a steamer trunk of a woman, loomed in the doorway to announce lunch was served.

While Madame, with Walter's help, installed Mother and her cast at the head of the table I took a detour via the pantry and poured another gin, which I had instead of the soup, an all-purpose vegetable and leftover potage nettoyage. Richard and Walter drank white wine, but Mother rang for tea. Only the astute observer would have noticed the absence of steam rising from the cup. From where I sat I couldn't tell whether it was dark rum or rye. Although she much prefers gin, Mother believes in keeping up appearances.

"I was watching those puppets on television the other day," began Mother rising to the obligation that a hostess entertain her guests. "One of them said to the other, If I fried potatoes in a monastery would they call me the French friar?' 'No,' said the other, 'they would call you the chip monk.' " Mother began to shake with laughter. "And one said to the other, 'How did you like the sketch?' And the other replied, 'Rare.' Or was it 'Medium'? Yes, that was it; the other replied, 'Medium. It wasn't rare and it wasn't well done.' " We all laughed politely. My laughter came largely from relief. Mother generally begins telling a joke with the punch line and works backwards.

The main course turned out to be a chicken, which as acting host, I had to carve. I rose to sharpen the knife on the steel, the way Father always did, conscious of two gins on an empty stomach. I drove the two-pronged carving fork deep into the breast and started to slice off a wing when I began to have the oddest sensation. The knife, no longer a knife, felt in my hand like a hacksaw; the wing, no longer a wing, turned into an arm. I put down the knife. "Richard, would you be so good as to finish carving. Excuse me." I went down the hallway to the bathroom and splashed cold water on my face. The feeling passed.

Never apologize; never explain. I returned to my place

at table. The chicken, no more than a chicken, lay neatly dismembered on the Aynsley plates. "Have you ever been to New York, Richard?" I asked, consciously not looking at the drumstick on my plate. "He's going down to buy a harpsichord," I added for Mother's benefit.

"No, I haven't."

"Don't dawdle on the streets, and carry twenty bucks' mugging money. And whatever the drawbacks it's still the most exciting place in the world."

"It's a strange city," added Walter. "In fact America is a strange country. I once drove to San Francisco via New York and Chicago. By the time I reached Los Angeles I realized Preston Sturges and Billy Wilder movies are documentaries."

"Now don't go criticizing the United States," began Mother into her cup of tea. "Everybody is always saying nasty things about the U.S. Goodness me, where would we be without them?"

Next door to Mexico, Constance," said Walter. "Instead of the Rio Grande, those wetbacks would be swimming the St. Lawrence, an awesome prospect."

"You shouldn't call them wetbacks," continued Mother, whose idea of an ideological stance was to stick up for the underdog. "It's not as if they were darkies."

"Of course not," said Walter poking diffidently at his chicken.

As I surveyed the group, ignored the food, and listened to the small talk, so small it sounded as if it had been pushed through a sieve, I decided Walter was getting a poor return on his carnations. Richard gamely ate his lunch. I had noticed he never spoke unless he had something to say. Few people understand the values of silence and immobility. Most people are far too eager to please. Like Labrador puppies they jump and frolic, begging to be liked. Richard did not have to please; his appearance compelled attention. I wondered anew if he realized how arresting the combination of beauty and silence could be, how he would kindle longings in strangers drawn to his cold chemical light like randy fireflies. Walter sat mesmerized; his dark brown eyes in their delta of wrinkles seldom left Richard's face.

"You know everything, Walter," began Mother, paying one of those extravagant compliments characteristic of her generation. "Is there anything really worth while coming up on television this week? I get so tired of sex and violence."

Walter thought for a minute. "There's always music on PBS. And this week there's an Emlyn Williams festival. *The Corn is Green*, that's the one about the schoolteacher who goes to a Welsh mining town. And they'll play *Night Must Fall*; that's the one about the murderer who keeps a head in a hatbox."

"A head in a hatbox?" echoed Mother. "I don't think I would want to watch that."

"It's a good film, Constance. I hope they play the first version, with Robert Montgomery. Did I say something funny, Geoffry?"

"No, Walter, but you may have just saved my life."

Before anyone could react, Madame bore down upon us with dessert, a trifle drenched in sherry. Having failed on the chicken I compensated by pouring coffee.

"Richard," began Walter, pouring cream from the silver jug, "there is no criticism implied in the question, but why would you want to switch from piano to harpsichord? Don't you consider the piano a more expressive instrument?"

"For certain kinds of music, yes. But the period that interests me predates the piano."

"True enough. But Sophocles preceded the proscenium theatre. We no longer sit out of doors to watch *Oedipus Rex*, especially in winter. Do you not believe in evolution of the arts? Let me put it another way. Can baroque music not be performed more expressively on a more evolved and sophisticated instrument?"

"Not if you want to serve the composer. Look at what has happened to opera. Singers have dropped all those self-indulgent cadenzas and sing the notes as the composer wrote them." Richard's tone was that of a schoolmarm quelling a minor insurrection rather than that of a true proselytizer.

"What you are talking about is style. The singers are still singing music written for the voice. What interests me is whether music written for one kind of instrument, in this instance the harpsichord, cannot perhaps find a truer expression on the piano. I don't mean one should romanticize Bach, rubatos and lots of loud pedal. But the sound of a piano has more nuance, it is capable of a wider range of colour than that of a plucked instrument."

"Yes, but if you're going to recreate the style of a medieval icon you don't use gooey paint from a tube and pile up impastoes."

"Nor do you have apprentices grinding up lapis lazuli and preparing panels with rabbit skin glue. You use the contemporary equivalent."

Richard shifted his position as he warmed to the argument. Walter pushed back his chair and crossed his legs, something I had been taught as a child was bad manners. On the point of making a flip remark about the wheel versus the runner, I glanced down the table. No one had noticed Mother was fast asleep in her chair. I slipped into the kitchen to find Madame, who had become a past mistress at getting Mother tidily into bed. I offered Walter a lift and suggested to Richard he might think of getting organized for his flight. Lunch ended without fanfare.

RICHARD AND I STOPPED AT Winnifred's house to pick up his luggage. I suggested he not carry his new record albums all the way down to New York and home to Toronto, "I'll be coming to Toronto in a week or so. I'll bring the records along. We can have dinner."

"Terrific! I'd like you to hear me play."

"I'd like to hear you play. I didn't ask you on this visit because I'm sure Winnifred's upright piano is dreadfully out of tune."

While he carried his things to the car I took a wallet of

cheques from my jacket pocket, wrote one for Richard, and slid it into an envelope. We drove in silence to the airport. Traffic was heavy and I have never been able to drive a car and chat at the same time. Driving, like sex, demands my full attention. "I'll just let you out at the entrance," I said, pulling up the ramp to the entrance marked Air Canada, "unless you want me to wave forlornly as you go through security check."

"That won't be necessary."

I pulled over to the curb. Reaching into my inside pocket I took out the envelope. "Richard, this is a cheque. It will pay your way to New York with something left over for a deposit on your harpsichord, should you decide to order it. There is no point in telling your parents; they probably wouldn't approve."

"I really don't know what to say."

"Then don't say anything. Let me hear from you when you get back to Toronto. I think you can spring for a long-distance call."

To my immense surprise the young man turned in his seat and threw his right arm around my neck. For a brief moment he pressed his cheek to mine. "Thanks for everything, Geoffry. I'll call." He lifted his gear from the back seat and crossed the sidewalk. At the door he turned, waved, and disappeared into the concourse.

# 11.

WITH WALTER'S UNWITTING SUGGESTION in my mind, I drove slowly back to my apartment building through rush hour traffic. I was surprised and touched by Richard's gesture. When had I last been embraced by a man in a manner not sexual but affectionate? Generally, whenever I touched another man it was either to shake hands or take him to bed, bent out of shape as I was by an upbringing that frowned on physical contact between men. Not that one couldn't have bodily contact, on the football field or hockey rink, in the boxing ring, on a wrestling mat; but heaven forbid a touch that was not cloaked in violence. One punched one's friends; one did not caress them. One could hold hands to arm wrestle, not when walking. A hug must disguise itself as a headlock; a hand on the nape must squeeze the neck painfully between thumb and middle finger. Adolescent males could press their tumescent bodies together in a struggle for supremacy; rough-housing it was called, rather than a search for self-transcendence. Buttocks could be felt, crotches grabbed, just so long as the gesture came across as aggressive. Christ, wasn't it boring.

I pulled into my parking space and took the elevator up

to my apartment. The answering tape held nothing but junk calls: the handicapped wanted to sell me light-bulbs and panty hose, neither of which I needed; one of the newspapers, to which I didn't even subscribe, wanted to know if service was satisfactory; someone else inquired about a used car he claimed was listed in the classified ads under this number. All promised faithfully to call back. I was just about to turn off the machine when a young woman's voice came onto the tape to announce herself as calling from the Montreal Veterinarian Clinic. "Mr. Chadwick, your cat is ready to pick up. She has been wormed, given a flea bath, as well as all her shots, and the tartar has been scraped from her teeth. The kittens have been cleared of fleas. The bill is seventy-five dollars; board is ten dollars a day, day in day out. Cash or Chargex. Thank you." I turned off the machine. Seventy-five bucks to ransom a family of strays – and rising. And then what the hell was I going to do with them? Place an ad in the local paper?

I picked up a pen and wrote idly on a pad. Sentimental approach: My name is Velvet Paws and I want to be your friend. So do my brothers and sisters.

Practical approach: Mother and five kittens available for babysitting and light housekeeping duties in exchange for room and board.

Titillating approach: Family of cats trained to do interesting and unusual things with their rough little tongues. Adults only.

I crumpled the sheet and turned to the mail, which was grim; a few late Christmas cards and the first of the December bills. But the main reason for my coming to the apartment had me carrying the small folding stepladder into the hall closet and reaching down a box from the very top shelf.

It was no ordinary box, not by a long shot. Made of the finest cowhide, kept supple by regular cleanings with saddle soap, the lid opened on two brass hinges riveted to the leather with brass studs. Two brass rings attached the leather handle to leather loops stitched onto the top while a pair of brass buckles held the lid shut with straps likewise stitched to the top. There was also a lock but the tiny key had disappeared years ago. Inside the box, upside down in a well of red velvet, sat a top hat made of beaver, sheared to the texture of satin, ringed with a moire band, lined in white silk, and bearing, inside the crown, the proud logo of a Bond Street hatter. The hat belonged to my grandfather, then to my father, now to me. I had never worn it; I never would. The hat fit me perfectly, and I must confess I looked distinguished, even handsome, wearing it. For some totally irrational reason the hat in its box was one of my favourite possessions, like my father's watch and a small jade goddess Winnifred bought me on one of her trips.

I placed the hatbox on my small dining table, undid the buckles, and lifted out the hat, pausing just a moment to brush the glossy surface with the tips of my fingers. Even more than the hat, its box caught my fancy, the improbable yet elegant combination of leather and velvet. It was the closest thing to a coffin Dale Lawton would ever have. His head strapped into the box, weighted, and dropped off a bridge, would find its final resting place at the bottom of the St. Lawrence River. Night must indeed fall. Had the ground not been frozen I would have taken the box somewhere into the country to bury. It seemed more fitting. But January dictated the river.

Why had I saved the head until the last? It was the easiest fragment to dispose of, but I knew that was not the real reason. In the head, severed crudely at the neck by a hacksaw, lay the core of the man; his spirit, his soul, had lurked behind those ordinary features. Whatever perceptions he had of the world entered through those mismatched eyes. Maybe I kidded myself that so long as I had not disposed of the head he still existed, no longer alive, nor yet completely dead, a creature in limbo condemned to total oblivion once the deep freeze stood empty. Why in the past have men made masks of the dead. Was it an attempt to capture the essence of the man, to push back the fact of death? Or was it no more than imprisoning a likeness, an earlier version of the tintype or fading studio photograph. The *memento mori* need not always be a skull.

Still the morbid side of man's imagination will always be fascinated by the skull beneath the living head, a solemn synecdoche, the part representing the whole. In no other part of the body does the substructure lie so close to the living surface. Teeth become suddenly terrifying, stripped of lips and tongue. Even those teeth duly admired in television commercials turn sinister seen in their naked setting. One shudders to think of bodies burned beyond recognition identified through dental records. The *danse macabre* stretches across the centuries from fourteenth to twentieth, even more fearful today than then. We will all grow very old; we yearn to remain young. But no longer do we hoard bits of the real person, a skull, a locket with a twist of hair, "a bracelet of bright hair about the bone." Instead we cling to photographs or jewellery or intimate possessions, a razor, a letter opener, a pair of glasses, objects frequently used and supposedly imbued with the spirit of the dead.

Think of the hue and cry that would be raised today were one to try and obtain the skull of a loved one to keep. I wouldn't really want a skull myself, but it might make an interesting test case bringing in everyone from public health authorities to psychiatrists. At a time when the skull has ceased to be an object of terror it is nearly impossible to obtain one. But, it is one thing to contemplate a skull; it is another thing to dispose of one.

The doorbell interrupted my speculations. I thought it odd, considering visitors are usually announced by the doorman. It could be someone who came and went so regularly the doorman no longer bothered or else someone going from apartment to apartment like a census taker. I never hesitated to open the door. I thought it highly unlikely that someone would force his way in to steal my purse after dragging me into the bedroom to force me to submit to gross indignities. Some people have all the luck.

I opened the door. "Chris – for Chrissake!"

"Hello, Geoffry. Long time no see – to coin a phrase."

"What are you doing here? Don't answer that. You are standing on the mat having just rung my bell. Why are you here?"

"To see you. Are you busy?"

"No. I might even stretch a point and ask you in."

Chris pulled off his shell rubbers; he was the only one I knew who still wore them, and came inside to drop his duffel coat, with its wooden pegs, onto a chair. Shell rubbers and a duffel coat, but then his clothes always did span the decades. "Drink?"

"Yes, please. Scotch, if you have it."

"You look wonderful. Such a tan. You must have been South, or else you've cornered the market on bronzer."

"Audrey and I took the family to St. Thomas for a week. Christmas in the Caribbean. Her mother cashed in a bond. The hitch was that she came along."

"Was it jolly? Did Santa Claus arrive by yacht?"

"No."

"I have scotch but are you sure you wouldn't prefer a piña colada?"

"No, thanks."

I carried two highballs into the living room. A small package on the coffee table caught my eye; wrapped, but not in Christmas paper. I surmised it must be for me and found myself embarrassed in anticipation. Chris smiled his irresistible smile; teeth that looked false in their white perfection and laugh lines making a triangle at the corner of each eye. The tan knocked five years off his age; sun and salt water had painted streaks in his thick auburn hair. On a scale of one to ten I thought he looked ten plus. He was here for a reason; of that I was certain. I also knew that given time the reason would surface. But, preoccupied as I was with the head of Dale Lawton, the last and most incriminating fragment, I found myself disinclined to chat. Maybe absence had not made the heart grow fonder, but it had served to emphasize the emotional vacuum through which I now moved. Still, I had an odd sensation as I looked at Chris, so close I could reach out and touch him, almost as if I were looking through the wrong end of a telescope at a part of my life that seemed very small and far away. New Year's Eve 1980 had changed all that. To hear Chris speak reminded me of a familiar voice heard on a tape recorder, one step removed. "Chris, you came here to tell me something. I'm listening."

He chuckled quietly. "You don't beat around the bush. I've missed you, Geoffry."

"I've missed you too, but that isn't what you came to tell me."

"Maybe it is, or at least partly. I never got the Cranbrook job."

Unable to think of anything to say I gave an all-purpose shrug, registering at least that I had heard what he said.

"My credentials were impeccable, my experience; but – get this – they wanted a younger man. They hired someone in his mid-thirties."

"Are you sure that's the real reason? Forty-five isn't exactly antique."

"It is when you're talking pension funds and retirement benefits, with option for early retirement." He laughed without mirth. "I must confess it's the first time I've really heard time's wingèd chariot, a sobering experience I might add."

"Join the club. There's a first time for all of us and it isn't very much fun." I saw no point in adding that breaking up with Chris had been my wingèd chariot, my realization that whatever shreds of youth remained had gone. Real or illusory youth, it didn't matter. Then after we split up I turned fifty, the big five-O, and faced the bleak idea that unless I live to be a hundred my life is more than half over. Had I learned of Chris not getting the job even some weeks before I might have taken perverse pleasure in the news along the lines of "Serves him fucking well right," but all I could feel now was a sense of overpowering regret that nobody's life seemed to work out as wished. Our love affair had ended because Chris wanted the job. Now he didn't have it. He was disappointed and I was no better off than before. Worse actually. Had Chris been around there would not have been the episode with Dale. And I knew that even if I succeeded in unloading the body I could never unburden myself of memory. Chris and I were both worse off as we sat sipping our scotches in my handsomely appointed room in my desirable apartment building. I knew Chris well enough to know how deeply he had been disappointed. The starch had gone out of his stiff upper lip. Two men, outwardly prosperous, well-dressed, one wearing the ultimate status symbol of a winter tan, the other pale from stress and lack of sleep; each condemned to live with himself and his sense of failure. Nor could I take comfort from the fact that I was not trapped in East Germany willing to risk my life to climb the wall, nor was I wading into shark infested waters off the Chinese coast prepared to hazard the swim to freedom. I did not rot in a Turkish jail, nor had my home been blown up during a raid by the PLO. The world teemed with people far worse off than I would ever be, but the knowledge didn't really help. Being less miserable does not make one feel less miserable. You don't get to heaven on other people's sins; you don't reach contentment on other people's misfortunes. If anything Chris's news made me feel worse, all that emotional upheaval, and for what.

"Anyhow, it's done," said Chris, breaking silence. "In the meantime, I missed your birthday. That's a little something from St. Thomas."

I reached gingerly for the package, almost as if it might detonate in my hand. But the paper, a montage of cigars, pipes, cigarettes, in suitably masculine browns and reds, seemed innocuous enough. Inside a small cardboard box; inside a velvet box; inside a gold watch of elegant simplicity. On a rectangular white face four tiny gold rectangles marked 3, 6, 9, 12. It was a watch I would have bought for myself. "It's beautiful, Chris. Thanks. I'll even spare you the 'Oh – you shouldn't have!' Does it have a movement?"

"Yes, you s.o.b." He grinned. "Now that you're all softened up by my lavish present I come to my next bit of news. It's a question rather than an announcement. Ergo: any chance at all of our getting back together again?"

To my surprise I was not surprised. "I don't know. I don't even know that I want to. Isn't it just a bit pat. We split up because you applied for the Cranbrook job. You didn't get it, and so you've had to face remaining in Montreal. Therefore why not warm up the old relationship. It's easier than breaking in a new one. Am I far off base?"

"No. You're dead on. As a footnote let me add that I've played around a bit since I saw you last. And all I have learned is that I want you back. All that sand and surf has given me a necessary perspective on what is really important in my life. I thought Cranbrook was; I'm not so certain now. You are. I understand now that I was totally unfair, but it's done. I am sorrier than perhaps you realize, but being sorry doesn't change a thing. I'll see you on your terms; you call the shots. I still love you; I always did. And regardless of what you decide you can keep the watch. It's a free gift."

By this time I had poured myself a second scotch, and I found myself giggling, yes giggling, into my glass. I was being courted; declarations and expensive presents. Ought I to hold out for a mink coat or a cruise? Pearls? Tupperware? However, Chris read my reaction, and things began to happen very quickly. He was tightly built and enormously strong. With ease he reached down and grasped me by both arms to lift me, unresisting, to my feet. Then he kissed me, his mouth a velvet vacuum cleaner. I was too surprised to resist, nor did I have much resistance to summon, returning his kiss as eagerly as it was offered. We kissed again, then again, prying ourselves apart only long enough to tear off our clothes. With one sharp pull I undid my carefully knotted tie. My vest flew onto a chair. A cuff link bounced off the coffee table to roll under the couch as the tail of my shirt billowed over my belt. I pulled off my shoes and socks still standing up. Unfastening belt and zipper I let my trousers slide to the floor and stepped out where they lay. I managed to peel off my jockey shorts as I hurried into the bedroom where a naked Chris was already turning back the covers.

We came together with a shock of recognition. Our bodies took over, reducing brain to nothing more than a switchboard for sensation. I had forgotten how good that supple brown body felt next to mine. Sensation has a short memory. With Chris each time had been a discovery. We kissed ravenously, our hands hungrily exploring each other's body. Then Chris rolled onto his stomach and spread his strong swimmer's legs, offering me his buttocks white and vulnerable against his smooth brown back and thighs. As I entered him with excruciating pleasure, as he raised his hips to meet me and find the rhythm of my thrusts, I knew my skin would love his skin for always. I came with a shudder, no longer aware of pleasure or pain, racked with a searing sweetness that left me collapsed and gasping across his body. At that moment Chris braced himself and contracted his sphincter. "Jesus Christ," I said almost yelling, "are you trying to kill me?"

"What a way to go. And you shouldn't take our Lord's name in vain."

"Just remember. Beware the blunted needle."

"True. But I did not fold, bend, staple, or mutilate."

I withdrew slowly. "Okay, wiseacre. Turn over."

"Attention. Contents under pressure. Handle with care. May explode if heated."

"Ask one who owns one." Kneeling between his legs I drew him into my mouth. It did not take long. "Oh my God," he moaned softly as his body went into spasm.

We lay together without speaking. Chris and I spoke little during lovemaking. Let your fingers do the walking; let your bodies do the talking. I dislike people who issue bulletins during sex. I do not wish to be informed it's like music-or poetry. It isn't. I grow impatient with people who announce the imminent arrival of their orgasm like an on-the-spot newscaster trying to hype the arrival of some celebrity or other. "I think she's coming now. No, not quite. Any minute now, Ladies and Gentlemen. No, not quite yet. Just a minute ... I think ... And here she comes!" Most of all I dislike what Larry calls the T.T.M.P.'s. Talk To Me Dirty's. Those who while having sex either wish you to abuse them verbally, not my trip; to describe clinically what you are presently engaged in doing to them, the quintessence of redundancy; or who wish you to describe sexual acts you have already performed with others. "Ever do it with a black? Was it good?" The answer remains nobody's business.

After a while Chris turned to me again. This time we were less frantic, less focussed on the groin. The keen edge of desire dulled we wallowed in each other's bodies, tasting, testing, exploring the entire person. We floated into popper land, sniffing butyl nitrate from a small amber bottle taken from the drawer of my night table. With hearts pounding and skins flushed we sank dizzily into a languorous sensuality where not an orifice remained unexplored. Release was a sweet shudder, not a jolting spasm.

As was so often the case in the past the clock became our chaperone. Chris was due at a dinner party. He dressed to go. "Can I see you again?"

"Yes."

"I'll call."

I gave him Winnifred's phone number.

"How does Audrey feel about not going to Toronto?"

Chris grew thoughtful. "She may still go. That's something we have to work out."

"Trouble in River City?"

"Bad day at Black Rock. Don't worry; you'll be the third to know." He glanced at his watch. "I've got to dash. I'll call tomorrow." On his way through the living room he paused, noticing the top hat for the first time. A top hat compels a head. "It's two a day for Keith; And three a day for Loew's," he sang, jumping to kick his heels together in mid-air and executing a buck and wing down the passageway. He moved beautifully, never a wasted gesture. At the door he gave a smile and a wave before disappearing down the hall for the elevator.

I carried my half-finished drink into the bathroom and stepped into the shower. "Shit!" I muttered as cold water left in the pipe from the last shower hit me in the chest. I soaped myself with Pears transparent, the soap that looks good enough to eat, enjoying the warm water spraying me clear of suds. Halfway through towelling myself dry I paused; something bothered me. Nothing really wrong, yet I felt vaguely uneasy. My mind groped toward the cause like someone in an unfamiliar room reaching for the light switch.

Then I realized quite simply I was no longer in love with Chris. A flat statement for a flat feeling. I was no longer in love. Simple to say; not simple to accept. Even in the depths of misery who would voluntarily cease to love, to abandon that condition and sink to a lower level of awareness? In a world drugged with nicotine, alcohol, valium, marijuana, cocaine, heroin – to name a few – being in love stands out as the last natural high. I discount joggers and those who hyperventilate. To be in love is to be more alive. We are preoccupied with something other than self. The highs that people pursue so single-mindedly through art, exercise, sex, drink, or drugs are no more than a temporary escape from the prison of self. Some manage to escape more regularly than others; either they have great talent or iron constitutions. After two drinks I can forget how bored I am with my work. After four I can accommodate myself to the fact of Dale Lawton. When I was in love with Chris, way back then through the wrong end of the telescope, my own world seemed a better place, not the world but my world. I drank less and enjoyed it more. I carried my high around with me. My total consciousness did not focus on myself, except perhaps when I had the flu, or stubbed my toe. I was not happy; I am not stupid enough to be happy, but the scale tipped upwards from discontent toward a state of well-being.

And even when we were separated, when I ached from his absence, I would not of my own free will have ceased to love him. Our low periods whet our consciousness just as much as our elations. To be down is not such jolly fun as to be up, but we are still more alive than when things go calmly according to schedule. Conditioned as I was during childhood to apply a damper of good manners to strong feelings I have always been afraid of love, an untidy, uncontrollable emotion. I feared the loss of my own autonomy, the dependence on another to help trap the chimera of happiness. Yet even more than love itself I feared its loss. Knowing it to be transient I longed for permanence. I knew falling in love to be like sculpting in ice, dependent on so many factors outside one's control. And this absence of control, particularly of myself, made me uneasy.

As a young man I discovered it was fashionable, even desirable, to be passionate about ideas but not about people. Imagine growing passionate over late forties' liberalism. Blacks have blood types too, and RH factors. Oriental eyes do not slant; orientals have an extra fold of skin on the lid. Otherwise they are just like us. Then there was the death penalty, always good for an argument. Bowdlerized books in schools was a pet peeve of my father's. Sacco and Vanzetti were beginning to fade from the national consciousness to be replaced by defecting spies. Today they have been replaced by baby harp seals. Ideological excesses could be allowed, even applauded; emotional excesses were bad form, in terrible taste, and self-indulgent in the extreme.

It went without saying that sexual drives stood out as the most unruly and the most in need of control. I speak not of sex tamed by society, marriage with an extremely eligible girl like Susan, perhaps even a discreet affair with an older woman, provided she were divorced, separated, widowed. But love is not a tidy emotion. I grew up at a time when there was still a sexual underground. The closet forties became the tentative fifties blossoming into the strident sixties. The shockproof seventies will fade into the mellow eighties.

But I collided with puberty during the forties, my adolescence influenced by the aftermath of the war, that last great romantic crusade. It started out just as medieval as any thirteenth-century attempt to liberate Jerusalem. Heroes opposed villains; good faced off against evil; issues stood clear. Khaki-clad knights rode off on trains instead of on chargers;

ladies waved goodbye from station platforms instead of castle walls. Love affairs were short, brief, intense, the lovers separated by forces far greater than they. The Casablanca Syndrome. No matter. The spirit of romance hung in the air. Then came saturation bombing and the Holocaust and Hiroshima and Nagasaki to soil the world. Romance cannot exist in radioactive air.

But I have a memory of that earlier time when the romantic spirit was a natural part of one's view of the world, before this same romantic view had degenerated into the narcissistic preoccupation of the Me Generation. As a result love always shimmered on the horizon like a distant castle circled by a deep, cold moat. A cauldron of oil bubbled continuously above the lowered portcullis behind the raised drawbridge. But high in the keep lay treasure of fabulous richness and beauty. When I met Chris the castle turned into a chateau, spacious and sunlit, and above all accessible. And even when the sun went behind a cloud, when the windows stood closed and shuttered and a chill wind from the garden blew drafts down the deserted corridors I would not willingly have left.

And suddenly I found myself evicted. I stood on the outside unable to get back inside with only a dim recollection of beautiful rooms. I was not unhappy, but I felt a sense of loss, a feeling of exclusion. Were I to go through that door again it would be as a visitor, a tourist, never again as keeper of the keys.

After a lapse of many months I had just made love with Chris, love which stirred my senses as deeply as they could be stirred, but which did not touch my mind. To be more legalistically precise we had just had sex, very good sex; but we used to make love. Maybe I'm quibbling. Who, at fifty, opens the door to a handsome, vital man dying to go to bed? For many no doubt that would be more than satisfactory.

But more pressing concerns crowded in on me. Tonight I would shed the last fragment of the corpse. I would awake to a brighter tomorrow, as I read somewhere once. The only tomorrow I have ever found to be perceptibly brighter is the day we go onto daylight saving time. I closed the hatbox and carried it down to my car for the short drive up the hill to Winnifred's house.

At the sound of the side door the cat shot down the basement steps erupting into a volley of snarls, yelps, and croons, which combined relief to see me with scolding my absence in a cacophony of yeowls. Even without kittens cats are natural mothers. I confess a growing attachment to the animal, a really spaced-out kitty. A decade ago I would have called her neurotic, but that buzz word has fallen from fashion. A useful word in its time. A neurotic was someone who disagreed with your point of view at cocktail parties; raging neurotic applied to the other person in a recently terminated affair. The word never seemed to be used in conjunction with those suffering from genuine neuroses. But poor little Norma, feline, fertile, unfulfilled, incarcerated in Winnifred's house with me as surly keeper, must surely have a clutch of conflicting drives pulling at her pea-sized brain. I fed her and watered the plants. The cat had done in two avocados and a large African violet lay on its side, the pot in shards.

I stood in the window of the guest bedroom, the one I had appropriated, and looked across rooftops, across the city shimmering with streetlights to a black void which must be the river. Canada's own St. Lawrence. The mighty St. Lawrence. It is not the longest nor the most historic, not even the most mysterious. It undoubtedly carries the most industrial pollution, but it is mine. My river, my city, my life. I don't ordinarily go on this way, but I was having yet another scotch on top of no breakfast and next to no lunch. Seen through a luminous haze of alcohol and neon Montreal struck me as beautiful beyond belief. I stood like an exile returning home, scanning the horizon for that first glimpse of the familiar shoreline. Indeed I was an exile; disposing of the head stood between me and landfall. A sudden impatience gripped me, to be rid of it all, every last goddamn piece. Did I really have to wait until the small hours? The hatbox was not large. To stop my car at the side of the bridge. To lift the hood, sug-

## SUNDAY'S CHILD

gesting motor difficulties. To open the trunk and drop the weighted hatbox over the railing in the dark. What could be simpler? What indeed?

I hurried to the basement. For just a second I paused in front of the deep freeze; the cat sat on the basement steps lashing her tail, waiting for something to happen. I raised the lid. The solitary package lying on the bottom of that large white box looked small and unprepossessing. It turned out to be heavy. Holding the frozen head of Dale Lawton in my two hands, the head of the man whose death I had caused, I was almost shocked at my ability to accommodate. What ought to have caused me waves of guilt and remorse had become a simple inconvenience. But true guilt like true love cannot be summoned on command. Instead of remorse I felt only relief that the final episode was at last under way.

I placed the head in the hatbox and fastened the buckles. As an extra precaution I wrapped several strands of heavy wire around the box, passing the strands under the handle. With the same wire I fastened a spring lock clip to the remaining cement block still in the trunk of my car. Back in the basement I put on my overcoat and overshoes, then carried the hatbox out to the garage.

For a reason I still cannot explain – the law makes few allowances for the irrational – I did not put the hatbox into the trunk with the cement block. Did I honestly believe the back seat more suitable for the final ride? I don't know. Hell, I was not operating from any precedent. I tilted the driver's seat forward; my car has only two unwieldy doors, and placed my grandfather's hatbox on the back seat. About to close the door I became aware of a dull, roaring sound coming from the next house. I peered cautiously outside to find the source. Winnifred's neighbour, the one who jogs in granny glasses, was vacuuming snow from his front steps with a large indoor-outdoor vacuum cleaner. He wore his jogging suit, the adult version of rompers. Catching sight of my startled face he flicked the switch. The roar faded. "Mr. Chadwick, I believe?"

## EDWARD O. PHILLIPS

More than a little tight, I killed the impulse to reply, "Dr. Livingstone, I presume." Instead I delivered a simple Yes.

"De-De, Deirdre, my wife, found out you were Winnifred's nephew. We thought you might drop by for a drink. I'm Tony Tyler, by the way."

"How do you do, Tony. I am Geoffry Chadwick. May I take a rain- or a snow-check on the drink? Unfortunately I have an appointment at the moment."

"How about tomorrow then? We're having a few people in around five. Eggnog and mince pie sort of thing."

The very thought of mince pie and eggnog made my fillings jump, but part of my caretaking mandate included maintaining good relations with the neighbours. "That would be very pleasant," I fibbed.

"Super." He waved and flicked the switch; with a roar the canister began to suck snow from the already shovelled strip of cocoa matting anchored to the steps with steel rods. I eased the car through the narrow door, built for earlier models, down to Sherbrooke Street, then turned west toward the Champlain Bridge. I wouldn't half-mind talking to Tony Tyler if he were bare-assed in bed. But across a cup of eggnog? Looking into those granny glasses sliding down a button nose with no bridge? And I had just missed out on a unique opportunity: to walk up to him carrying the hatbox and ask him if he would like to have some head.

I HAVE NEVER FOR A MOMENT believed life imitates art; sometimes it imitates craft; more frequently it imitates television. I was just pulling away from an intersection, keeping well within the speed limit, when a young man dashed heedlessly in front of my car. Jamming on the brakes I skidded to a halt as his body fell across the hood and slid off to land inches from the front wheels. Without even pausing to turn off the motor I jumped out to see how badly he was hurt. As I knelt beside him he made a recovery that bordered on miraculous. A violent push in the chest sent me backwards onto the sidewalk as the young man climbed nimbly into my car. I scrambled to my feet just in time to catch a glimpse of a bearded profile before the automobile took off in a squeal of tires. But that great director in the sky saw fit to introduce a passing cab. Without even pausing for the commercial I sprang in beside the driver and barked the deathless line, "Follow that car!" To which I added, "There's fifty bucks – no make it seventy-five – if you can head him off." So quickly did the driver gun his engine that I was literally flung against the back of the seat. "Jesus!" I exclaimed.

"That is my name, *señor*," replied the driver with a grin. "Jesùs-Domingo Lopez."

"Mexico?" I asked.

"Si, señor."

I knew that with a Mexican driver I would either overtake my stolen car or die in the attempt. Only the Israelis can match the Mexicans for crazy on the road. Small matter if I was killed. If I didn't get that hatbox back I was a dead or extremely compromised duck: my licence plate, my car registration in the glove compartment. I wondered what was the current going rate for a head in a hatbox on the blackmail market. "That's it; that's my car," I shouted. "The bastard's turning onto the expressway."

"Got him!" replied Jesùs-Domingo.

I tore my eyes from the road for a quick look at my Mexican chauffeur. He drove like a fiend, but he knew how to drive. Small, quick, well-co-ordinated, he handled his cab like a real pro. By now the driver of my car had picked us up in his rear-view mirror. With a burst of acceleration he veered off toward the bridge. Once off the island he could hit the autoroute hard. And the gas tank in my car was three-quarters full.

We darted in and out of lanes in a sonata of honking horns, above which the faint but unmistakable wail of a police siren pierced the air. To think I might have been sipping a quiet drink with Tony and De-De. A mass of steel girders supporting the central span of the bridge loomed ahead.

Then something happened. The driver of my car sideswiped a panel truck and skidded out of control into the concrete barrier separating east and west lanes. The car ricocheted across the double lane into the bridge railing and rolled over completely to right itself just in time to hit the concrete median once again. The hood flew up as the motor exploded into crimson and yellow flame. Cars and trucks skidded to a collective halt. So did my taxi; so sharply I was thrown against the dashboard. I had to reach my car. Pushing open the door of the cab I raced toward the burning vehicle. "Come back, *señor*," I heard the driver call. "She will explode." Ignoring the intense heat I wrenched open the driver's door sprung ajar from force of impact. The young man lay collapsed onto the steering wheel. I had just room to reach in behind the seat and grope for the hatbox which had fallen to the floor. My fingers found the handle; I lifted the box through the door. Then with the strength of desperation I hurled it. Light from the burning motor allowed me to see my grandfather's hatbox with the head of Dale Lawton describe a low ellipse to disappear over the railing of the bridge into the darkness beyond. Grasping the young man under the arms I pulled him free of the car. Fortunately he had not had time to fasten his seat belt. I remember thinking he needed to wash his hair. Stumbling backwards I half-dragged, half-lifted the limp body back toward the line of cars when a roar filled my ears and the car erupted into orange brilliance. Backwards I went. The explosion tore the body from my arms and drove my feet sideways. Pavement rushed up to meet me as the giant ball of excoriating crimson grew smaller and smaller until it vanished into a tiny pinpoint of unconsciousness.

# 12.

I WAS LUCKY: THREE CRACKED RIBS and a large bump on the head. It throbbed, but I even escaped a concussion, or so the intern assured me. My left side was stiff with tape. It only hurt to breathe. I sincerely hoped no one around me will be too funny for the next little while. I couldn't wait for my first sneeze.

I was pretty groggy when I talked to police and reporters. The two officers struck me as oddly reassuring with their spit and polish uniforms and gallic courtesy. They asked me questions – they had to – and for the first time I was able to tell the truth. My car had been stolen, and I chased the thief in a taxi. For the crash and subsequent explosion there were any number of witnesses. One of the officers, whose English was fluent, told me my car was a total wreck, a charred hull. The young man who stole the car died in the crash. I saved a dead man from the explosion. It seems he was a small-time hood with a police blotter a yard long, mugging, breaking and entering, trafficking. A punk pure and simple, but he was dead. The bodies pile up.

When the two police officers had finished questioning me they wished me goodnight and a speedy recovery. I thanked them and my thanks were genuine. Two reporters who had been waiting in the wings came at me with more questions. The reporter from the French press was fascinated by an establishment English lawyer risking his life to save a French hood from a burning car. The English reporter, pale and intense, seemed to favour the humanity in crisis slant. Language, race, religion fail to figure in extreme situations. He personally intended to make sure I was awarded a Medal of Bravery, perhaps even a Star of Courage. Although he seemed to speak through a fog I hoped he would not seriously press the issue. Did Gertrude Pringle's *Etiquette in Canada* inform one how gracefully to refuse a medal one did not merit? I certainly was no hero, just someone who pulled a fast one and got away with it. My head ached; my ribs hurt; I longed to go home.

I pried the English reporter loose by promising to talk with him the following day, when my head was clear. Rising unsteadily to my feet I slid my jacket onto my shoulders without putting my arms into the sleeves, like a 1940s lounge lizard, and walked with extreme care to the exit. My cab driver, Jesùs-Domingo Lopez, had waited all that time to drive me home. He helped me ease myself into the cab and drove me back to my apartment building. Although groggy and sore I was more touched by this simple kindness than I could express. When I asked him how much he had lost in fares because of me he smiled and shrugged, holding up his hands palm outward in a gesture of dismissal. It was a brave thing I had done, he said; it was an honour to chauffeur me. I felt an awful fraud. When I asked him if he would permit me to send him a cheque through the mail he replied it wouldn't be necessary. But I made a mental note of the cab company. A Mexican driver shouldn't be difficult to trace. Money is an arid and sterile way of saying thank you, but it is the only way I know.

My apartment had never looked as good as it did when I flicked the switch beside the door. Back in my lair I could lick my wounds in private. I washed down three codeine aspirins with a stiff highball and tried to decide whether sitting or reclining was less uncomfortable than lying down. The telephone rang. Any time after 11:00 p.m. the telephone is a terrifying experience; my first reaction was, Mother has done it again. I walked stiffly into the bedroom and slowly reached out my right hand for the receiver. "Hello?" A brief pause followed, almost as if the sound of my voice surprised the caller. Then an all too familiar voice spoke.

"I used to believe in the tooth fairy but then I stopped dating my dentist."

"Larry!" Pain made me wince. "It's a very informal hour for a telephone call." Though why was I surprised.

"*Mea culpa*. I expected to get your recorded tape. I'm not even drunk but I'm having a bad attack of the insomnias. I just got rid of a bodybuilder. Disaster; total disaster. He made me feel like Jane but it turned out he wanted me to be Tarzan. Oh, well, when do pectorals become tits? When are you coming to Toronto?"

"Good question. Not until Winnifred gets back. Then I may decide to go somewhere warm for a week."

"Why don't you come down to Key West with me? You can watch me do my dance of desire under a full moon with a frangipani blossom clenched in my teeth."

"It's a thought."

"I was naughty, wasn't I?"

"I guess you were. Hell, who knows? It isn't my house. I overreacted."

"I've never seen you like that. I was really scared for a minute."

"I must confess I surprised myself."

"Never mind. I just said to myself, 'It's pretty Geoffry's way.' And I must admit it's kind of flattering to be slapped. You certainly have the other person's full attention."

"Are you angry with me?"

"Yes and no. Not for the body blows; I guess I had those coming to me. Yes because you carry on as though your shit doesn't smell. Anything the least bit physical is bad form. That parka I found on New Year's Eve didn't belong to Mother Cabrini. Fair's fair. I don't care what you do, but just don't be too hard on us poor girls. Remember, every madame was once a whore."

Forgetting my ribs I started to laugh, but not for long, "I'll take out that deathless *perçu* in cross-stitching as I recover from three cracked ribs I just got in a car accident. Don't press for details. I haven't decided which of several versions I plan to tell you. Suffice it to say until my ribs mend I won't be going anywhere."

"Answer me one question: are you all right, yes or no?"

"Yes. It will be in the papers tomorrow. I'll send you a clipping. What the hell; it's not every day I have a printed alibi to get me out of eggnog and mince pie with the neighbours. For once I won't have to lie. I only wish I hadn't agreed to see that reporter."

"You sound a bit dazed. Are you really okay?"

"Yes, honestly."

"Good. You can fill me in over a cup of tea. You're a crazy bastard but I'd hate anything to happen to you. There are so few of us left. Why don't I call in a couple of days?"

"Good idea. By that time I'll be off the drink and dangerous drugs. Ciao."

Sleep was out of the question. Codeine was beginning to dull the pain but my mind jumped. I stood beside the window in the darkened bedroom, looking down at the empty parking lot. Fine particles of snow undulated across the concrete space in the wake of a mean winter wind. A good metaphor for my life: the view of a deserted parking lot at midnight on a cold winter night. A good metaphor, if only I could believe it and overlook that the view from my living room window across the sweep of city to the river is superb. In spite of cracked ribs and a throbbing head I refused to allow myself to start feeling sorry for Geoffry Chadwick. Pain passes; it is only another sensation, after all. And the balance sheet looked not too bad at the moment.

First the good news: Larry still a friend. I would have called him eventually, but I underestimated his resilience.

Nor will he hold the episode over my head as a weapon. For Larry today is already yesterday, and he lacks the true instinct for malice. An infuriating man at times, but a friend nevertheless.

My nephew Richard: possibly to become another friend. In spite of, maybe because of, differences in age and outlook we may have something to offer one another. I am in a position to give him some financial help with his career. If he goes to Europe to study I could use his being there as a perfect excuse for a trip. Geoffry Chadwick, patron. Why not? I intend to give it a try.

Christopher: suddenly back in my life, if I want him. I'm not so sure I do. There is a time to be born and a time to die; a time to love and a time to let go. Fifty is too old for romantic attachments. Romantic love is for the young with their limitless reserves of energy and time. At my age love ought not to be a castle, not even a chateau. At fifty love should be a condominium, to be lived in on a daily basis, comfortable, convenient, and a sound investment. Nor do I wish any more trouble – for myself, for Chris, for Audrey, for anybody. Maybe I have grown up. When I met Chris I was a middle-aged emotional adolescent. To grow up always means relinquishing something, usually an illusion, in my case the illusion of love. I'm not the first to make the discovery; I won't be the last. It was a lovely illusion. I regret letting it go.

Finally the car: a total wreck. Maybe that is the best news of all. I have never enjoyed owning a car, just about the poorest investment one can make. Something minor is always going wrong and I am too compulsive to let it slide. Even the lighter has to work and I don't smoke. A car keeps you poor; I will never own another. Considering insurance and repairs and gas – which will soon be selling by the ounce, like Arpège – I would be far better off taking cabs. And taxi drivers have to make a living too. The insurance settlement will buy me a much needed vacation. I have a big glossy promotional photo of my ex-car which I will frame and hang above my desk as a remembrance of things past. "That's my last Pontiac hanging on the wall, looking as if it were to drive."

I walked stiffly into the kitchen and poured myself another highball. Now the bad news: Two young men, both dead. One a street hustler, the other a common thief – not your pillars of society – but I would not have wished them dead. Two other young men, a pair of sadistic punks; but they paid dearly for the hundred or so odd dollars in my pocket. Major dental work for one, possibly semi-blindness for the other. Why could they not have left me alone, or simply taken my money and gone? But they wanted violence; and violence breeds violence, feeding on itself like a cancer. And would to God the sanitation department cleans up the lane and carts off the suitcase to a dump before someone decides to salvage it. No one could possibly trace it to me; but I would wish no one to discover what was inside – just as I did not wish the two young men dead, the other two maimed. What was that phrase from long ago at law school? *"Actus non facit ream, nisi mens sit rea."* The act is not criminal unless the intent is criminal. Latin saws offer small comfort. I must learn to live with what I have done. Learn? I was living with the fact this very minute, this very second. Maybe scotch and codeine are not the best aids to logical introspection, but my principal awareness was a feeling of deep regret: regret for Dale; regret for the car thief, who would at least be decently buried; regret for the two leather punks with damaged faces; regret at my own inability to feel deeply – love, hate, remorse. Time had slowed down my body; worse it had tamed my ability to react.

Finally, where was the hatbox now? Where would it end up? Mercifully it would find its water-logged way to the bottom of the river. Maybe it would bob its way downstream past Quebec City, past Anticosti Island to the wide sweep of the Atlantic. I could only wish that nobody might be prompted by curiosity to fish the box from the water for a look inside. But it was out of my hands now. Everything was. Perhaps I should list the complete disposal of the corpse on the plus side of the ledger. But I couldn't.

Supposing I had called the police on New Year's Eve? Would the squalid experience of confession, inquest, arraignment, trial have purged me? Would a suspended sentence or even acquittal have brought a surge of gratitude to my heart? Would I have stood on the other side of the consequences a better person? No. Nor was I going to indulge myself in endless rounds of self-recrimination. I remember Father saying to me as a child. "I am not pleased with the way you have behaved. Do not let it happen again."

I will not let it happen again. Nothing more. *No obiter dictum.* The rest is silence.

I switched on the light and sat at my desk. Sorting mail can be soothing, bills in one pile, Christmas cards in another, junk mail in the basket. A postcard from Winnifred pictured locks on the Panama Canal. "Geoffry, Interesting trip, once enough. Good luck with table mates, bad luck with bridge foursome. Will be home probably Jan. 10. When I get my head together I will have much to tell. Fondly, W."

I smiled as I thought of Winnifred getting her head, firmly clamped in its coronet of iron-grey braids, together. "When I sort out my impressions" makes more sense, but that's our Winnifred. At the bottom of the pile lay the still unanswered wedding invitation: "Mr. and Mrs. Richard D. Hamilton announce the marriage of their daughter Leslie Ann ..."

I took a sheet of notepaper and began to write: "Mr. Geoffry Chadwick accepts with pleasure ..." I paused, then drew a line through "with pleasure." To watch a young woman who might have been my own daughter walk in white down the nave would not be a pleasure. To stand there reminded of Allison and Susan and sharply aware of my own fifty years would indeed not be a pleasure. But one pays one's dues to the next generation. Was I not about to make room in my life for my nephew Richard? The invitation was no more than one of a thousand tiny details forming the surface texture of my life. And I had just committed unspeakable acts to keep that texture smooth and free from cracks and tears. I would not accept the invitation "with pleasure," but I would accept.

## EDWARD O. PHILLIPS

Taking a fresh sheet of paper I wrote. "Mr. Geoffry Chadwick accepts the kind invitation of Mr. and Mrs. Richard D. Hamilton to be present at the marriage of their daughter Leslie Ann on Saturday, March 1, at three o'clock."

THE MONDAY AFTER THE ACCIDENT I took my father's watch to the jeweller for cleaning and oiling. I intended to give it to my nephew Richard on his twenty-first birthday. My sister was giving Richard Father's signet ring, and I tried not to dwell on how much my present would upstage hers. Sooner or later the watch would go to Richard. Why not sooner? I didn't need a watch to remind me of my father, any more than I needed photographs to remind me of Susan. People you have loved become part of you; they remain with you forever independent of any objects they may have left behind.

That same night while I checked Winnifred's house my apartment was burgled. Taken were a Persian lamb coat, which I never wore, my small television set, which I intended to replace, my dress studs and cuff links, which I didn't much like, and a gold identification bracelet, which made the wearer look as if he were allergic to penicillin. The thief or thieves also took a silver baby's mug with the initials A.C. I very much wanted it back. They also took the two watches, the one I kept from Dale and the present from Chris. I could not honestly say I wanted Dale's watch returned. I would have kept it certainly, as *memento mori*; but perhaps it was better gone. I felt equally ambivalent about the watch from Chris. Like the man it was beautiful. But I knew now I no longer wanted the man. As a result I would never have worn the watch; it too was a *memento mori*. And maybe it too was better gone. While listing stolen items in triplicate for police and insurance I did not mention the watches. I knew there was little or no chance of their ever being found. And they belonged after all to another time.

**EDWARD O. PHILLIPS**

Edward O. Phillips' first novel *Sunday's Child* was published to extraordinary acclaim in 1981. It was followed by *Where There's A Will, Buried on Sunday*, and *Hope Springs Eternal.* His short stories have appeared in many Canadian magazines, and one, "Matthew and Chauncey", was produced as a French Canadian television film.

Born in 1931, Phillips has lived most of his life in Montreal. His educational credits boast a law degree from the University of Montreal, a Master's degree in teaching from Harvard, and a second Master's degree in English Literature from Boston University. For several years, Edward was a teacher, but later devoted all of his time to writing. He passed away on 30 May 2020.

# About ReQueered Tales

In the heady days of the late 1960s, when young people in many western countries were in the streets protesting for a new, more inclusive world, some of us were in libraries, coffee shops, communes, retreats, bedrooms and dens plotting something even more startling: literature – highbrow and pulp – for an explicitly gay audience. Specifically, we were craving to see our gay lives – in the closet, in the open, in bars, in dire straits and in love – reflected in mystery stories, sci-fi and mainstream fiction. Hercule Poirot, that engaging effete Belgian creation of Agatha Christie might have been gay ... Sherlock Holmes, to all intents and purposes, was one woman shy of gay ... but where were the genuine gay sleuths, where the reader need not read between the lines?

Beginning with Victor J Banis's "Man from C.A.M.P." pulps in the mid-60s – riotous romps spoofing the craze for James Bond spies – readers were suddenly being offered George Baxt's Pharoah Love, a black gay New York City detective, and a real turning point in Joseph Hansen's gay California insurance investigator, Dave Brandstetter, whose world weary Raymond Chandleresque adventures sold strongly and have never been out of print.

Over the next three decades, gay storytelling grew strongly in niche and mainstream publishing ventures. Even with the huge public crisis – as AIDS descended on the gay community beginning in the early 1980s – gay fiction flourished. Stonewall Inn, Alyson Publications, and others nurtured authors and readers ... until mainstream success seemed to come to a halt. While Lambda Literary Foundation had started to recognize work in annual awards about 1990, mainstream publishers began to have cold feet. And then, with the rise of e-books in the new millennium which enabled a new self-publishing industry ... there was both an avalanche of new talent coming to market and burying of print authors who did not cross the divide.

The result?

Perhaps forty years of gay fiction – and notably gay and lesbian mystery, detective and suspense fiction – has been teetering on the brink of obscurity. Orphaned works, orphaned authors, many living and some having passed away – with no one to make the case for their creations to be returned to print (and e-print!). General fiction and non-fiction works embracing gay lives, widely celebrated upon original release, also languished as mainstream publishers shifted their focus.

Until now. That is the mission of ReQueered Tales: to keep in circulation this treasure trove of fantastic fiction. In an era of ebooks, everything of value ought to be accessible. For a new generation of readers, these mystery tales, and works of general fiction, are full of insights into the gay world of the 1960s, '70s, '80s and '90s. For those of us who lived through the period, they are a delightful reminder of our youth and reflect some of our own struggles in growing up gay in those heady times.

We are honored, here at ReQueered Tales, to be custodians shepherding back into circulation some of the best gay and lesbian fiction writing and hope to bring many volumes to the public, in modestly priced, accessible editions, worldwide, over the coming years.

So please join us on this adventure of discovery and rediscovery of the rich talents of writers of recent years as the PIs, cops and amateur sleuths battle forces of evil with fierceness, humor and sometimes a pinch of love.

## The ReQueered Tales Team

*Justene Adamec • Alexander Inglis • Matt Lubbers-Moore*

# *Mysteries from* ReQueered Tales

**Buried on Sunday**
*Edward O. Phillips*

**A Geoffry Chadwick Misadventure, Book 2** – "One of the problems with weekends in the country" says Geoffry Chadwick's genial host in *Buried on Sunday*, "is that people feel free to drop in unannounced." And drop in they do. No sooner has our lovable lawyer hero settled in with a spicy Bloody Mary, than hardened criminals on the lam burst in and take Chadwick and his hosts hostage in their own beautiful home.

The tale brims with poignant and comic drama: one of the other hostages, now married, had once been Chadwick's lover. As the hours of their forced confinement turn into days, a flood of bittersweet memories engulf Chadwick: of an affair whose painful end he could never forget, of a lover who had changed the course of his life. Chadwick reckons with the road he has taken and the quite different path of marriage and convention chosen by his early love.

Published in 1986, it won the coveted Arthur Ellis Best Novel Award from the Crime Writers of Canada. This edition contains a contemporary interview on Phillips' reception of his work and a reminiscence of his 80th birthday celebration by author Nancy Wigston.

And don't miss ...

**Sunday Best**: Geoffry gets roped into planning a wedding for his niece Jennifer, but the groom has closet issues and a sexy latino chauffeur has a mixed agenda. Then there is widowed Montreal socialite Lois, mother to the groom, who casts her net for Geoffry ...

**Working on Sunday**: Geoffry Chadwick has a stalker. But between avoiding Christmas parties, gift shopping, moving his mother into a senior living facility, handling his recently widowed sister, and dealing with the loss of his long-term boyfriend Patrick, Geoffry Chadwick does not have time for a stalker.

# SUNDAY'S CHILD

## A Body to Dye For
*Grant Michaels*

**A Stan Kraychik Mystery, Book 1** – Stan "Vannos" Kraychik isn't your everyday Boston hairdresser. Manager of Snips Salon, which is owned by best bud (and occasional nemesis) Nicole, Stan thought this day was an ordinary one. A delivery van backed into the salon's rear driveway and accidentally spilled gallons of conditioner, leaving Stan and hunky Roger) embracing in a gooey mess trying to staunch the flow, with little success as they slid and slipped with Nicole watching on with rolling eyes. Later Roger is found murdered.

Stan's client, Calvin Redding, who owns the apartment where Roger's body was found, can't explain why the body is dressed in little more than bowties. Enter Lieutenant Branco, dark, muscular, Italian, (straight) of Boston PD Homicide who immediately suspects everyone, especially Stan. In an attempt to clear his name, Stan travels to California, takes up mountain climbing, eavesdropping, spying, schmoozing, and a little bit of schtupping, all in an attempt to find the truth.

Grant Michaels' zany series of adventures starring Stan Kraychik garnered multiple Lambda Literary Awards including a 1991 nomination for Best Gay Men's Mystery. For this new edition, Carl Mesrobian reminisces about his brother Grant in an exclusive foreword, and Neil S. Plakcy provides an introduction of appreciation.

And don't miss ...

**Love You to Death**: Stan visits a chocolate factory after a patron drops dead at a chi-chi cocktail party

**Dead on Your Feet**: Stan's new boyfriend, choreographer Rafik, is accused of murder

**Mask for a Diva**: Stan nabs a gig as wig master to a summer opera festival but the final curtain for one star comes down early

**Time to Check Out**: Stan takes a holiday to Key West but a dead bodies turns up anyway

**Dead as a Doornail**: In the midst of renovating his new Boston brownstone, Stan becomes the (unintended?) murder target

# EDWARD O. PHILLIPS

## In the Game
*Nikki Baker*

**A Virginia Kelly Mystery, Book 1** – When businesswoman Virginia Kelly meets her old college chum Bev Johnson for drinks late one night, Bev confides that her lover, Kelsey, is seeing another woman. Ginny had picked up that gossip months ago, but she is shocked when the next morning's papers report that Kelsey was found murdered behind the very bar where Ginny and Bev had met. Worried that her friend could be implicated, Ginny decides to track down Kelsey's killer and contacts a lawyer, Susan Coogan. Susan takes an immediate, intense liking to Ginny, complicating Ginny's relationship with her live-in lover. Meanwhile Ginny's inquiries heat up when she learns the Feds suspected Kelsey of embezzling from her employer.

"The auspicious debut of a black writer who brings us a sharp, funny and on-the-mark murder mystery."
— *Northwest Gay & Lesbian Reader*

"An entertaining assortment of female characters makes Baker's debut promising" — *Publishers Weekly*

"It has adventure, romance, and some of the best internal dialogue anywhere." — Megan Casey

Nikki Baker is the first African-American author in the lesbian mystery genre and her protagonist, Virginia Kelly is the first African-American lesbian detective in the genre. Interwoven into the narrative are observations on the intersectionality of being a woman, an African-American, and a lesbian in a "man's" world of finance and life in general.

First published to acclaim in 1991, this new edition features a foreword by the author.

## The Always Anonymous Beast
*Lauren Wright Douglas*

**A Caitlin Reece Mystery, Book 1** – Val Frazier, Victoria's star TV anchorwoman, is Caitlin's newest client. She is the victim of a viciously homophobic blackmailer who has discovered her relationship with Tonia Konig. Tonia is a lesbian-feminist professor, an outspoken, passionately committed proponent of nonviolence. She is enraged by her own helplessness, she is outraged by Caitlin's challenge to her most fundamental beliefs, and by Caitlin herself, whom she considers "a thug".

As Caitlin stalks the blackmailer and his accomplices through the byways of the city of Victoria, she uncovers ever darker layers of danger surrounding Tonia. And she struggles against a new and altogether unwanted complication: she is increasingly attracted to the woman who despises her.

> "A very accomplished first novel, which is distinguishable by an elegant flair for description and an obvious love of the language." — Karen Axness, *Feminist Bookstore News*

> "Douglas' book is snappily written, peppered with wit and literary allusions, and filled with original characters."
> — Sherri Paris, *The Women's Review of Books*

Douglas's debut novel in 1987 began a six part series for Caitlin Reece. This new edition includes an introduction by the author and a foreword by legendary Katherine V. Forrest.

And don't miss ...

**Ninth Life**: Caitlin is hired by a woman code-named Shrew, to pick up a package. Caitlin is sickened to the depths of her being by the contents of the package: a blind and maimed cat, and photographs of animal experimentation. And now Shrew is dead. As a member of the militant animal rights organization Ninth Life, she had infiltrated Living World, a cosmetics company. The other members of Ninth Life suspect she was betrayed by someone within their own ranks and murdered because of what she learned.

# EDWARD O. PHILLIPS

## Let's Get Criminal
*Lev Raphael*

**A Nick Hoffman / Academic Mystery, Book 1** – Nick Hoffman has everything he has ever wanted: a good teaching job, a nice house, and a solid relationship with his lover, Stefan Borowski, a brilliant novelist at the State University of Michigan. But when Perry Cross shows up, Nick's peace of mind is shattered. Not only does he have to share his office with the nefarious Perry, who managed to weasel his way into a tenured position without the right qualifications, he also discovers that Perry played a destructive role in Stefan's past. When Perry turns up dead, Nick wonders if Stefan might be involved, while the campus police force is wondering the same about Nick.

"*Let's Get Criminal* is a delightful romp in the wonderfully petty and backbiting world of academia. Well-drawn characters make up a delicious list of suspects and victims." — Faye Kellerman

"Reading *Let's Get Criminal* is like sitting down for a good gossip with an old friend. Its instant intimacy and warmth provides clever and sheer fun." — Marissa Piesman

Originally published in 1996, the first book in the Nick Hoffman Academic Mystery series is now back in print. This edition contains a new foreword by the author.

And don't miss ...

**The Edith Wharton Murders:** Nick has been saddled with a thankless task: coordinating a conference on Edith Wharton that will demonstrate how his department and his university supports women's issues. He's forced to invite two warring Wharton societies, and the conflict between rival scholars escalates from mudslinging to murder.

**The Death of a Constant Lover:** The son of a professor is murdered on a campus bridge and Nick's presence puts him in the middle of trouble.

**Little Miss Evil:** When cryptic messages in Nick's mailbox escalate into another corpse on campus, the reluctant sleuth is back on the case.

## Simple Justice
*John Morgan Wilson*

**A Benjamin Justice Mystery, Book 1** – It's 1994, an election year when violent crime is rampant, voters want action, and politicians smell blood. When a Latino teenager confesses to the murder of a pretty-boy cokehead outside a gay bar in L.A., the cops consider the case closed. But Benjamin Justice, a disgraced former reporter for the Los Angeles Times, sees something in the jailed boy others don't. His former editor, Harry Brofsky, now toiling at the rival Los Angeles Sun, surprises Justice from his alcoholic seclusion to help neophyte reporter Alexandra Templeton dig deeper into the story. But why would a seemingly decent kid confess to a brutal gang initiation killing if he wasn't guilty? And how can Benjamin Justice possibly be trusted, given his central role in the Pulitzer scandal that destroyed his career?

Snaking his way through shadowy neighborhoods and dubious suspects, he's increasingly haunted by memories of his lover Jacques, whose death from AIDS six years earlier precipitated his fall from grace. As he unravels emotionally, Templeton attempts to solve the riddle of his dark past and ward off another meltdown as they race against a critical deadline to uncover and publish the truth.

> "Wilson keeps the emotional as well as forensic suspense up through the very last sentence. The final scene is not only a satisfying explanation of the crime, but a riveting study of the erotic cruelty of justice." — *The Harvard Gay and Lesbian Review*

Awarded an Edgar by Mystery Writers of America for Best First Novel on initial release, this 25th Anniversary edition has been revised by the author. A foreword for the 2020 edition by Christopher Rice (*Bone Music*) is included.

# *More from* ReQueered Tales

### Like People in History
*Felice Picano*

Solid, cautious Roger Sansarc and flamboyant, mercurial Alistair Dodge are second cousins who become lifelong friends when they first meet as nine-year-old boys in 1954. Their lives constantly intersect at crucial moments in their personal histories as each discovers his own unique – and uniquely gay – identity. Their complex, tumultuous, and madcap relationship endures against 40 years of history and their involvement with the handsome model, poet, and decorated Vietnam vet Matt Loguidice, whom they both love. Picano chronicles and celebrates gay life and subculture over the last half of the twentieth century: from the legendary 1969 gathering at Woodstock to the legendary parties at Fire Island Pines in the 1970s, from Malibu Beach in its palmiest surfer days to San Francisco during its gayest era, from the cities and jungles of South Vietnam during the war to Manhattan's Greenwich Village and Upper East Side during the 1990s AIDS war.

> "It's the heroic and funny saga of the last three decades by someone who saw everything and forgot nothing." — Edmund White

> "Harrowing and sad, and very funny, *Like People in History* manages to bridge the unnerving chasm between the queer present and the gay past." — Andrew Holleran

In a book that could have been written only by one who lived it and survived to tell, Picano weaves a powerful saga of four decades in the lives of two men and their lovers, relatives, friends, and enemies. Tragic, comic, sexy, and romantic, filled with varied and colorful characters, *Like People in History* is both extraordinarily moving and supremely entertaining.

Published to acclaim in 1995, winner of the Ferro-Grumley Award for Best Novel, this 25th Anniversary edition for 2020 features a new foreword by Richard Burnett and an afterword by the author.

# Mountain Climbing in Sheridan Square
*Stan Leventhal*

A series of discrete episodes among friends provide snapshots of one gay man's life. There are parties, concerts, dinners with everyday life – and death – interwoven in the rich story-telling. An actress, a painter, a set designer, a writer – all sweating and surviving in Manhattan, all scoring their first successes. Part autobiography and part documentary, artfully written, it details the lives of these creative people. Young and professional, they know there is more to life than money. There is trust and the sort of love that trades in deeds of kindness.

> "Stan was a literary activist who always gave to, built and endorsed literature and writers. I can see still see Stan in his apartment window on Christopher Street, next door to the Stonewall Inn, overlooking Sheridan Square as he typed away." — Michele Karlsberg, LGBTQ publicist and friend

Leventhal's debut novel was welcomed warmly as a Lambda Literary Awards Finalist in 1988. This new edition features a foreword by Christopher Bram (*Gods and Monsters*).

And don't miss ...

**The Black Marble Pool** – There's a dead body at the bottom of a pool in the backyard of a guest house in Key West. Who is he? And what caused his untimely demise? Maybe it's suicide. Or an accident. But more likely – murder! And who's responsible? One of the guests, the people who run the guest house or one of those mysterious women in town?

> "The pace is brisk: the plot keeps twisting, as no one is at all who they seem." — Keith John Glaeske, *Out In Print*

# EDWARD O. PHILLIPS

### The Family of Max Desir
*Robert Ferro*

It was a family dealing with old values, acceptance and death. Max Desir loved his Italian roots and he loved his American family. As he came of age, Max Desir found love in Italy. Now, at age 40, his American family is split: Max and Nick are accepted as a stable, long-term couple by mother and siblings, but his father John does not. When a needlepoint family tree is to be hung at Christmas, acceptance of family is re-examined. In this beautiful, haunting tale, told in a clear, impassioned narrative, Robert Ferro created a classic. His highly celebrated breakthrough novel is not to be missed.

> "An honest, eloquent and entirely original novel ... at once realistic and mythological, intensely personal and public ... a triumph."
> — Edmund White

> "Nobody has told this story before, and Robert Ferro has the power to make his telling definitive ... his clear, impassioned narrative moves with wit and sensuous energy. It has shaken and excited me more than any recent American fiction. I want to give it to people. I want everyone to read it." — Walter Clemons

> "A stunning achievement ... not limited to the gay experience, but touches upon the very nature of the human condition ... renews faith in the American novel ... One of the finest (and certainly most moving) novels of the year." — *The Advocate*

Originally published in 1983, this new edition includes a foreword by fellow author and friend Felice Picano.

## Life Drawing
*Michael Grumley*

Born in Iowa to the sounds of Bob and Bing Crosby and the Dorsey brothers, Mickey grows up to the comforting images of his living room TV and the reassuring ruts of his parents' life. During the restless summer of his senior year in high school, drifting away from the girlfriend he could never quite love, Mickey spends a night with another boy, and his world will never be the same.

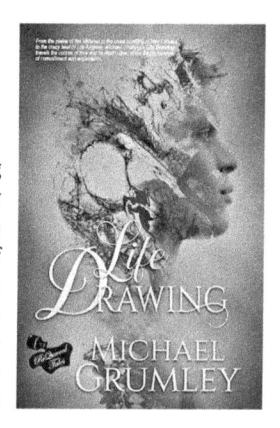

On a barge floating down the Mississippi, he falls in love with James, a black card player from New Orleans, and in time the two of them settle, bristling with sexual intensity, in the French Quarter – until a brief affair destroys James's trust and sends Mickey to the drugs and sordid life of Los Angeles.

> "A simple, classic, engaging, and beautifully written tale of a boy who ran away from home, a man who didn't make it in the movies, an artist who found himself earlier than most and did it all west of the Mississippi, in places which, while very American, few Americans have ever been." — Andrew Holleran

> "*Life Drawing* affirms the rich complexity of passion in the story of a small-town boy's difficult journey to manhood. Michael Grumley's crisp, direct language brings to life the demanding wonder of sexuality and the delicate tightrope of love between black men and white men." — Melvin Dixon

Originally published in 1991, it was Grumley's only novel, completed in the month's leading to his death from AIDS as he was cared for his lover Robert Ferro. This new edition contains the original foreword by Edmund White (*A Saint from Texas*) and afterword by George Stambolian (*Gay Men's Anthologies Men on Men*), close friends of the couple.

# EDWARD O. PHILLIPS

## Murder and Mayhem
*Matt Lubbers-Moore*

**An Annotated Bibliography of Gay and Queer Males in Mystery, 1909-2018.**

Librarian and scholar Matt Lubbers-Moore collects and examines every mystery novel to include a gay or queer male in the English language starting with Arthur Conan Doyle's "The Man with the Watches". Authors, titles, dates published, publishers, book series, short blurbs, and a description of how involved the gay or queer male character is with the mystery are included for a full bibliographic background.

*Murder and Mayhem* will prove invaluable for mystery collectors, researchers, libraries, general readers, aficionados, bookstores, and devotees of LGBTQ studies. The bibliography is laid out in alphabetical order by author including the blurb and author notes, whether a hard boiled private eye, an amateur cozy, a suspenseful romance, or a police procedural. All subgenres within the mystery field are included: fantasy, science fiction, espionage, political intrigue, crime dramas, courtroom thrillers, and more with a definition guide of the subgenres for a better understanding of the genre as a whole.

A ReQueered Tales Original Publication.

## The Male Homosexual in Literature: A Bibliography *and* The Male Homosexual in Literature: Supplement (2020)
*Ian Young*

Ian Young's bibliography has served as a basic guide to English-language works of fiction, drama, poetry and autobiography concerned with male homosexuality or having male homosexual characters. Entries include titles published through 1980. Works are identified by author, title, place of publication, publisher, and date. For easy reference, entries are numbered and a title index is provided. Five highly acclaimed essays on gay literature by Ian Young, Graham Jackson and Dr. Rictor Norton, including essay on gay publishing, round out the listings. A title index of gay anthologies completes the work.

The present *Supplement* includes titles overlooked in the *Bibliography* Second Edition, plus works written before the 1981 cut-off date but published later, including works published for the first time in book form.

**If you enjoyed this book,
please help spread the word
by posting a short,
constructive review at
your favorite social media site
or book retailer.**

**We thank you, greatly,
for your support.**

**And don't be shy! Contact us!**

*For more information about current and future releases, please contact us:*

E-mail: *requeeredtales@gmail.com*
Facebook (Like us!): www.facebook.com/ReQueeredTales
Twitter: @ReQueered
Instagram: www.instagram.com/requeered
Web: www.ReQueeredTales.com
Blog: www.ReQueeredTales.com/blog
Mailing list (Subscribe for latest news): https://bit.ly/RQTJoin